NOAH'S COMPASS

If Morning Ever Comes

The Tin Can Tree

A Slipping-Down Life

The Clock Winder

Celestial Navigation

Searching for Caleb

Earthly Possessions

Morgan's Passing

Dinner at the Homesick Restaurant

The Accidental Tourist

Breathing Lessons

Saint Maybe

Ladder of Years

A Patchwork Planet

Back When We Were Grownups

The Amateur Marriage

Digging to America

NOAH'S COMPASS

ANNE TYLER

CHATTO & WINDUS
LONDON

Published by Chatto & Windus 2009

Published in the United States of America by Alfred A. Knopf in 2009

4 6 8 10 9 7 5 3

First published in Great Britain in 2009 by
Chatto & Windus
Random House, 20 Vauxhall Bridge Road,
London SW1V 2SA
www.rbooks.co.uk

Addresses for companies within The Random House Group Limited can be found at:
www.randomhouse.co.uk/offices.htm

The Random House Group Limited Reg. No. 954009

A CIP catalogue record for this book
is available from the British Library

Hardback ISBN 9780701184230
Trade Paperback ISBN 9780701184247

The Random House Group Limited supports The Forest Stewardship
Council (FSC), the leading international forest certification organisation. All our titles
that are printed on Greenpeace approved FSC certified paper carry the FSC logo.
Our paper procurement policy can be found at:
www.rbooks.co.uk/environment

Mixed Sources
Product group from well-managed
forests and other controlled sources
www.fsc.org   Cert no. TT-COC-2139
© 1996 Forest Stewardship Council
FSC

Printed and bound in Great Britain by
Clays Ltd, St. Ives plc

Noah's
Compass

1

In the sixty-first year of his life, Liam Pennywell lost his job. It wasn't such a good job, anyhow. He'd been teaching fifth grade in a second-rate private boys' school. Fifth grade wasn't even what he'd been trained for. *Teaching* wasn't what he'd been trained for. His degree was in philosophy. Oh, don't ask. Things seemed to have taken a downward turn a long, long time ago, and perhaps it was just as well that he had seen the last of St. Dyfrig's dusty, scuffed corridors and those interminable after-school meetings and the reams of niggling paperwork.

In fact, this might be a sign. It could be just the nudge he needed to push him on to the next stage—the final stage, the summing-up stage. The stage where he sat in his rocking chair and reflected on what it all meant, in the end.

He had a respectable savings account and the promise of a pension, so his money situation wasn't out-and-out desperate. Still, he would have to economize. The prospect of economizing interested him. He plunged into it with more enthusiasm than he'd felt in years—gave up his big old-fashioned apartment within the week and signed a lease on a smaller place, a one-bedroom-plus-den in a modern complex out toward the Baltimore Beltway. Of course this meant paring down his possessions, but so much the better. Simplify, simplify! Somehow he had accumulated far too many encumbrances. He tossed out bales of old magazines and manila envelopes stuffed with letters and three shoe boxes of index cards for the dissertation that he had never gotten around to writing. He tried to palm off his extra furniture on his daughters, two of whom were grown-ups with places of their own, but they said it was too shabby. He had to donate it to Goodwill. Even Goodwill refused his couch, and he ended up paying 1-800-GOT-JUNK to truck it away. What was left, finally, was compact enough that he could reserve the next-smallest-size U-Haul, a fourteen-footer, for moving day.

On a breezy, bright Saturday morning in June, he and his friend Bundy and his youngest daughter's boyfriend lugged everything out of his old apartment and set it along the curb. (Bundy had decreed that they should develop a strategy before they started loading.) Liam was reminded of a photographic series that he'd seen in one of those magazines he had just thrown away. *National Geographic? Life?* Different people from different parts of the world had posed among their belongings in various outdoor settings. There was a progression from the contents of the most primitive tribesman's hut (a cooking pot and a blanket, in Africa or some such) to a suburban American family's football-field-sized assemblage of furniture and automobiles, multiple TVs and sound systems, wheeled racks of clothing, everyday china and company china, on and on and on. His own collection, which had seemed so scanty in the gradually emptying rooms of his apartment, occupied an embarrassingly large space alongside the curb. He felt eager to whisk it away from public view. He snatched up the nearest box even before Bundy had given them the go-ahead.

Bundy taught phys ed at St. Dyfrig. He was a skeletal, blue-black giraffe of a man, frail by the looks of him, but he could lift astonishing weights. And Damian—a limp, wilted seventeen-year-old—was getting paid for this. So Liam let the two of them tackle the heavy stuff while he himself, short and stocky and out of shape, saw to the lamps and the pots and pans and other light objects. He had packed his books in small cartons and so those he carried too, stacking them lovingly and precisely against the left inner wall of the van while Bundy singlehandedly wrestled with a desk and Damian tottered beneath an upside-down Windsor chair balanced on top of his head. Damian had the posture of a consumptive—narrow, curved back and buckling knees. He resembled a walking comma.

The new apartment was some five miles from the old one, a short jaunt up North Charles Street. Once the van was loaded, Liam led the way in his car. He had assumed that Damian, who was below the legal age for driving a rental, would ride shotgun in the van with Bundy, but instead he slid in next to Liam and sat in a jittery silence, chewing on a thumbnail and lurking behind a mane of lank black hair. Liam couldn't think of a single thing to say to him. When they stopped for the light at Wyndhurst he contemplated asking how Kitty was, but he decided it might sound odd to inquire about his own daughter. Not until they were turning off Charles did either of them speak, and then it was Damian. "Swingin' bumper sticker," he said.

Since there were no cars ahead of them, Liam knew it had to be his own bumper sticker Damian meant. (*BUMPER STICKER*, it read—a witticism that no one before had ever seemed to appreciate.) "Why, thanks," he said. And then, feeling encouraged: "I also have a T-shirt that says *T-SHIRT*." Damian stopped chewing his thumbnail and gaped at him. Liam said, "Heh, heh," in a helpful tone of voice, but still it seemed that Damian didn't get it.

The complex Liam was moving to sat opposite a small shopping mall. It consisted of several two-story buildings, flat-faced and beige and bland, placed at angles to each other under tall, spindly pines. Liam had worried about privacy, seeing the network of paths between buildings and the flanks of wide, staring windows, but during the whole unloading process they didn't run into a single neighbor. The carpeting of brown pine needles muffled their voices, and the wind in the trees above them made an eerily steady whispering sound. "Cool," Damian said, presumably meaning the sound, since he had his face tipped upward as he spoke. He was under the Windsor chair again. It loomed like an oversized bonnet above his forehead.

Liam's unit was on the ground floor. Unfortunately, it had a shared entrance—a heavy brown steel door, opening into a dank-smelling cinderblock foyer with his own door to the left and a flight of steep concrete steps directly ahead. Second-floor units cost less to rent, but Liam would have found it depressing to climb those stairs every day.

He hadn't given much thought beforehand to the placement of his furniture. Bundy set things down any old where but Damian proved unexpectedly finicky, shoving Liam's bed first one way and then another in search of the best view. "Like, you've got to see out the window first thing when you open your eyes," he said, "or how will you know what kind of weather it is?" The bed was digging tracks across the carpet, and Liam just wanted to leave it where it stood. What did he care what kind of weather it was? When Damian started in on the desk—it had to be positioned where sunlight wouldn't reflect off the computer screen, he said—Liam told him, "Well, since I don't own a computer, where the desk is now will be fine. That about wraps things up, I guess."

"Don't own a computer!" Damian echoed.

"So let me just get you your money, and you can be on your way."

"But how do you, like, communicate with the outside world?"

Liam was about to say that he communicated by fountain pen, but Bundy said, chuckling, "He doesn't." Then he clapped a hand on Liam's shoulder. "Okay, Liam, good luck, man."

Liam hadn't meant to dismiss Bundy along with Damian. He had envisioned the two of them sharing the traditional moving-day beer and pizza. But of course, Bundy was providing Damian's ride back. (It was Bundy who'd picked up the U-Haul, bless him, and now he'd be returning it.) So Liam said, "Well, thank you, Bundy. I'll have to have you over once I'm settled in." Then he handed Damian a hundred and twenty dollars in cash. The extra twenty was a tip, but since Damian pocketed the bills without counting them, the gesture felt like a waste. "See you around," was all he said. Then he and Bundy left. The inner door latched gently behind them but the outer door, the brown steel one, shook the whole building when it slammed shut, setting up a shocked silence for several moments afterward and emphasizing, somehow, Liam's sudden solitude.

Well. So. Here he was.

He took a little tour. There wasn't a lot to look at. A medium-sized living room, with his two armchairs and the rocking chair facing in random directions and filling not quite enough space. A dining area at the far end (Formica-topped table from his first marriage and three folding chairs), with a kitchen alcove just beyond. The den and the bathroom opened off the hall that led back to the bedroom. All the floors were carpeted with the same beige synthetic substance, all the walls were refrigerator white, and there were no moldings whatsoever, no baseboards or window frames or door frames, none of those gradations that had softened the angles of his old place. He found this a satisfaction. Oh, his life was growing purer, all right! He poked his head into the tiny den (daybed, desk, Windsor chair) and admired the built-in shelves. They had been a big selling point when he was apartment hunting: two tall white bookshelves on either side of the patio door. Finally, finally he'd been able to get rid of those glass-fronted walnut monstrosities he had inherited from his mother. It was true that these shelves were less spacious. He'd had to consolidate a bit, discarding the fiction and biographies and some of his older dictionaries. But he had kept his beloved philosophers, and now he looked forward to arranging them. He bent over a carton and opened the flaps. Epictetus. Arrian. The larger volumes would go on the lower shelves, he decided, even though they didn't need to, since all the shelves were exactly, mathematically the same height. It was a matter of aesthetics, really—the visual effect. He hummed tunelessly to himself, padding back and forth between the shelves and the cartons. The sunlight streaming through the glass door brought a fine sweat to his upper lip, but he postponed rolling up his shirtsleeves because he was too absorbed in his task.

After the study came the kitchen, less interesting but still necessary, and so he moved on to the boxes of foods and utensils. This was the most basic of kitchens, with a single bank of cabinets, but that was all right; he'd never been much of a cook. In fact here it was, late afternoon, and he was only now realizing that he'd better fix himself some lunch. He made a jelly sandwich and ate it as he worked, swigging milk straight from the carton to wash it down. The sight of the six-pack of beer in the refrigerator, brought over the day before along with his perishables, gave him a pang of regret that took a moment to explain. Ah, yes: Bundy. He must remember to phone Bundy tomorrow and thank him at greater length. Invite him to supper, even. He wondered what carry-out establishments delivered within his new radius.

In the living room he arranged the chairs in what he hoped was a friendly conversational grouping. He placed a lamp table between the two armchairs and the coffee table in front of them, and the other lamp table he set next to the rocker, which was where he imagined sitting to read at the end of every day. Or *all* day, for that matter. How else would he fill the hours?

Even in the summers, he had been accustomed to working. St. Dyfrig students could be counted on to require an abundance of remedial courses. He had taken almost no vacation—just one week in early June and two in August.

Well, think of this as one of those weeks. Just proceed a day at a time, is all.

On the kitchen wall, the telephone rang. He had a new number but he had kept his existing plan, which included caller ID (one of the few modern inventions he approved of), and he checked the screen before he lifted the receiver. *ROYALL J S.* His sister. "Hello?" he said.

"How's it going, Liam?"

"Oh, fine. I think I'm just about settled."

"Have you made up your bed yet?"

"Well, no."

"Do it. Now. You should have done it first thing. Pretty soon you're going to notice you're exhausted, and you don't want to be hunting for sheets then."

"Okay," he said.

Julia was four years his senior. He was used to receiving orders from her.

"Later in the week I may stop by and visit. I'll bring you a pot of beef stew," she said.

"Well, that's very nice of you, Julia," he said.

He hadn't eaten red meat in thirty-some years, but it would have been useless to remind her.

After he hung up he obediently made his bed, which was easily navigated since Damian had positioned it so there was walking space on either side. Then he tackled the closet, where clothes had been dumped every which way. He nailed his shoe bag to the closet door and fitted in his shoes; he draped his ties on the tie rack that he found already installed. He'd never owned a tie rack before. Then, since he had the hammer out, he decided to go ahead and hang his pictures. Oh, he was *way* ahead of the game! Picture hanging was a finishing touch, something that took most people days. But he might as well see this through.

His pictures were unexceptional—van Gogh prints, French bistro posters, whatever he'd chosen haphazardly years and years ago just to save his walls from total blankness. Even so, it took him a while to find the appropriate spot for each one and get it properly centered. By the time he'd finished it was after eight and he'd had to turn all the lights on. The ceiling globe in the living room had a burnt-out bulb, he discovered. Well, never mind; he'd see to that tomorrow. All at once, enough was enough.

He wasn't the slightest bit hungry, but he heated a bowl of vegetable soup in his miniature microwave and sat down at the table to eat it. First he sat facing the kitchen alcove, with his back to the living room. The view was uninspiring, though, so he switched to the end chair that faced the window. Not that he had much to see even there—just a sheet of glossy blackness and a vague, transparent reflection of his own round gray head—but it would be nice in the daytime. He would automatically settle in that chair from now on, he supposed. He had a fondness for routine.

When he stood up to take his empty bowl to the kitchen, he was ambushed by sudden aches in several parts of his body. His shoulders hurt, and his lower back, and his calves and the soles of his feet. Early though it was, he locked his door and turned off the lights and went into the bedroom. His made-up bed was a welcome sight. As usual, Julia had known what she was talking about.

He skipped his shower. Getting into his pajamas and brushing his teeth took his last ounce of energy. When he sank onto the bed, it was almost beyond his willpower to reach over and turn off the lamp, but he forced himself to do it. Then he slid down flat, with a long, deep, groaning sigh.

His mattress was comfortably firm, and the top sheet was tucked in tightly on either side of him as he liked. His pillow had just enough bounce to it. The window, a couple of feet away, was cranked open to let the breeze blow in, and it offered a view of a pale night sky with a few stars visible behind the sparse black pine boughs—just a scattering of pin-pricks. He was glad now that Damian had taken such trouble to situate the bed right.

Most probably, he reflected, this would be the final dwelling place of his life. What reason would he have to move again? No new prospects were likely for him. He had accomplished all the conventional tasks—grown up, found work, gotten married, had children—and now he was wind-ing down.

This is it, he thought. The very end of the line. And he felt a mild stirring of curiosity.

Then he woke up in a hospital room with a helmet of gauze on his head.

2

He knew it was a hospital room because of the medical apparatus crowded around his bed—the IV pole and the tubes and the blinking, chirping monitor—and because of the bed itself, which was cranked to a half-sitting position and had that uniquely uncomfortable, slick, hard hospital mattress. The ceiling could only be a hospital ceiling, with its white acoustic tiles pocked and cratered like the moon, and nowhere else would you find the same sterile taupe metal furniture.

He knew his head was bandaged even before he reached up a hand to touch it, because the gauze covered his ears and turned the chirping of the monitor into a distant peep. But not until he reached did he realize that his hand was bandaged also. A wide strip of adhesive tape encircled his left palm, and in fact his palm stung sharply across the padded part now that he thought about it. Exactly where his head was injured, though, he couldn't tell. It ached uniformly all over, a relentless, dull throbbing that seemed connected to his vision, because looking at the blinking lights of the monitor made it worse.

He knew from the square of pearly white sky framed by the plate-glass window that it must be daytime. But *which* day? And what hour of the day?

Any second now an explanation would occur to him. There had to be one. He had fallen down some stairs or he'd been in a car wreck. But when he searched his mind for his last available memory (which took a distressingly long moment), all he could find was the image of going to sleep in his new apartment. His new apartment's address was 102C Windy Pines Court; what a relief to be able to produce that. His new phone number was . . . oh, Lord. He couldn't recall.

But that was understandable, wasn't it? The number had been assigned to him only a week ago.

The exchange was 882. Or maybe 822. Or 828.

He gave up the search for his phone number and returned to the image of falling asleep. He tried to invent a next act. So: in the morning he had awakened, let's say. He might have wondered where he was for an instant, but then he'd oriented himself, gotten out of bed, headed toward his new bathroom . . .

It didn't work. He drew a blank. All he could remember was lying on his back in the dark, appreciating his sheets.

A nurse came in, or maybe an aide; hard to tell, these days. She was young and plump and freckled, and she wore baby-blue pants and a white smock printed with teddy bears. She punched a button on the monitor and it stopped chirping. Then she leaned over his face, too close. "Oh!" she said. "You're awake."

"What happened?" he asked her.

"I'll tell them at the desk," she said.

She went off again.

He could see now that a tube ran from the IV pole to his right arm. He sensed that he had a catheter, too. He was fastened down like Gulliver, trapped by cords and wires. A flutter of panic started rising in his chest, but he subdued it by gazing steadily out the open door, where a blond wooden handrail followed the corridor wall in a predictable and calming way.

Surgery. Maybe he'd had surgery. Anesthesia could do this to you—wipe out any sense that time had passed while you were unconscious. He remembered that from his tonsillectomy, fifty-odd years ago. But he had awakened from the tonsillectomy with a clear recall of going under, and of the hours leading up to it. It had been nothing like this.

Another nurse, or some such person, entered so swiftly that she set up a breeze. This was an older woman but her smock was equally ambiguous, patterned all over with smiley faces. "*Good* afternoon!" she said loudly. It turned out that hearing stabbed his head just as much as seeing. She took something from her pocket, a little penlight kind of thing, and shined it painfully into his eyes. He forced himself not to close them. He said, "It's afternoon?"

"Mmhmm."

"What's wrong with me?"

"Concussion," she said. She slipped the penlight back in her pocket and turned to check the monitor. "You got a little bump on the noggin."

"I don't remember anything about it," he told her.

"Well, there you are, then. That's what concussion does to people."

"I mean I don't remember being in a situation where I could *get* a concussion. All I remember is going to bed."

"Did you maybe fall out of bed?" she asked him.

"Fall out of bed! At my age?"

"Well, I don't know. I just came on duty. Let's ask your daughter."

"I have a daughter here? Which one?"

"Dark hair? A little bit curly? I think she went to the cafeteria. But I'll try and track her down for you."

She checked something at the side of the bed—his catheter bag, he supposed—and then left.

It was absurdly comforting to know that a daughter was here. The very word was comforting: *daughter.* Someone who was personally acquainted with him and cared about more than his blood pressure and his output of pee.

Even if she *had* absconded to the cafeteria without a backward glance.

He closed his eyes and fell off a cliff, into a sleep that felt like drowning in feathers.

When he woke up, a bearded man was prying open his eyelids. "*There* you are," the man said, as if Liam had stepped out of the room for a moment. Liam's oldest daughter was standing at the foot of the bed, her sensible, familiar face almost startling in these surroundings. She wore a sleeveless blouse that must not have been warm enough for this refrigerated air, because she'd wrapped her solid white arms around her rib cage.

"I'm Dr. Wood," the bearded man told Liam. "The hospitalist."

Hospitalist?

"Mr. Pennywell, do you know where you are?"

"I have no idea where I am," Liam said.

"What day is it, then?"

"I don't know that either," Liam said. "I just woke up! You're asking impossible questions."

Xanthe said, "Dad, *please* cooperate," but Dr. Wood raised a palm in her direction (never fear; he knew how to handle these old codgers) and said, "You're quite right, of course, Mr. Pennywell," in a soothing, condescending tone. "So," he said. "The president. Can you tell me who our president is."

Liam grimaced. "He's not *my* president," he said. "I refuse to acknowledge him."

"Dad—"

Liam said, "Look here, Dr. Wood, I should be asking the questions. I'm completely in the dark! I went to bed last night—or some night; I wake up in a hospital room! What happened?"

Dr. Wood glanced at Xanthe. It was possible that he didn't know himself what had happened—or had already forgotten, in the crush of his other patients. At any rate, Xanthe was the one who finally answered. "You were injured by an intruder," she told Liam.

"An intruder?"

"He must have gotten in through the patio door, which, incidentally, you left unlocked for any passing Tom, Dick, or Harry to waltz through as the whim overtook him."

"An intruder was in my *bedroom*?"

"I guess you struggled or shouted or something, because the neighbors heard a commotion, but by the time the police came the man had fled."

"I was there for this? I was conscious? I was fighting off an attack?"

He felt a deep chill down the back of his neck, and it wasn't from the air conditioning.

"They need to keep you here a while for observation," Xanthe told him. "That's why they've been waking you so often to ask you questions."

It was news to Liam that he had been awakened often, but he didn't want to admit to yet another failure of memory. "Have they caught the man?" he asked her.

"Not yet."

"He's still out there?"

Before she could answer, Dr. Wood said, "Sit up for me, please, Mr. Pennywell." Then he led Liam through a series of exercises that made him feel foolish. Raise this arm; raise that arm; touch his own nose; follow Dr. Wood's finger with his eyes. Xanthe stood to one side, narrowly watchful, as the soles of his bare feet were scraped with a pointed object. During the whole process, Dr. Wood remained expressionless. "How am I?" Liam was forced to ask finally.

Dr. Wood said, "We'll need to keep you here another night just to be on the safe side. But if all goes well, we can release you tomorrow."

"Tomorrow!" Xanthe said. "Are you serious? Look at him! He's weak as a kitten! He looks like death warmed over!"

"Oh, that will change," the doctor said offhandedly. He told Liam, "Nothing to eat today but liquids, I'm afraid, in case we have to take you very suddenly to the OR." Then he nodded in Xanthe's direction and left the room.

"Typical," Xanthe muttered when he'd gone. "First he says

they're booting you out and then in the same breath he says you may need emergency brain surgery."

She spun away with a flounce of her skirt. Liam feared for a moment that she was leaving too, but she was only going over to the corner for a green vinyl chair. She dragged it closer to his bed and plunked herself down in it. "I hope you're satisfied," she told Liam.

"Well, not completely," he said drily.

"I knew you shouldn't have moved to that place. Didn't I tell you when you signed the lease? A sixty-year-old man in a rinky-dink starter apartment directly across from a shopping mall! And then to leave your door wide open! What did you expect?"

He hadn't left his door wide open. And he hadn't meant to leave it unlocked. He hadn't known it *was* unlocked. But it was his policy not to argue. (An infuriating policy, his daughters always claimed.) Arguing got you nowhere. He smoothed down his bedclothes with his good hand, accidentally tugging the tube that ran from his arm to the IV pole.

"A sixty-year-old man," Xanthe said, "who can still move all his belongings in the very smallest size U-Haul."

"Next smallest," he murmured.

"Whose so-called car is a Geo Prizm. A *used* Geo Prizm. And who, when he gets hit on the head, nobody knows where his people are."

"How *did* they know?" he asked. It only now occurred to him to wonder. "Who called you?"

"The police called. They'll be in to question you later, they said. They got my number from your address book; I was the only entry with the same last name as yours. I had to hear it over the phone! At two o'clock in the morning! If you don't think *that's* an experience . . ."

He was accustomed to Xanthe's rants. They were sort of a hobby of hers. Funny: she was so completely different from her mother, his first wife—a waifish, fragile musician with a veil of transparent hair. Millie had taken too many pills when Xanthe was not yet two. It was his second wife who'd ended up raising Xanthe, and his second wife whom she resembled—brown haired and sturdy and normal-looking, pleasantly unexceptional-looking. He wondered sometimes if genetic traits could be altered by osmosis.

"And here's the worst of it," Xanthe was saying. "You invite a known drug addict into your home and give him total access."

"Excuse me?" he said. He was startled. Had there been some whole other episode he had lost to his amnesia?

"Damian O'Donovan. What were you *thinking*?"

"Damian . . . *Kitty's* Damian? Kitty's boyfriend?"

"Kitty's drug-addict, slacker boyfriend whom none of us trust for an instant. Mom won't even let them be alone in the house together."

"Well, of course she won't," Liam said. "They're seventeen years old. But Damian's not a drug addict."

"Dad. How can these things slip your mind? He was suspended last year for smoking pot backstage in the school auditorium."

"That doesn't make him an addict."

"He was suspended for a week! But you: you're such a patsy. You choose to forget all about it. You say, 'Oh, here, Damian, let me show you where I live. Let me point out my flimsy patio door that I plan to leave unlocked.' In fact I wouldn't be surprised if he unlocked that door himself while he was there, just so he could get back in and mug you."

"Oh, for heaven's sake," Liam said. "He's a perfectly harmless kid. A little . . . vacant, maybe, but he would never—"

"I don't want to say you had it coming," Xanthe said, "but mark my words, Dad: 'Those who cannot remember history are condemned to repeat it.' Harry Truman."

"The past," Liam said reflexively.

"What?"

" 'Those who cannot remember the *past* are condemned to repeat it.' And it's George Santayana."

Xanthe gazed at him stonily, her eyes the same opaque dark brown as her stepmother's. "I'm going to find someplace where my cell phone works and let the others know how you're doing," she said.

Even though she could be a bit wearing, he was sorry to see her leave.

His head was pounding so hard that it made a sound inside his ears like approaching footsteps. His injured palm was stinging, and something seemed to be wrong with his neck. A twisty pain ran down the left side.

He had fought with someone? Physically struggled?

Let's try this again: he had gone to bed in his new bedroom. He had felt grateful for his firm mattress, his resilient pillow, his tightly tucked top sheet. He had looked out the window and seen the stars sprinkled above the pine boughs.

Then what? Then what? *Then what?*

His lost memory was like a physical object just beyond his grasp. He could feel the strain in his head. It made the throbbing even worse.

Okay, just let it go. It would come to him in good time.

He closed his eyes and slid toward sleep, almost all the way but not quite. Part of him was listening for Xanthe. What was she telling her sisters? It would be nice if she were saying, "Such a scare; we almost lost him. I've been out of my mind with worry." Although more likely it was "Can you believe what he's done *this* time?"

But it wasn't his fault! he wanted to say. For once, he wasn't to blame!

He knew his daughters thought he was hopeless. They said he didn't pay attention. They claimed he was obtuse. They rolled their eyes at each other when he made the most innocent remark. They called him Mr. Magoo.

At St. Dyfrig once, invited to view a poem on the English department's computer, he had clicked on *How to listen* and been disappointed to find mere technical instructions for playing the audio version. What he had been hoping for was advice on how to listen to poetry—and, by extension, how to listen, *really* listen, to what was being said all around him. It seemed he lacked some basic skill for that.

He was hopeless. His daughters were right.

He reached for sleep as if it were a blanket that he could hide underneath, and finally he managed to catch hold of it.

When he opened his eyes, a policeman was standing at his bedside—a muscular young man in full uniform. "Mr. Pennywell?" he was saying. He already had his ID card in hand, not that one was needed. Nobody would mistake him for anything but a cop. His white shirt was so crisp that it hurt to look at it, and the weight of his gun and his radio and his massive black leather belt would have sunk him like a stone if he had fallen into any water. "Like to ask a few questions," he said.

Liam struggled to sit up, and something like a brick slammed into his left temple. He groaned and eased himself back against his pillow.

The policeman, oblivious, was tucking away his ID. (If he had given his name, he must have done so before Liam woke up.) He took a small notebook from his breast pocket, along with a ballpoint pen, and said, "I understand you left your back door unlocked."

"That's what they tell me."

"Pardon?"

"That's what they tell me, I said!"

He had thought he was speaking quite loudly, but it was hard to know for sure inside all that gauze.

"And when did you retire?" the man asked, writing something down.

"I'm not exactly calling it retirement yet."

"Pardon?"

"I'm not exactly calling it retirement yet! I'll have to see how my money holds out."

"When did you go to *bed*, Mr. Pennywell. On the night of the incident."

"Oh." Liam reflected for a moment. "Wasn't that last night?"

The policeman consulted his notebook. "Last night, yes," he said. "Saturday, June tenth."

"You called it 'the night of the incident.' "

"Right," the man said, looking puzzled.

"It was your wording, you see, that caused me to wonder."

"Caused you to wonder what, Mr. Pennywell?"

"I meant . . ."

Liam gave up. "I don't know when I went to bed," he said. "Early, though."

"Early. Say eight?"

"Eight!" Liam was scandalized.

The policeman made another notation. "Eight o'clock. And how soon after that would you guess you fell asleep?" he asked.

"I would never go to bed at eight!"

"You just said—"

"I said 'early,' but I didn't mean *that* early."

"Well, when, then?"

"Nine, maybe," Liam told him. "Or, I don't know. What: you want me to make something up? I don't know what time! I'm completely at a loss here, don't you see? I don't remember a thing!"

The policeman crossed out his last notation. He closed his notebook in an ostentatiously patient and deliberate way and slid it into his pocket. "Tell you what," he said. "We'll check with you in a few days. Oftentimes a thing like this comes back to folks by and by."

"Let's hope so," Liam said.

"Pardon?"

"Let's hope it comes back!"

The policeman made a sort of gesture, half wave and half salute, and left.

Let's hope so, dear Lord in heaven. Even if it were some

violent, upsetting scene (well, of course it would be violent and upsetting), he needed to retrieve it.

He thought of those slapstick comedies where a character is beaned and conks out and forgets his own name; then he's somehow beaned again and magically he remembers.

Although even the thought of another blow to his head caused Liam to wince.

Too late, he realized that he should have asked the policeman some questions of his own. Had any of his belongings been stolen? Damaged? What state was his apartment in? Maybe Xanthe would know. He turned cautiously onto his side so that he was facing the doorway, watching for her return. Where *was* the girl? And how about her sisters? Weren't they going to visit? He seemed to be all alone, here.

But the next steps he heard were the squeegee soles of a tall skinny aide with a tray. "Supper," she told him.

"What time is it?" he asked. (The sky outside his window was still bright.)

She threw a glance at a giant wall clock that he somehow hadn't noticed before. Five twenty-five, she did not bother saying. She set his tray on a wheeled table and rolled it toward him. Jell-O, a steel pot dangling a tea-bag tab, and a plastic cup of apple juice. She left without another word. Inch by inch he hauled himself up and reached for the juice. It was sealed with a tight foil lid that turned out to be beyond him. Pulling it completely off took more strength than he could muster just now, and the harder he tried the more mess he made, because he had to squeeze the cup with his bandaged hand and the plastic kept squashing inward and spilling. Finally he lay back, exhausted. He wasn't hungry, anyhow.

The distressing thing about losing a memory, he thought, was that it felt like losing control. Something had happened, something significant, and he couldn't say how he'd comported himself. He didn't know if he had been calm, or terrified, or angry. He didn't know if he'd acted cowardly or heroic.

And here he'd always taken such pride in his total recall! He could quote entire passages from the Stoics—in the original Greek, if need be. Although remembering a personal event, he supposed, was somewhat different. He had never been the type who dwelt on bygones. He believed in moving on. (He used to tell his daughters, any time they threw one of those tiresome blame-the-parents fits, that people who are true adults do not keep rehashing their childhoods.) Still, this was the first time he had experienced an actual gap. A hole, it felt like. A hole in his mind, full of empty blue rushing air.

He had lain down in his new bedroom. He had felt grateful for his firm mattress and his bouncy foam-rubber pillow. His tucked-in top sheet, the open window, the stars beyond the pines . . .

By morning, the ache in his head had grown more localized. It was specific to his left temple. He believed he could detect a goose egg there, not from the contour of it, since his bandage was so thick, but from the way a certain spot leapt into full-blown pain before the surrounding area when he pressed tentatively with his fingers.

There was still no sign of Xanthe. Had she come and gone again while he was sleeping? A stream of other people passed through, though. A woman took his vital signs; another brought him breakfast. (Toast and eggs and cornflakes; he must have graduated to solids.) A third woman freed him of his IV tube and his catheter, after which he tottered into the bathroom on his own. In the mirror, he looked like a derelict. The white gauze helmet gave his skin a yellowish cast, and he had a stubble of gray whiskers on his cheeks and bags under his eyes.

Of course his scalp wound was impossible to see, but once he was safely in bed again he set to work unwinding the adhesive tape from his hand. Underneath he found blood-spotted gauze. Under that, two inches of coarse black stitches curved across his swollen and discolored palm. He was sorry now that he'd looked. He replaced the tape as best he could and lay back and stared at the ceiling.

If his attacker had knocked him out while he slept, the knot on his head would have been his only injury. It was clear, then, that he must have been awake. Either that, or he had awakened as soon as he heard a noise. He must have raised a hand to protect himself.

The woman who'd brought his breakfast tray returned for it and tut-tutted. "Now, how you going to get your strength back, not eating more than this?" she asked him.

"I did drink the coffee."

"Right; *that's* a big help."

Encouraged, he said, "I wonder if I could have a phone in my room."

"You don't have no phone?"

"No, and I need to call my daughter."

"I'll tell them at the desk," she said.

But the next woman who entered carried a compartmented box of medical supplies. "I'm Dr. Rodriguez," she told him. "I'm going to change your dressings before we send you home."

"Well, but my daughter's not here," he said.

"Your daughter."

"How will I get home on my own?"

"You won't. You're not allowed. Somebody has to drive you. And somebody has to keep an eye on you for the next forty-eight hours."

She set her supplies on his table and selected a pair of scissors sealed in cellophane. Liam doubted that she was past thirty. Her glowing olive skin lacked the slightest wrinkle, and her hair was inky black. Maybe you needed to be older to realize that it wasn't always easy to find someone who would stick around for forty-eight hours at a stretch.

He closed his eyes while she snipped at the gauze around his head, and then he felt a coolness and lightness as she pried it away. "Hmm," she said, once it was off. She peered closely, pursing her lips.

"What's it look like?"

She slid a drawer from beneath his table. For a moment he thought she was leaving his question unanswered, but it turned out she wanted to show him his reflection in a little pop-up mirror. He saw first a flash of his neck (old!) and then the side of his head, his short gray hair shaved away to reveal a purple swelling on his scalp and a shallow V of black threads dotted with dried blood.

"Fairly clean edges," the doctor said, folding away the mirror. "That's good." She unwrapped a square of gauze and stuck it in place with adhesive tape—no more helmet. "Your primary-care physician can take the stitches out. We'll give you written instructions when you leave. Now let me see your hand."

He held it up, and she unwound the tape without much interest and applied a fresh strip. "I'll write a prescription for pain pills too," she said, "just in case you need them."

She dumped the old dressings, the paper wrappers, and even the scissors into a red plastic bin. The scissors clattered so loudly that they hurt his head. Such wastefulness! Not even recycled! But he had more important things to discuss. "Is it all right to go home in a taxi?" he asked.

"Absolutely not. Somebody should be with you. Do you not have anybody? Should we be getting in touch with the social worker?"

For a minute he thought she was referring to Xanthe, who happened to be a social worker herself. When he realized his mistake, he flushed and said, "Oh, no, that won't be necessary."

"Well, good luck," she told him. She picked up her box of supplies and walked out.

As soon as she was gone, he pressed the call button on his bed rail.

"Yes?" a voice crackled from some invisible spot.

"Could I have a telephone, please?"

"I'll ask."

He sank back on his pillow and closed his eyes.

How could he have ended up so alone?

Two failed marriages (for he had to count Millie's death as a failure), three daughters who led their own lives, and a sister he seldom spoke to. The merest handful of friends— more like acquaintances, really. A promising youth that had somehow trailed off in a series of low-paying jobs far beneath his qualifications. Why, that last job had used about ten percent of his brain!

And he should have stood up for himself when they fired him. He should have pointed out that if they really needed to reduce the two fifth-grade classes to one, he ought to be the teacher they kept. He was way, way senior to Brian Medley. Brian was hired just two years ago! But instead he'd tried to put a good face on it. He'd tried to make Mr. Fairborn feel less guilty for letting him go. "Certainly," he had said. "I understand completely." And he had packed up his desk drawers when no one else was around to feel discomfited by the sight. Why make a scene? he had asked when Bundy voiced his outrage. "No sense clinging to resentments," he'd said.

He must not even have clothes to go home in. Not day clothes, at least; just pajamas. He was naked and alone and unprotected and unloved.

Well, this was just a mood he was in, created by current circumstances. He knew it wouldn't last.

Before they could bring him a telephone—if they ever planned to—his ex-wife arrived. Cheery and purposeful, hugging a paper grocery bag from which his favorite blue shirt poked forth, she breezed in already talking. "My goodness, what it takes to track a person down in this place! The switchboard said one room, the reception desk said another . . ."

Liam felt so relieved he was speechless. He stared round-eyed from his bed, clinging to the sight of her.

She was a medium sort of woman, medium in every way. Medium-length curly brown hair finely threaded with gray, medium-weight figure, and that lipstick-only makeup style that's meant not to draw attention to itself. Her clothes always looked slightly unkempt—the belt of her shirtwaist dress, today, rode inches above her waistline—but she would have gone unremarked in almost any gathering. He used to have trouble recalling her face when they were dating. This had seemed a plus, he remembered. Enough of those lovely, poetic, ethereal women who haunted a person's dreams!

"It's good to see you, Barbara," he told her finally. Then he had to clear his throat.

"How are you feeling?"

"I'm okay."

"*Awful* experience," she said blithely. "I can't imagine what the world is coming to." She sat down on the green vinyl chair and started rummaging through her bag, producing first the blue shirt and then a pair of over-the-calf black silk socks, not what he would have chosen to wear with the khakis she drew out next. "If you can't sleep safely in your own bed—"

Liam cleared his throat again. He said, "I don't think it was Damian, though."

"Damian?"

"Xanthe believes Damian was the one who clobbered me."

Barbara waved a hand and then bent to set his black dress shoes on the floor beside the bed. "I'm sure I brought underpants," she murmured, peering into the bag. "Ah. Here they are. Well, you know Xanthe. She thinks pot's the first step to perdition."

Barbara used to smoke a bit of pot herself, Liam recalled. She could surprise you sometimes. For all her medium looks and her stodgy school-librarian job, she'd had a fondness for rock music and she used to dance to it like a woman possessed, pumping the air with her soft white fists and sending her bobby pins flying in every direction. This was back in the days when they were still together, before she gave up on him and filed for divorce. Strange how distinctly, though, that image all at once presented itself. Maybe it was a side effect of the concussion.

"Do you still like Crack the Sky?" Liam asked her.

"What?" she said. "Oh, mercy, I haven't listened to Crack the Sky in ages! I'm sixty-two years old. Put your clothes on, will you? Heaven only knows when they'll spring you, but you might as well be ready once they do."

From the way she held out his underpants, stretching the waistband invitingly and cocking both her pinkies, it seemed she might be expecting him to step into them then and there. But he took them from her and gathered the rest of his clothes and padded off to the bathroom, clutching his hospital gown shut behind him with his free hand.

"After we get you settled at home," she called from her chair, "the girls and I will keep in touch by telephone to see that you're okay."

"Just by telephone?" he asked.

"Well, and Kitty's going to come spend the night with you as soon as she gets off work. She's found herself a summer job filing charts in our dentist's office."

"Your dentist's open on Sunday?"

"It's Monday."

"Oh."

"We'll phone and ask if you know your name, just to make sure you're *compos mentis*. Or where you live, or what day it is . . ." There was a sudden pause. Then she said, "You thought it was Sunday?"

"That could happen to anyone! I just lost track, is all."

He had to sit on the toilet lid to put his socks on; his balance seemed a bit off. And bending down made his head throb.

"They told us you should be under constant observation, but this is the best we can manage," he heard through the slit in the door. "Xanthe works such impossible hours, and Louise of course has Jonah."

She didn't say why *she* couldn't do it, with her luxurious summer schedule, but Liam didn't point that out. He shuffled from the bathroom in his stocking feet, holding up his trousers. (Barbara seemed to have forgotten his belt.) "Could you hand me my shoes, please?" he said as he sat on the edge of the bed.

"Forty-eight hours is the amount of time they told us," she said. She bent for a shoe and, without being asked, fitted it onto his foot and tugged the laces snug and tied them. He felt well-tended and submissive, like a child. She said, "I did call your sister. Has she been in touch?"

"This room doesn't have a phone."

"Well, she'll probably call once you're home. I told her you'd be discharged today. She wants you to get a burglar alarm as soon as possible."

He nodded, not bothering to argue, and raised his other foot.

Then there was a period of limbo while they waited for his paperwork. Barbara took a crossword puzzle from her grocery bag, and Liam lay back on the bed, shoes and all, and stared at the ceiling.

The few times he'd been hospitalized before, he could hardly wait to leave, he remembered. He'd pressed his call button repeatedly and kept sending whoever was with him out to the nurses' station to see what the holdup was. But now he was grateful for the delay. At least here, he wasn't alone. He felt lazy and content, and the sound of Barbara's pencil whispering across the paper almost put him to sleep.

Imagine he was a man who lived in the hospital permanently. He'd been born here and he had somehow never left. His meals, his clothes, his activities—all taken care of. No wonder, therefore, he had forgotten how he had arrived! He had been here all along; this was the sum of his world. There was nothing more to remember.

Eventually, though, a nurse came with his prescriptions and instructions. She perched on the very edge of his bed, giving off a smell of mouthwash, and went over the doctor's orders line by line. "You can't be alone for the next two days, and you can't drive your car for a week," she said.

"A week!"

"Longer than that if you experience the slightest sense of vertigo."

"You're being unreasonable," Liam told her.

"And it's crucial to complete the full course of antibiotics. There is nothing on earth more septic than the bite of another human being."

"A what?" he said. "A bite?"

"The bite on your hand."

"I was *bitten?*"

A sickish zoom hit the bottom of his stomach, as if an elevator had dropped. Even Barbara looked taken aback.

"Well, not on purpose, maybe," the nurse said. "But from the shape of the wound, they think you must have flailed out and made contact with the other guy's teeth."

She gave him a smile that was probably meant to be reassuring. "So it is very, very important to take these pills for the full ten days," she said. "Not nine days, not eight days . . ."

Liam lay back and covered his eyes with his good hand. On purpose or not, there was something so . . . intimate about a stranger's biting him.

After that they had the usual endless wait for a wheelchair, and Barbara used the time to go off to the hospital pharmacy and get his prescriptions filled. Liam picked up her crossword puzzle and studied it while she was gone. *Famous WWII battlefield* and *Birthplace of FDR* and *Palindromic Ms. Gardner*—she had known them all, good librarian that she was, and so did Liam, or at least he recognized her answers as correct once he saw them. But *Stressful occupation?* gave him an itch of anxiety deep inside his skull, the way riddles used to when he was a child. *Poet*, Barbara had answered, so confidently that the cross of the *T* flew tip-tilted across the upright. He felt overcome with discouragement, and he dropped the puzzle onto the bed.

It was nearly eleven a.m.—Barbara long back from the pharmacy and deep in a novel—before an orderly arrived with a wheelchair and they were free to go. Shifting from the bed to the wheelchair made Liam realize that he didn't have his wallet. He missed the pressure of that slight bulge in his rear pocket when he sat. "How did they admit me?" he asked Barbara.

"What do you mean?" she said. She was trotting down the hall behind him, keeping pace with the orderly.

"I mean, without my insurance card and ID."

"Oh, Xanthe gave them the information once she got here. I have your insurance card now in my purse; don't let me forget to return it."

He pictured how it must have been—his flaccid, unaware form heaved onto a stretcher, loaded into an ambulance, trundled through the emergency room. It was the most unsettling sensation. "Depending on the kindness of strangers," he said.

"Excuse me?"

"Nothing."

But as soon as they were alone—as soon as she'd brought her car around and the orderly had settled him inside it—he told her, "I hate, hate, hate not remembering how this happened."

"It's probably just as well," she said.

She was fumbling in her pocketbook, and she sounded distracted. He waited until she'd paid at the parking booth before he spoke again. "It is *not* just as well," he said. "I'm missing a piece of my life. I lie down one night; I go to sleep; I wake up in a hospital room. Can you imagine how that feels?"

"You don't have any recollection whatsoever? Like, hearing a suspicious noise? Seeing somebody in the doorway?"

"Nothing."

"Maybe it will come back to you when you get into bed tonight."

"Ah," he said. He thought about it. "Yes, that makes sense."

"You know how sometimes you dream about someone, and you forget you dreamed at all but then you happen to see that person and this sort of inkling will flit across your mind . . ."

"Yes, it's possible," Liam said.

They stopped for a traffic light, and he suddenly felt impatient to be home. He would lie down on his bed immediately and see if the memory wafted up from his pillow the way his past dreams often did. Probably nothing would come until dark, but it wouldn't hurt to try earlier.

"If it were me, though," Barbara said, "I'd be happier not knowing."

"You say that now. I bet you wouldn't feel that way if it really happened."

"And how about your nerves? Do you really think you'll be able to sleep comfortably in that apartment again?"

"Of course," he said.

She sent him such a long doubtful glance that the car behind them honked; the light had changed to green. "I'd be terrified, myself," she said as she stepped on the gas.

"Well, I *will* lock the patio door from now on. Do you know how you would lock one of those plate-glass doors that slides sideways?"

"There's a thingamajig, I believe. We'll look."

This implied that she would be coming in with him, and he was happy to hear it. It wasn't fear of another break-in he felt so much as distrust of his own capabilities. He had lost his self-confidence. He wasn't sure anymore that he was fully in charge. Intruders were the least of his worries.

Barbara parked in the proper lot without his directing her. Obviously she had grown familiar with his apartment. And she had his keys in her purse—his worn calfskin key case with his car key and his door key. She took them out as she was waiting for him to inch forth from the passenger seat. (Standing up too fast made his head go spacey.) "Want an arm?" she asked him, but he said, "I'm all right." And he was, once he'd waited for the amoebas to clear from his vision.

The pine needles gave off a nice toasty scent in the sunshine, but the foyer smelled as cold and basement-like as ever. Barbara unlocked his front door and then stood back to let him go first. "Now, the girls and I did clean up a little," she said.

"Did it need it?"

"Well, somewhat."

He wasn't sure what she meant when he first entered, because the living room looked just the way he'd left it: more or less in order if you didn't count the few unpacked cartons lined up along one wall. He moved down the hall past the den, Barbara close on his heels, and saw nothing different there, either. But when he reached the bedroom, he found a runner of brown wrapping paper on the carpet leading toward the bed. And the bed was fitted with linens that he had never seen before—an anemic light-blue blanket, slightly pilled, and sheets sprinkled with flowers. He had avoided patterned sheets ever since a childhood fever in which the polka dots on his sheets had swarmed like insects.

"We rented one of those carpet shampooers from the supermarket," Barbara said. "But the carpet's not completely dry yet; you'll have to walk on the paper a while. And your sheets and blanket were, well, I'm sorry; we put them in the trash. I didn't know where you kept your extras."

"Oh," he said. "I see."

He stood there in a daze, looking slowly from bed to window to closet. Everything seemed benign and ordinary and somehow not quite his own. But maybe that was because it *wasn't* quite his own; he had so recently moved in.

"Was anything taken?" he asked.

"We don't think so, but you're the only one who'll be able to say for sure. The police are going to come back and interview you later. We did see that the drawer was yanked out in that table between the armchairs, and there wasn't anything in it but we didn't know if that meant something was missing or you just hadn't filled it yet."

"No, it was empty," he said.

He walked into the room, his shoes scuffing across the brown paper, and sat on the edge of the bed and continued gazing around him. Barbara watched from the doorway. "Are you all right?" she asked him.

"Yes, fine."

"Really the police made more mess than the burglar, I think. And the ambulance people."

"Well, it was nice of you to clean up," he said. His lips moved woodenly, as if they too were not quite his own.

"Louise was the one who rented the carpet shampooer; Louise and Dougall. You might want to offer to pay them back; you know they're not rolling in money."

"Yes, certainly," Liam said.

"Are you sure you're all right, Liam?"

"Of course."

"I'd be happy to get you something before I go."

She was going?

"A cup of coffee, or tea," she said. "Or maybe a bowl of soup."

"No, thanks," he said. The thought of food made him want to gag.

"Okay, then. I'll put your insurance card here on the bureau. Don't forget to take your pills."

"I'll remember."

She hesitated. Then she said, "Well, so, Kitty should be here around six. And meanwhile you have my number in case anything goes wrong."

"Thank you, Barbara."

She left.

He sat motionless until he heard the front door shut, and then he lifted his feet onto the bed and lay back. His pillow-case smelled of some unfamiliar detergent. And the pillow inside was unfamiliar as well—filled with feathers or goose down, something that sank in and stayed there.

He knew that he should be thankful to Barbara for even this much. It wasn't as if she were responsible for him any longer.

But hadn't she promised to check the lock on the patio door?

Outside his window he saw pine boughs, almost black even in daylight, and a sky as blue as bottle glass. No stars, of course. Nothing connected with that night.

He must get up. He had things to do. He would fix himself a nice lunch and force himself to eat it. He would find out which box his linens were in and set them out on the daybed for Kitty. Maybe finish his unpacking, too. Break down the last of the cartons for the recycling bin.

But he went on lying there, looking not at the window now but at the bedroom door, and summoning up the image of a hulking figure emerging from darkness. Or a small, slight, sneaky figure. Or maybe two figures; why only one?

Nothing came. His mind was a blank. He had heard that expression a thousand times, *mind was a blank*, but only now did he understand that a mind really could be as blank and white and textureless as a sheet of unused paper.

3

Kitty arrived with a duffel bag almost bigger than she was. She carried it slung over her shoulder, and the weight forced her to stand at a steep slant in the doorway—a tiny person in a halter top and minuscule denim shorts, with chopped-looking, sand-colored hair and a quick, alert little face. "Poppy!" she said. (She was the only daughter who called him that.) "You look like you've been run over!"

Even so, she shucked off her bag and heaved it into his arms. His knees buckled as he received it. "What's in here, the kitchen sink?" he asked, but secretly, he was pleased. She must be planning to stay a while.

He stood still for a fleeting kiss on the cheek and then followed her into the living room, where she threw herself into an armchair. "I am so, so tired of old ladies," she said. "There's not a patient in that office who's under ninety, I swear."

"Oh, and, ah, is that how you dress for work?" he asked.

"Huh? No, I changed before I left. You would not believe my uniform. It's polyester! And pink!"

He set her bag on the floor beside her. (In his current condition, he couldn't imagine lugging it all the way to the den.) Then he lowered himself into the other armchair. "What do you think of my apartment?" he asked.

"Your old one had a fireplace."

"I never used it, though."

"And your old one didn't have homicidal maniacs climbing through the window."

"Door," he said. He pressed his hands between his knees. "But one assumes that won't be an everyday occurrence."

Kitty didn't look convinced. "Anyway," she said. "Let's see: what am I supposed to ask. Do you know what year this is? Can you tell me your last name?"

"Yes, yes . . ."

"And you don't feel dizzy or sleepy?"

"Certainly not," he said.

In fact, he had slept for most of the afternoon, waking only for check-up calls from Louise, Louise again, and his sister. He had been troubled by strange, vivid dreams and some sort of olfactory hallucination—a smell of vinegar—but he had answered each of the calls in his brightest voice. "Yes, *fine*, thanks! *Thank* you for calling!" Louise had seemed reassured, but his sister, who knew him better, was harder to deceive. "Are you positive you're all right?" she had asked. "Do you think I ought to come over?"

"That would be a waste of your time. I'm fine. And Kitty's due here shortly," he'd said.

"Oh. Well, okay."

She was glad to be let off the hook, he could tell. (He knew her pretty well, too.) They didn't actually set eyes on each other more than once or twice a year.

Kitty was examining the lamp table next to her chair. She pulled out the drawer and peered inside. "What was in here?" she asked Liam. "Any valuables?"

"Nothing."

"Nothing at all?"

"It's usually got, you know, pens and pencils and memo pads, but I hadn't unpacked them yet. In fact, as far as I can tell, I'm not missing a single thing. My wallet was still on the bureau, even—the first place you'd think a burglar would look. I guess he just didn't have time."

"Lucky," Kitty said.

"Lucky, right. Except . . ."

Kitty was bending over now to rummage in the outside pocket of her duffel bag. She drew forth a flat, silvery computer of the type that Liam believed was called a "notebook," a rather attractive pink iPod, and finally a cell phone no bigger than a fun-size candy bar. (So much equipment, these young people seemed to need!) She flipped the phone open and put it to her ear and said, "Hello?" And then, after a moment, "Well, *sorry*! I had it on Vibrate. Yes, of course I'm here. Where else would I be? *Yes.* He's fine. You want to talk to him?"

Liam sat forward expectantly, but Kitty said, "Oh. Okay. Bye." She snapped the phone shut and told Liam, "Mom."

"She didn't want to talk to me?"

"Nope. That woman is eternally checking up on me. She thinks I might be with Damian."

"Ah."

"This business about me staying with you? It's just an excuse. Really she wants to make sure I'm properly chaperoned every everlasting minute, and now that she's got a boyfriend she's too busy to do it herself, so she ships me off to you."

"Your mom has a boyfriend?" Liam asked.

"Or something like that."

"I didn't realize."

But Kitty was punching phone keys. "Hey," she said. "What's up."

Liam collected himself with some effort and rose to see about supper.

The smell of vinegar persisted. It seemed to emanate from his own skin. He asked Kitty over supper (canned asparagus soup and saltines), "Do I smell like vinegar to you?"

"Huh?"

"I keep thinking I smell like vinegar."

She fixed him with a suspicious stare and said, "Do you know what year this is?"

"Stop asking me that!"

"Mom told me to. It's not *my* idea."

"Half the time I don't know what year it is anyhow," he said, "unless I take a minute to think. The years have started flying past so fast that I can't keep track. You'll see that for yourself, by and by."

But Kitty appeared to have lost interest in the subject. She was crushing saltines into her soup with the back of her spoon. Her fingers were long and flexible, ending in nail-bitten nubbins—lemur fingers, Liam thought. He wasn't sure she had taken so much as a mouthful of soup yet. When she felt his eyes on her, she looked up. "I'm going to have to sleep in the room he broke into, aren't I," she said.

"Pardon?"

"The room where the burglar came in. I saw that door! That's the one he entered through, isn't it."

"Well, but then it wasn't locked. Now it is," Liam said. He had checked the lock himself, earlier. It was a little up-and-down lever arrangement, not complicated at all. "If you like, though," he said, "I can sleep there."

So much for letting his memory come back to him in the dark. But already he had begun to admit that that wasn't likely to happen.

"Seems to me you'd be scared too," Kitty told him. "I would think you'd have the heebie-jeebies forever after! Living in the place where you were attacked."

"Now that I *have* been attacked, though, I somehow feel that means I won't be attacked again," he said. "As if a quota has been reached, so to speak. I realize that's not logical."

"Durn right it's not logical. Guy breaks in, sees all the loot, doesn't have time to grab it . . . More logical is, he decides to come back for it later."

"What loot?" Liam asked. "I don't have any jewels, or silver, or electronics. What would he come back for, except that wallet with seven dollars in it?"

"*He* doesn't know it's seven dollars."

"Well, I hardly think—"

"Is seven dollars *it*?"

"What?"

"Is that all you've got in the world?"

Liam began to laugh. "You've heard of banks, I trust," he said.

"How much do you have in the bank?"

"Really, Kitty!"

"Mom says you're a pauper."

"Your mother doesn't know everything," he said. And then, "Who is this so-called boyfriend of hers?"

Kitty batted the question away with a flick of her hand. "She's worried you'll end up on the streets, what with getting fired and all."

"I wasn't fired, I was ... downsized. And I have a perfectly adequate savings account. You tell her that. Besides which," he said, "I did turn sixty in January." He let a significant pause develop.

The pause was for Kitty to realize that she had forgotten his birthday. His whole family had forgotten, with the exception of his sister, who always sent a Hallmark card. But Kitty just said, "What's that got to do with it?"

"After fifty-nine and a half, I'm allowed to draw on my pension."

"Right; I bet that's a fortune."

"Well, it's not as if I need very much. I've never been an acquirer."

Kitty dropped another saltine in her soup and said, "I'll say you're not an acquirer. When I went into the den I was like, 'Whoa! Oh, my God! The burglar guy stole the TV!' Then I remembered you don't even own a TV. I mean, I knew that before but I just never put it all together. I'm going to miss all my shows while I'm here! There isn't a single TV anywhere in this apartment!"

"I don't know how you're going to survive," Liam said.

"I'll bet the burglar looked around and thought, Great; someone's beaten me to it. Everything's already been ripped off, he thought."

"Funny how people always assume a burglar's a he," Liam said. "Aren't there any women burglars? Somehow you never hear of them."

Kitty tipped part of her milk into her soup. Then she started stirring her soup around and around, dreamily.

"I keep trying to put a face on him. Or her," Liam said. "I'm sure it must be somewhere in my subconscious, don't you think? You can't imagine how it feels to know you've been through something so catastrophic and yet there's no trace of it in your mind. I almost wish you all hadn't cleared away the evidence. Not that I don't appreciate it; I don't mean that. But it's as if I've been excluded from my own experience. Other people know more about it than I do. For instance, how bad were my bed sheets? Were they *soaked* with blood, solid red? Or just spattered here and there."

"Yuck," Kitty said.

"Well, sorry, but—"

A throaty rasp started up, like the sound a toad or a frog would make. Kitty lunged out of her chair and grabbed her cell phone from the coffee table. "Hello?" she said. And then, "Hey."

Liam sighed and set his spoon down. He hadn't made much headway with his soup, and Kitty's bowl was fuller than when she had started—a disgusting mush of crackers and swirled milk. Maybe tomorrow they should eat out someplace.

"Oh . . ." she was saying. "Oh, um . . . *you* know"—clearly responding in code.

Liam's hands had a parched look that he had never noticed before, and his fingers trembled slightly when he held them up. Also, the vinegar smell was still bothering him. He was sure it must be obvious to other people.

This was not his true self, he wanted to say. This was not who he really was. His true self had gone away from him and had a crucial experience without him and failed to come back afterward.

He knew he was making too much of this.

Liam had once had a pupil named Buddy Morrow who suffered from various learning issues. This was back in the days when Liam taught ancient history, and he had been paid an arm and a leg to come to Buddy's house twice a week and drill him on his reading about the Spartans and the Macedonians. Anyone could have done it, of course. It didn't require special knowledge. But the parents were quite well off, and they believed in hiring experts. The father was a neurologist. A very successful neurologist. A world-renowned authority on insults to the brain.

Liam liked the phrase "insults to the brain." In fact it might not be a phrase that Dr. Morrow himself had used; he might have said "*injuries* to the brain." He'd said neither one to Liam, in any case. They'd talked only about Buddy's progress, on the few occasions they'd spoken.

Still, on Tuesday morning at 8:25 Liam telephoned Dr. Morrow's office. He chose the time deliberately, having given it a good deal of thought in the middle of the night when Dr. Morrow's name first occurred to him. He reasoned that there must be a patients' call-in hour, and that probably this was either prior to nine a.m. or at midday. Eight a.m. until nine, he was betting. But he had to wait till after Kitty left for work, because he didn't want her overhearing. She left at 8:23, walking to the bus stop beside the mall. He was on the phone two minutes later.

He told the receptionist the truth: he was Dr. Morrow's son's ex-teacher, not an official patient, but he was hoping the doctor might be able to answer a quick question about some aftereffects of a blow to his head. The receptionist—who sounded more like a middle-aged waitress than the icy young twit he'd expected—clucked and said, "Well, hold on, hon; let me check."

The next voice he heard was Dr. Morrow's own, tired and surprisingly elderly. "Yes?" he said. "This is Dr. Morrow."

"Dr. Morrow, this is Liam Pennywell. I don't know if you remember me."

"Ah, yes! The philosopher."

Liam felt gratified, even though he thought he detected an undertone of amusement. He said, "I'm sorry to phone you out of the blue, but I was recently knocked unconscious and I've been experiencing some very troubling symptoms."

"What sort of symptoms?" the doctor asked.

"Well, memory loss."

"Short-term memory?"

"Not short, exactly. But not long-term either. More like . . . intermediate."

"*Intermediate* memory?"

"I can't remember being hit."

"Oh, that's very common," Dr. Morrow said. "Very much to be expected. Are you currently under medical care?"

"Yes, but . . . In the hospital I was, but . . . Dr. Morrow, I hate to presume, but could I come in and talk to you?"

"Talk," the doctor said thoughtfully.

"Just for a couple of minutes? Oh, I do have insurance. I have health insurance. I mean, this would be a purely professional consultation."

"What are you doing right now?" the doctor asked.

"Now?"

"Could you make it here before nine fifteen?"

"Certainly!" Liam said.

He had no idea if he could make it; the phone book had listed a downtown address and he was way, way up near . . . oh, Lord, he should never have moved. He was way up near the Beltway! But he said, "I'll be there in half a second. Thank you, Dr. Morrow. I can't tell you how I appreciate this."

"Half a second exactly," the doctor said, and the undertone of amusement seemed to have returned to his voice.

Liam had on a more casual outfit than he would normally wear in public: a stretched-out polo shirt and khakis with one torn belt loop. No time to change, though. All he did was switch his slippers for sneakers. Bending down to tie them made his head throb, which he welcomed. He wanted as many symptoms as possible if he was presenting his case to a doctor.

In the parking lot, the throbbing in his head was bothersome enough to make him try to slide straight-backed into his car, bending only at the knees. He had just made it onto the seat when a woman shrieked, "What are you *doing?*"

He turned to find an aged blue sedan pulled up behind

him. His middle daughter was glaring at him through her open side window, and his grandson sat in the back. "Why, Louise," Liam said. "Good to see you! Sorry, but I'm in a bit of a—"

"You know you're not supposed to be driving!"

"Oh."

"They told you at the hospital! I came all the way over here in case you needed some errands run."

"Well, isn't that nice of you," he said. "Maybe you could take me to the neurologist's office."

"Where's that?"

"Down on St. Paul," he said. He was climbing out of his car now, trying once again not to lower his head by so much as an inch. It was lucky Louise had happened along; he hadn't realized how woozy he felt. He shuffled around the hood of her car to the passenger side and got in.

"It's going to pull like anything when you yank that bandage off," Louise said, peering at his scalp.

She had Barbara's dark coloring but not her softness; there was always a sort of edge to her, especially when she squinted like this. Liam shrank away from her gaze and said, "Yes, well." He began fumbling through his pockets. "Now, somewhere or other—" he muttered. "Aha." He held up a torn-off corner from a Chinese menu. "Dr. Morrow's address."

Louise glanced at it briefly before putting her car in gear. Liam turned to look at his grandson. "Jonah!" he said. "Hey, there!"

"Hi."

"What've you been up to?"

"Nothing."

In Liam's opinion, the child lacked verve. He was . . .

what, three years old? No, four; four and a half, but he still sat in one of those booster seats, docile as a little blond puppet, with a teddy bear clutched to his chest. Liam considered starting on a whole new subject but it didn't seem worth the effort, and eventually he faced forward again.

Louise said, "I was thinking you might need groceries brought, or a prescription filled. Nobody mentioned a doctor's appointment."

"This was sort of last-minute," Liam told her.

"Is something wrong?"

"No, no."

Louise made a wide U-turn and headed out the entranceway, ignoring several arrows pointing in the opposite direction. Liam gripped the dashboard but made no attempt to set her straight.

"Although I do, ah, seem to be having a little trouble with my memory," he said finally.

He was hoping they might get into a discussion about it, but instead she said, "I guess it was pretty creepy staying in the apartment last night."

"Not at all," he said. "Kitty was a bit nervous, though. I had to give her the bedroom."

This reminded him; he said, "I believe I owe you some money for the rug shampooer."

"Don't worry about that," Louise said.

"No, I insist," he said. "How much was it?"

"You can pay me back when you get a job," she told him.

"A job. Well . . ."

"Have you filled out any applications yet?"

"I'm not sure I even want to," he said. "It's possible I'll retire."

"Retire! You're sixty years old!"

"Exactly."

"What would you do with yourself?"

"Why, there's plenty I could do," he said. "I could read, I could think . . . I'm not a man without resources, you know."

"You're going to sit all day and just *think*?"

"Or also . . . I have options! I have lots of possibilities. In fact," he said spontaneously, "I might become a zayda."

"A what?"

"It's an adjunct position at a preschool out on Reisterstown Road," he said. He was proud of himself for coming up with this; he hadn't thought of it in weeks. "One of the parents at St. Dyfrig mentioned there was an opening. They use senior citizens as, so to speak, grandparent figures in the younger children's classrooms. Zayda is the Jewish word for grandfather."

"You aren't Jewish, though."

"No, but the preschool is."

"And you aren't a senior citizen, either. Besides, this sounds to me like a volunteer position. Are you sure it's not volunteer?"

"No, no, I would be paid."

"How much?"

"Oh . . ." he said. Then he said, "What *is* it with you girls? All of a sudden you seem to think you have a right to pry into my finances."

"For good reason," Louise told him. She slowed for a light. She said, "And don't even get me started on the obvious irony, here."

"What's that?"

"Grandfather!" she said. "You, of all people!"

He raised his eyebrows.

"Do you even *like* small children?" she asked.

"Of course I like them!"

"Huh," she said.

Liam turned once more to look at Jonah. Jonah sent back a milky blue gaze that gave no indication what he was thinking.

They entered the city limits and traveled through Liam's old neighborhood—dignified, elderly buildings grouped around the Hopkins campus. Liam felt a pang of homesickness. Resolutely, he steered his thoughts toward the new place: its purity, its stripped-down angularity. Louise (a mind reader, like both of her sisters) said, "You could always move back."

"Move back! Why would I want to do that?"

"I doubt your old apartment's been rented yet, has it?"

"I'm very content where I am," he said. "I have a refrigerator now that dispenses water through the door."

Louise just flicked her turn signal on. Behind her, Jonah started singing his ABCs in a thin, flat, tuneless voice. Liam turned to flash what he hoped was an appreciative smile, but Jonah was looking out his side window and didn't notice.

Imagine naming a child Jonah. That was surely Dougall's doing—Louise's husband. Dougall was some kind of fundamentalist Christian. He and Louise had dated all through high school and married right after graduation, over everyone's objections, and then Dougall went into his family's plumbing business while Louise, a straight-A student, abandoned any thought of college and gave birth in short order to

Jonah. "Why Jonah?" Liam had asked. "What's next: Judas? Herod? Cain?" Louise had looked puzzled. "I mean, Jonah's was not a very *happy* story, was it?" Liam asked.

All Louise said was, "I do know someone named Cain, in fact."

"Does he happen to have a brother?" Liam asked.

"Not that I ever heard of."

"*Inn*-teresting," Liam said.

"Hmm?"

Joining the Book of Life Tabernacle had done nothing for her sense of humor.

Dr. Morrow's office turned out to be just below Fender Street, in an ornate old building squeezed between a dry cleaner's and a pawnshop. Parking, of course, was impossible. Louise said, "You hop on out and I'll find a space around the block." Liam didn't argue. According to his watch, it was 9:10. He wondered if Dr. Morrow would restrict him to a mere five minutes.

The lobby had a high, sculptured ceiling and a marble floor gridded with seams of brass. An actual person—an ancient black man in full uniform—operated the elevator, sitting on a wooden stool and sliding the accordion door shut with a white-gloved hand. Liam was amazed. When the only other passenger, a woman in a silk dress, said, "Three, please," he felt he had been transported back to his childhood, to one of the old downtown department stores where his mother could spend hours fingering bolts of fabric. "Sir?" the operator asked him.

"Oh. Four, please," Liam said.

Four was jarringly modern, carpeted wall to wall in businesslike gray and lined overhead with acoustical tiles. A disappointment, but also a relief. (You wouldn't want your neurologist to be *too* old-fashioned.)

An entire column of doctors' names marched down the plate-glass door of Suite 401, beneath larger lettering that read *ST. PAUL NEUROLOGY ASSOCIATES*. Even at this early hour, there were quite a few patients in the waiting room. They sat on molded plastic chairs under the bank of receptionists' windows—a separate window for each doctor. Dr. Morrow's receptionist had dyed black hair that made her look less cozy than she had sounded on the phone. The minute Liam gave her his name, she handed him a clipboard with a form to fill out. "I'll need to make a copy of your insurance card, too, and your driver's license," she said. Liam had been sincere when he told Dr. Morrow he intended to pay, but somehow he still felt taken aback by the woman's crass commercialism.

The other patients were in terrible shape. Good Lord, neurology was a distressing specialty! One man shook so violently that his cane kept falling to the floor. A woman held an oversized child who seemed boneless. Another woman kept wiping her blank-faced husband's mouth with a tissue. Oh, Liam should not be here. He had no business frittering away the doctor's time on such a trivial complaint. But even so, he continued printing out his new address in large, distinct block letters.

Louise and Jonah came in and settled across from him, although there were seats free on either side of him. Nobody would have guessed they had anything to do with him. They didn't look his way, and Louise immediately started searching through the magazines on the table to her left. Eventually she came up with a children's magazine. "Look!" she told

Jonah. "Baby rabbits! You love baby rabbits!" Jonah clutched his teddy bear tightly and followed her pointing finger.

To be honest, Liam thought, the Pennywells were a rather *homely* family. (Himself included.) Louise's hair was too short and her face too angular. She had on boxy red pedal pushers, not a flattering style for anyone, and flip-flops that showed her long white bony feet. Jonah was breathing through his mouth and he wore a slack, stunned expression as he gazed down at the page.

In a low, clear voice just inches from Liam's right ear, a woman said, "Verity."

Liam started and turned.

This was someone young and plump and ringleted, wearing a voluminous Indian-print skirt and cloddish, handmade-looking sandals. One hand was linked through the arm of an old man in a suit.

Liam said, "What?"

But she had already passed him by. She and the old man—her father?—were approaching Dr. Morrow's receptionist. When they reached the window, she dropped the old man's arm and stepped back. The old man told the receptionist, "Why, Verity! Good morning! Don't you look gorgeous today!"

The receptionist said, "Thank you, Mr. Cope," and she lifted a hand to her dyed hair. "Just have a seat and Dr. Morrow will see you shortly."

When the couple turned from the window, Liam lowered his eyes so they wouldn't know he'd been watching them. They took the two chairs next to Jonah. Louise was saying, "Just then, a big, big lion came out from behind the tree," and neither she nor Jonah glanced in their direction.

"Mr. Pennywell?" a nurse called from the far end of the room.

Liam rose and went over to where she stood waiting. "How are *you* today?" she asked him.

"Fine, thanks," he said. "Or, I mean, *sort* of fine . . ." but she had already turned to lead him down a corridor.

At the end of the corridor, in a tiny office, Dr. Morrow sat writing something behind an enormous desk. Liam would not have known him. The man had aged past recognition— his red hair a tarnished pink now, and his many freckles faded into wide beige splotches across his face. He wore a sports jacket rather than a white coat, and the only sign of his profession was the plaster model of a brain on the bookcase behind him. "Ah," he said, setting down his pen. "Mr. Penny-well," and he half rose in a creaky, stiff way to shake hands.

"It's good of you to make time for me," Liam said.

"No trouble at all; no trouble at all. Yes, you do have a bit of a nick there."

Liam turned the wounded side of his head toward the doctor, in case he might like to examine it more closely, but Dr. Morrow sank back onto his chair and laced his fingers across his shirtfront. "Let's see: how long has it been?" he asked Liam. "Nineteen eighty, eighty-one . . ."

"Eighty-two," Liam told him. He was able to say for sure because it had been his last year at the Fremont School.

"Twenty-some years! Twenty-four; good God. And you're still teaching?"

"Oh, yes," Liam said. (No sense getting sidetracked by any long involved explanations.)

"Still hoping to stuff a little history into those rascally Fremont boys," Dr. Morrow said, chuckling in his new elderly way.

"Well, ah, actually it's St. Dyfrig boys now," Liam admitted.

"Oh?" Dr. Morrow frowned.

"And, um, fifth grade."

"Fifth grade!"

"But anyway," Liam said hastily. "Tell me how Buddy's doing."

"Well, these days we call him Haddon, of course."

"Why would you do that?"

"Well, Haddon is his name."

"Oh."

"Yes, Haddon's all grown up now—turned forty back in April, would you believe it? Has his own trucking company. Statewide. *Very* successful, considering."

"I'm delighted to hear it."

"You were awfully kind to him," Dr. Morrow said, and all at once his voice sounded different—not so bluff and pompous. "I haven't forgotten the patience you showed."

"Oh, well," Liam said, shifting in his seat.

"Yours was about the only course he managed to get fired up about, as I recall. Seneca! Wasn't that who he wrote his paper on? Yes, we used to hear quite a lot about Seneca at the dinner table. Seneca's suicide! Big news, as if it happened yesterday."

Liam gave a little laugh that came out sounding oddly like Dr. Morrow's chuckle.

"I'll have to tell him I saw you," Dr. Morrow said. "Haddon will get a kick out of that. But enough chitchat; let's hear about your injury."

"*Oh* yes," Liam said, as if that had not been uppermost on

his mind the whole time. "Well, evidently I was struck on the head and knocked unconscious."

"Is that so! By someone you knew?"

"Why, no," Liam said.

"Lord, Lord, what's the world coming to?" Dr. Morrow asked. "Have they caught the assailant?"

"Uh, not that I've heard," Liam said.

The word *assailant* momentarily derailed him. It was one of those words you saw only in print, like *apparel*. Or *slain*. Or . . . what was that other word he'd noticed?

"And yet they claim they're working to make this city safer," Dr. Morrow said.

"Actually, I live in the county," Liam told him.

"Oh, really."

Exclaimed. That was another word you saw only in print.

"But the point is," Liam said, "I was hit and knocked unconscious, and I don't remember anything more till I woke up in a hospital bed."

"They did a CT scan, I assume."

"That's what I'm told."

"And they found no sign of intracranial bleeding."

"No, but . . ."

Barbara used to say that he didn't phrase things strongly enough when he visited his doctor. She'd ask, "Did you tell him about your back? Did you tell him you were in agony?" and Liam would say, "Well, I mentioned I was experiencing some discomfort." Barbara would roll her eyes. So now he leaned forward in his chair. "I have a very, very serious concern," he said. "I really need to talk about this. I feel I'm going crazy."

"Crazy! You told me memory loss."

"I'm going crazy over my memory loss."

"What is it you don't remember, exactly?"

"Anything whatsoever involving the attack," Liam said. "All I know is, I went to bed, I slid under my covers, I looked out the window . . . and *pouf*! There I am in a hospital room. A whole chunk of time has vanished. Someone broke into my apartment and I must have woken up, because they say I got this hand injury fighting off the . . . assailant. Then a neighbor called 911, and the police came and the ambulance, but every bit of that is absent from my mind."

"You do remember other things, though," Dr. Morrow said. "The time before you went to bed. The time after you woke in the hospital."

"Yes, all of that. Just not the attack."

"Nor will you ever, I venture to say. People always hope for some soap-opera moment where everything comes back to them. But the memories surrounding a head trauma are gone forever, in most cases. As a matter of fact, you're fairly unusual in recalling as much as you do. Some victims forget days and days leading up to the event, and they have only spotty recollections of the days afterward. Consider yourself fortunate."

"Fortunate," Liam said, with a twist of his mouth.

"And why would you even *want* to remember such an experience?"

"You don't understand," Liam said.

He knew he had used up his time. A new tension had crept into the room's atmosphere; the doctor's posture had grown more erect. But this was important. Liam gripped his knees. "I feel I've lost something," he said. "A part of my life has been stolen from me. I don't care if it was unpleasant; I need to know what it was. I want it back. I'd give anything to get it back! I wish I had someone like the . . . rememberer out in your waiting room."

Dr. Morrow said, "The what?"

"The young woman who's bringing in her, I don't know, her father, I guess, to see you. He seems to need reminding of names and such and she's right there at his elbow, feeding him clues."

"Ah, yes," Dr. Morrow said, and his expression cleared. "Yes, couldn't we *all* use a rememberer, as you call her, after a certain age. And wouldn't we all like to have Mr. Cope's money to pay her with."

"He pays her?"

"She's a hired assistant, I believe," the doctor said. But then he must have worried that he had committed an indiscretion, because he rose abruptly and came around to the front of his desk. "I'm sorry I can't be more helpful, Mr. Pennywell. There's really nothing I can do. But I think you'll find that over time, this issue will seem less important. Face it: we forget things every day of our lives. You're missing *lots* of chunks! But you don't dwell on those, now, do you?"

Liam rose too, but he couldn't give up so easily. He said, "You don't think I could maybe, for instance, get hypnotized or some such?"

"I wouldn't advise it," the doctor said.

"Or how about drugs? Some sort of pill, or truth serum?"

Dr. Morrow had a firm clasp on Liam's upper arm now. He was guiding him toward the door. "Trust me: this whole concern will fade away in no time," he said, and his voice had taken on the soothing tone of someone dealing with a minor pest. "See Melanie at the cashier's window on your way out, will you?"

Liam allowed himself to be ejected. He mumbled something or other, something about thank you, appreciate your time, say hello to Buddy, or Haddon . . . Then he went to the cashier's window and wrote a check for more than he normally spent on a month's groceries.

In the waiting room, Louise was nodding and tsk-tsking as she listened to a sallow girl in overalls—a new arrival who had taken Liam's old seat. "I'm just watering the perennials," the girl was saying. "I work at the Happy Trowel Nursery, out on York Road; know where that is? And all at once I start hearing this song playing way too fast. It doesn't sound real, though. It sounds like . . . tin. All tinny and high-speed. So I say to this guy Earl, who's hauling in the petunias, I say, 'Do you hear Pavement singing?' Earl says, 'Come again?' I say, 'It seems to me I hear Pavement singing "Spit on a Stranger." ' Earl looks at me like I'm nuts. Well, especially since it turns out he had no *i*-dea Pavement was a musical group. He figured I meant York Road was singing."

"Where has he been all this time?" Louise asked. "Everyone knows who Pavement is."

"But he'd have thought I was nuts anyhow, because there wasn't no music of any kind playing. It was all in my brain. This big old tangled clump of blood vessels in my brain."

Liam jingled the coins in his pocket, but Louise didn't look up. "That must feel so weird," she said.

"Dr. Meecham thinks they can, like, zap it with a beam of something."

"Well, you know I'm going to be praying for you."

Liam said, "I'm ready to go, Louise."

"Right; okay. This is my father," Louise told the girl. "He got hit on the head by a burglar."

"He didn't!"

Louise told Liam, "Tiffany here has a tangled clump of—"

"Yes, I heard," Liam said.

But he wasn't looking at the girl; he was looking at the old man sitting next to Jonah, the one with the hired rememberer. You couldn't tell, at the moment, that anything was wrong with him. He was reading a *New Yorker*, turning the pages thoughtfully and studying the cartoons. His assistant was gazing down at her lap. She seemed out of place next to the old man, with his well-cut suit and starched collar. Her face was round and shiny, her horn-rimmed spectacles smudged with fingerprints, her clothes hopelessly dowdy. Liam wondered how he could ever have taken her for the old man's daughter.

Well, but consider his own daughter, rising now to grasp both of the overalled girl's hands. "Just keep in your heart the Gospel of Mark," she was saying. *"Thy faith hath made thee whole. Go in peace and be whole of thy plague."*

"I hear you, sister," the girl told her.

Liam said, "Could we please leave now?"

"Sure, Dad. Come along, Jonah."

They passed between the two facing rows of patients, all of whom (Liam was convinced) were giving off waves of avid curiosity, although nobody looked up.

"Must you?" Liam asked Louise the minute they reached the hall.

Louise said, "Hmm?" and pressed the call button for the elevator.

"Do you have to air your religion everywhere you go?"

"I don't know what you're talking about," she said. She turned to Jonah. "You were such a good boy, Jonah! Maybe we can get you an ice cream on the way home."

"Mint chocolate chip?" Jonah said.

"We could get mint chocolate chip. What did the doctor have to say?" she asked Liam.

But he refused to be diverted. He said, "Suppose that girl happened to be an atheist? Or a Buddhist?"

The elevator door clanked open and Louise stepped smartly inside, one arm around Jonah's shoulders. She told the operator, "No way am I going to apologize for my beliefs."

The operator blinked. The other two passengers—an older couple—looked equally surprised.

"*Let your light so shine before men,*" Louise said, "*that they may see your good works and glorify your Father which is in heaven.*"

"Amen," the operator said.

"Matthew five, sixteen."

Liam faced front and stared fixedly at the brass dial above the door as they rode down.

As soon as they were out of the elevator, Louise said, "I don't expect much of you, Dad. I've learned not to. But I do request that you refrain from denigrating my religion."

"I'm not denigrating your—"

"You're dismissive and sarcastic and contemptuous," Louise said. (Anger seemed to broaden her vocabulary—a trait that Liam had noticed in her mother as well.) "You seize every opportunity to point out how wrongheaded true Christians are. When I am trying to raise a child, here! How can I expect him to lead any kind of moral life with you as an example?"

"Oh, for God's sake; I mean, for heaven's sake," Liam said, trotting after her through the revolving door. Out on the sidewalk, the sudden sunlight jarred his head. "I lead a *perfectly* moral life!"

Louise sniffed and drew Jonah closer, as if she felt he needed protecting.

She didn't speak again until they reached the car. Even then, she was all motherly fuss and bustle. "Climb into your seat, Jonah; don't dawdle. Here, let me straighten that strap."

Liam settled himself in front with a sigh. He was forcing himself to say no more, although it always annoyed him when people implied you had to have a religion in order to hold to any standards of behavior.

And then out of nowhere, as Louise was flinging herself into her seat with an indignant little bounce, it came to him who that old man in the waiting room was. Why, of course: Mr. Cope. Ishmael Cope, of Cope Development—the billionaire whose office buildings and luxury condominiums and oversized shopping malls despoiled the entire area. His picture popped up in the paper almost weekly, his heron-like figure bending forward to shake hands with some accomplice over his latest environmentally ruinous project.

Billionaires could buy anything, evidently, including better memories. Liam saw Mr. Cope's assistant once again in his mind—her owlish glasses and earnest, slightly sweaty face. What a notion: paying someone else to experience your life for you! Because that was what she'd been hired for, really.

A new ache shot through his left temple as Louise gunned the engine, and he closed his eyes and rested his head against the side window.

4

Over the next few days, Liam often found his thoughts returning to the hired rememberer. It wasn't that he wanted to hire her for himself, exactly. What good would that have done? He had already lived through the one event he needed reminding of. No, it was just the concept that intrigued him. He wondered how it worked. He wondered *if* it worked.

On Wednesday evening he asked Kitty if he could use her computer. She was using it herself at the time, sitting on the edge of his bed with the computer resting on her knees, and she shielded the screen in a paranoid way when he walked into the room. "I'm not looking!" he told her. "I just wanted to know if I might do a little research once you're finished."

"Research . . . on my computer?"

"Right."

"Well, sure, I guess so," she said. But she looked dubious. His aversion to computers was common knowledge. There'd been numerous complaints from St. Dyfrig parents when they couldn't reach him by e-mail.

He retreated to the kitchen, where he was warming a pizza for his supper. (Kitty would be going out with Damian, she'd said.) A few minutes later, he heard her call, "It's all yours." When he walked into the bedroom, she was stepping into a pair of rhinestone-trimmed flip-flops. "Do you know how to log off when you're done?" she asked him. "Do you know how to work this, even?"

"Certainly I know how!"

Her computer sat on the nightstand, attached to the phone line there. He assumed this meant that no one could call in, which didn't trouble him as much as it might have. He settled on the edge of the bed and rubbed his hands together. Then he looked up at Kitty. "Did you want something?" he asked.

"No, no," she said, and she gave an airy wave. "I'm off," she told him.

"Okay."

She didn't mention when she'd be back. Was she supposed to have a curfew?

As of noon, they'd passed the forty-eight-hour mark since his release from the hospital, but she had said nothing about going home. Well, none of *his* affair.

He waited until she had left the room, and then he typed *Ishmael Cope* in the Search window. It was true that he knew how to work a computer—he'd taken a mandatory teachers' training course—but the smaller keyboard gave him some difficulty and he had to hit Delete several times.

There were 4,300-some references to Ishmael Cope. Liam knew from experience that many of these would be false leads—whole paragraphs in which *Ishmael* and *cope* coincidentally appeared at widely separated points, or even (amazingly enough) other Ishmael Copes in other cities— but still, he was impressed.

Ishmael Cope was buying up farmland in Howard County. Ishmael Cope and his wife had attended a gala for juvenile diabetes. Ishmael Cope's plan to build a strip mall on the Eastern Shore was meeting with stiff opposition. Pass on, pass on. Aha: a newspaper profile, dating from just this past April. Mr. Cope had been born on Eutaw Street in 1930, which would make him . . . seventy-six. Younger than Liam's father, although Liam had taken him for much older. He had only a high school diploma; he'd started his working life assisting in his parents' bakery. His first million had come from the invention of an "edible staple" to fasten filled pastries and crepes. (Liam allowed himself a brief grin.) The rest of his career was fairly run-of-the-mill, though: the million parlayed into two million, four million, then a billion as he swept across his own personal Monopoly board. Married, divorced, married again; two sons in the business with him . . .

Nothing about any memory problems.

The next entry dealt with a question of sewage disposal for a golf community that Mr. Cope was proposing near the Pennsylvania border. In the next, he was merely a name on a list of donors to Gilman School. Liam signed off and closed the computer. He might have known he would come up empty. The whole point of hiring a rememberer, after all, was to conceal the fact that one was needed.

And anyhow, what had he hoped to accomplish even if he had found what he was looking for?

On Thursday morning he had another visit from the police. There were two of them, this time—a man and a woman. The woman did all of the questioning. She wanted to know if Liam recalled any recent conversations in which he had publicly mentioned some valuable possession. Liam said, "Absolutely not, since I have no valuable possessions."

She said, "Well, maybe not by *your* standards, but . . . a high-definition TV, say? For lots of folks, that's a hot property."

"I don't even have a low-definition TV," Liam told her.

She looked annoyed. She was an attractive young woman, petite and towheaded, but a little W of wrinkles between her eyebrows marred the overall impression. She said, "We're just trying to figure out why your place would have been targeted, and on the very first night you lived here."

"Well, it wasn't Damian, if that's what you're thinking."

"Damian?"

He regretted bringing the name to her attention. He said, "It wasn't the guys who moved me in."

"No. Those were friends, as I understand."

"Right."

"How about the man's voice? Did you hear him speak?"

He felt a sudden sense of despair. He said, "Didn't they tell you I don't remember? I don't remember a thing!"

"Just checking."

"What: do you imagine you'll trip me up?"

"No need to get excited, sir."

He forced himself to take a deep breath. No need at all; she was right, but somehow he felt accused. To this woman he looked inattentive, sloppy, lax. He decided to go on the offensive. "So what will you do next?" he asked her.

"Well, we have the case in our records now."

"Is that *it?*"

She stared him down.

"How about fingerprints? Did they find any fingerprints?" he asked.

"Oh, well, fingerprints. Fingerprints are overrated," she said.

Then she told him to take care (an expression he hated; take care of *what?*), and she and her partner walked out.

Back during Liam's first marriage, when all their friends were having babies, he and Millie knew a woman who experienced some terrible complication during labor and lay in a coma for several weeks afterward. Gradually she returned to consciousness, but for a long time she had no recollection of the whole preceding year. She didn't even remember being pregnant. Here was this infant boy, very sweet and all that but what did he have to do with *her?* Then one day, a neighbor climbed her porch steps and trilled out, "Yoo-hoo!" Evidently that was the neighbor's trademark greeting, uttered in a high fluty voice with a Southern roundness to the vowels. The woman rose slowly from her chair. Her eyes widened; her lips parted. As she described it later, it was as if the neighbor's "Yoo-hoo" had provided a string for her to grab hold of, and when she tugged it, other memories came trailing in besides—not just the previous "Yoo-hoos," but how this neighbor brought homemade pies to people at the drop of a hat, and how she always labeled her pie tins with her name on a strip of masking tape, and how in fact she'd contributed a pie to the final, celebratory meeting of the childbirth class that they had both attended. Childbirth! And bit by bit, over the course of the next few days, more and more came back, until the woman remembered everything.

Wouldn't it be wonderful if Liam could find such a string?

"Good afternoon, Dr. Morrow's office," the voice on the telephone said.

Liam said, "Ah, hello. Verity? I'm calling on behalf of Ishmael Cope. Mr. Cope has mislaid his appointment card, and he asked me to find out when he's due in next."

"Cope," the receptionist said. There was a series of clicking sounds. "Cope. Cope. Ishmael Cope. He's *not* due in."

"He's not?"

"Did he say he was?"

"Well, ah . . . yes, he seemed to believe so."

"But he was just here," the receptionist said.

"Was he? Oh, his mistake, then. Never mind."

"Ordinarily he waits till closer to the actual time to make the next appointment, since we see him just every three months is all, but if you'd prefer to set something up for him—"

"I'll find out and call you back. Thanks."

Liam replaced the receiver.

That evening his sister arrived bearing a cast-iron pot. "Stew," she announced, and she swept past him into the apartment and stopped short and looked around. "Goodness," she said. Liam didn't know why. All his boxes were unpacked now and he thought the place was looking fairly decent. But: "You know," she said, "just because you live alone doesn't mean you have to live miserably."

"I'm not living miserably!"

She turned and skinned him with a glance. "And don't think I can't see what you're up to," she said. "You're trying to come out even with your clothes."

"Come out . . . ?"

"You suppose if you play your cards right, you won't have to buy more clothes before you die."

"I don't suppose any such thing," Liam said. Although it was true that the idea had crossed his mind once or twice, just as a theoretical possibility. "What's wrong with what I'm wearing?" he asked her.

"Your pants are losing a belt loop and that shirt is so old it's transparent."

He had hoped nobody would notice.

Julia herself was, as always, impeccably put together. She wore what she must have worn to work that day: a tailored navy suit and matching pumps. It was obvious she and Liam were related—she had Liam's stick-straight gray hair and brown eyes, and she was short like him although, of course, smaller boned—but she'd never allowed herself to put on so much as an extra ounce, and her face was still crisply defined while Liam's had grown a bit pudgy. Also, she had a much more definite way of speaking. (This may have been due to her profession. She was a lawyer.) She said, for instance, "I'm going to stay and eat with you. I trust you have no plans," and something in her tone suggested that if he did have plans, he would naturally be canceling them.

She marched on into the kitchen, where she set the pot on the stove and slid a canvas grocery bag from her shoulder. "Where do you keep your silverware?" she asked.

"Oh, um . . ."

Just then Kitty sauntered down the hallway from the bedroom, clearly summoned by the sound of their voices. "Aunt Julia!" she said.

"Hello, there, Kitty. I've brought your dad some beef stew."

"But he doesn't eat red meat."

"He can just pluck the meat out, then," Julia said briskly. She was pulling drawers open; in the third, she found the silverware. "Will you be joining us?"

"Well, sure, I guess so," Kitty said, although earlier she'd told Liam not to count on her for supper. (All three of his daughters seemed drawn to Julia's company, perhaps because she made herself so scarce.)

Kitty was wearing one of those outfits that showed her abdomen, and in her navel she had somehow affixed a little round mirror the size of a dime. From where Liam stood, it looked as if she had a hole in her stomach. It was the oddest effect. He kept glancing at it and blinking, but Julia seemed impervious. "Here," she said, handing Kitty a fistful of silver. "Set the table, will you." No doubt she saw all sorts of get-ups in family court. She slapped a baguette on a cutting board and went back to searching through drawers, presumably hunting a bread knife, although Liam could have told her she wouldn't find one. She settled on a serrated fruit knife. "Now, I trust you're researching burglar alarms," she told Liam.

"No, not really," he said.

"This is important, Liam. If you insist on living in unsafe surroundings, you should at least take steps to protect yourself."

"The thing of it is, I don't think this place *is* unsafe," Liam told her. "I think what happened was just a fluke. If I hadn't left the patio door unlocked, and if some drugged-up guy hadn't come fumbling around on the off chance he could get in somewhere . . . But at least I seem to have neighbors who will call the police, you notice."

He had met the neighbors that morning—a portly, middle-aged couple heading out to their car just as he was dropping a bag of garbage into the bin. "How's your head?" the husband had asked him. "We're the Hunstlers. The folks who phoned 911."

Liam said, "Oh. Glad to meet you." He had to force himself to proceed through the proper steps—thank them for their help, give a report on his injuries—before he could ask, "Why *did* you phone, exactly? I mean, what was it that you heard? Did you hear me say any words?"

"Words, well, no," the husband said. "Just, like, more of a shout. Just a shout like 'Aah!' or 'Wha?' and Deb says, 'What was *that?*' and I look out our bedroom window and see this guy running away. Kind of a darker shape in the dark, was all I could make out. Afraid I wouldn't be much of a witness if it ever came to trial."

"I see," Liam said.

"It was a medium-sized guy, though; I will say that. Medium-sized individual."

Liam said, "Hmm," barely listening, because why would he care what size the man was? It was his own words he'd hoped to hear about. That was *it?* "Aah!" and "Wha?" Surely he had said more. He felt a flash of exasperation with the Hunstlers.

As Julia said, setting the bread plate on the table, "You'd be a fool to rely on neighbors."

"Well, maybe you're right," Liam said. "I'll give some thought to an alarm."

But he knew he wouldn't.

"And have any arrests been made?" she asked once they'd taken their seats.

"Not that I've heard of."

"Any leads, at least?"

"Nobody's told me of any."

"Here's what *I* think," she said. "I think it was somebody in this complex."

"A neighbor?"

"You can see this is a down-and-outers' kind of place. Flimsily built rental units, opposite a shopping mall—imagine the sort of people who live here."

"*I* live here, for one," Liam said. He started buttering a slice of bread. "And so do the Hunstlers."

"Who are the Hunstlers?"

"Julia, you're missing the point," Liam said.

"What *is* the point, then? Surely you want to see justice done."

"This is more about me," he said. "Why can't I remember what happened?"

"Why would you want to?"

"Everybody asks me that! You don't understand."

"No, evidently not," Julia said, and then she turned to Kitty and, in an obvious changing-the-subject tone of voice, started quizzing her about her college plans.

Which wasn't much more successful, really. Kitty said, "I don't have any plans. I've just finished my junior year."

"I thought you were a senior."

"Nope."

"Shouldn't she be a senior?" Julia asked Liam.

"Nope."

Julia turned back to Kitty. "But still you must have visited some campuses," she said.

"Not yet. I might not even be going to college. I might decide to travel a while."

"Oh? Where would you travel to?"

"Buenos Aires is supposed to be fun."

Julia looked at her blankly for a moment. Then she shook her head and told Liam, "I thought she was a senior."

"Just goes to show," Liam said cheerfully. "This is the kind of thing that happens when you don't keep in touch with your family."

"I keep in touch!"

Liam raised his eyebrows.

"I phoned you just this past Saturday, when you were moving in!"

"So you did," Liam said.

"And I've brought you this nice beef stew, which you haven't even tasted!"

"Sorry," Liam said.

It was true; all he had on his plate was the one slice of bread. He helped himself to some stew. There were carrots, potatoes, and celery chunks along with the meat—enough to make a meal of, if he just scraped off the gravy.

"Your father's been a picky eater all his life," Julia told Kitty.

"It's not so much that I'm picky as that I'm out of the habit," Liam said. "If I went back to eating meat now, I doubt I'd have the enzymes anymore to digest it."

"See what I mean?" Julia asked Kitty. "There was a period in his childhood when he would eat nothing but white things. Noodles and mashed potatoes and rice. Our mother had to fix him an entire separate meal."

Liam said, "I don't remember that."

"Well, you were little. And another period, you would eat only with chopsticks. For one solid year, you insisted on eating everything including soup with these pointy ivory chopsticks they shipped back with Uncle Leonard's belongings after he died in the War."

"Chopsticks?" Liam said.

"And you had to have this old record played every night before you went to bed: 'It's Been a Long, Long Time,' with Kitty Kallen. Whatever happened to Kitty Kallen? *Kiss me once, and kiss me twice*," Julia sang, in an unexpectedly pretty soprano. "It was how Mother taught you to kiss us good night. You would blow kisses in tempo. Kiss to the right, kiss to the left . . . big smacking sounds, huge grin on your face. Wearing those pajamas with the feet and the trap-door bottom."

"How come you always remember so much more than me?" Liam asked.

"You were only two, is why."

"Yes, but you come up with so many details. And some are from when I was ten or twelve, when supposedly I was a fully conscious being; but still they're all news to me."

Although total recall was not an unmixed blessing, he had noticed. His sister could hold a grudge forever. She collected and polished resentments as if it were some sort of hobby. For over half a century now, she hadn't spoken to their father. (He'd left them to marry a younger woman back when they were children.) Even when he suffered a heart attack, a few years ago, Julia had refused to visit him. Let him go ahead and kick the bucket, she'd said; good riddance if he did. And she insisted on using their mother's maiden name, although their mother herself had stayed a Pennywell till she died. It may have been this bitter streak that kept Julia single. She had never even seriously dated, as far as Liam knew.

"I can see you plain as day," she said now. "Your little red cheeks, your sparkly eyes. Your fat little fingers flinging kisses. Don't tell me you didn't know exactly how cute you were being."

There was an acid edge to her voice, but even so, Liam envied how she envisioned this picture so clearly, hovering in the air above the table.

Cope Development's offices were on Bunker Street, near the train station, according to the telephone book. You would think Ishmael Cope could have sprung for a better address— something around Harborplace, say. But that was how the rich were, sometimes. It might be *why* they were rich.

Shortly before noon on Friday, defying medical orders, Liam drove down to Bunker Street. When he reached Cope Development he pulled over to the curb and shut off the ignition. He had hoped for a little park of some sort, or at least a strip of grass with a bench where he could sit, but clearly this was not that kind of neighborhood. All the buildings were scrunched together, and their wooden doors were chewed-looking, the paint on their trim dulled and scaling, their bricks crumbling like biscuits. The place to the right of Cope Development sold plumbing supplies; the place to the left was a mission for indigent men. (That was how the sign in the window phrased it. Would indigent men know the word "indigent"?) Apart from a hunched old woman dragging a wheeled shopping tote behind her, there wasn't a pedestrian in sight. Liam's original plan—to blend in with the crowd on the sidewalk, trailing Ishmael Cope and his assistant unobserved as they strolled to some nearby café— seemed silly now.

He sat low behind the steering wheel, arms folded across his chest, eyes on the Cope building. It looked as dismal as the others, but the plaque beside the door was brass and freshly polished. Twice the door opened and people emerged—a boy with a messenger bag, two men in business suits. Once a woman approached the building from the direction of St. Paul Street and paused, but she moved on after consulting a slip of paper she took from her purse. It was a warm, muggy, overcast day, and Liam had rolled his window down, but even so, the car began to grow uncomfortable.

He hadn't planned what he would do after he'd followed them to lunch. He had imagined finagling a table next to them and then, oh, just worming his way in, so to speak. Joining them. Becoming a member.

It was just as well that they weren't showing up, because this would never have worked.

Still, he went on waiting. He noticed that although he was watching for the two of them, it was the assistant he wanted to talk to. Mr. Cope himself had nothing to teach him; Liam knew all there was to know about forgetting. The assistant, on the other hand . . . Unconsciously, he seemed to be crediting the assistant with specialized professional skills, as if she were a psychologist or a neurologist. Or something more mysterious, even: a kind of reverse fortune teller. A predictor of the past.

It was this thought that made him come to his senses, finally. Not for the first time, he wondered if the blow to his head had somehow affected his sanity. He gave himself a little shake; he wiped his damp face on his shirt sleeve. Then he started the car and, after one last glance at the door (still closed), he pulled out into traffic and drove home.

Barbara called on Saturday morning and said she wanted to come get Kitty. "I'll stop by for her in, say, half an hour," she said. "Around ten or so. Is she still asleep?"

"Yes, I think so."

"Well, wake her up and tell her to pack. I've got a busy day today."

"Okay, Barbara. How have *you* been?" Liam asked, because he felt a little hurt that she hadn't inquired about his injuries.

But she just said, "Fine, thanks. Bye," and hung up.

He would be sorry to see Kitty go, in some ways. Having another person around was oddly cheering. And unlike her two sisters, who seemed to adopt a tone of high dudgeon whenever they talked to him, Kitty often behaved as if she might actually enjoy his company.

On the other hand, it would be good to have his own bed

back. He noticed when he stuck his head in to wake her that already the room had taken on her scent—various perfumed cosmetics mingling with the smell of worn clothing—and it was strewn with far more possessions than could have fit into that one duffel bag, surely. Bottles and jars covered the bureau; T-shirts littered the floor; extension cords trailed from the outlets. The bed itself was shingled with glossy magazines. He didn't know how she could sleep like that.

"Kitty, your mother will be here in half an hour," he said. "She's coming to take you home."

Kitty was just a feathery tousle of hair on the pillow, but she said, "Mmf," and turned over, so he felt it was safe to leave her.

He laid out breakfast: toasted English muffins and (against his principles) the Diet Coke she always claimed she needed to get her going. For himself he brewed coffee. He was starting on his second cup, seated at the table watching the English muffins grow cold, before she emerged from the bedroom. She still had her pajamas on, and a crease ran down one cheek and her hair was sticking up every which way. "What *time* is it?" she asked, pulling out her chair.

"Almost ten. Do you have your things packed?"

"No," she said. "Hello-o, did anyone warn me? All at once I'm yanked out of bed and told I'm being evicted."

"I guess it's the only time your mother can come," Liam said. He helped himself to an English muffin. "She said she had a busy day today."

"So she couldn't inform me ahead? Maybe ask me if it was convenient?"

Kitty popped the tab on her Diet Coke and took a swig.

Then she stared moodily down at the can. "I don't know why she wants me back anyway," she said. "We're not getting along at all."

"Well, everybody has their ups and downs."

"She's this, like, rule-monger. Nitpicker. If I'm half a minute late it's, whoa, grounded forever."

"I would have supposed," Liam said, picking his way delicately between words, "that she would be less concerned with all that now that she has a . . . boyfriend, did you say?"

"Howie," Kitty said. "Howie the Hound Dog."

"Hound dog!"

"He has these droopy eyes, like this," Kitty said, and she pulled down her lower lids with her index fingers till the pink interiors showed.

Liam said, "Heh, heh," and waited to hear more, but Kitty just reached for the butter.

"So, are they . . . serious, do you suppose?" Liam asked finally.

"How would I know?"

"Ah."

"They go to these movies at the Charles that all the artsy people go to."

"I see."

"He has permanent indigestion and can't eat the least little thing."

Liam said, "Tsk." And then, after a pause, "That must be hard for your mother. She's such an enthusiastic cook."

Kitty shrugged.

This was the first boyfriend Liam had heard about since Madigan died—Barbara's second husband. He had died of a stroke several years ago. Liam had always viewed Madigan as temporary, ersatz, a mere *substitute* husband; but in fact Madigan had been married to Barbara longer than Liam himself had, and it was Madigan who had occupied the Father of the Bride role at Louise's wedding. (Everything but the actual walking her down the aisle; that much they had oh-so-graciously allowed Liam.) At Madigan's funeral the girls had shed more tears than they ever would for Liam, he would bet.

"I'm just thankful your Grandma Pennywell didn't live to see your mother marry Madigan," he told Kitty. "It would have broken her heart."

"Huh?"

"She was very fond of your mother. She always hoped we'd reconcile."

Kitty sent him a look of such blank astonishment that he said, hastily, "But anyhow! Shouldn't you be packing?"

"I've got time," Kitty said. And even though the doorbell rang at the very next instant, she continued licking butter off each finger in a catlike, unhurried way.

Before he could get all the way to the door, Barbara walked on in. She wore a Saturday kind of outfit—frumpy, wide slacks and a T-shirt. (No doubt she would have dressed differently for what's-his-name. For Howie.) She was carrying a lidded plastic container and a cellophane bag of rolls. "How's the head?" she asked, striding right past him.

"Nobody seems to inquire about it anymore," he said sadly.

"I just did, Liam."

"Well, it's better. It doesn't ache, at least. But I still can't remember what happened."

"When do you get the stitches out?"

"Monday," he said. He was disappointed that she had ignored the reference to his failed memory. "I'm hoping maybe when I'm sleeping in my own bed again, it will all come back to me. Do you think?"

"Maybe," Barbara said absently. She was putting the container in his refrigerator. "This is homemade vegetable soup for your lunch. Where's Kitty?"

"She must be packing. Thanks for the soup."

"You're welcome."

"Guess what Julia brought: beef stew."

"Ha!" Barbara said. But he could tell her heart wasn't in it. She said, "How late did Kitty stay out nights?"

Liam didn't have time to answer (not that he'd have been able to, since he was generally sound asleep when Kitty got home) before Kitty called from the bedroom, "I heard that!"

"I was only wondering," Barbara said.

"Then why don't you ask *me*?" Kitty said. She appeared in the hallway, struggling under the weight of her duffel bag, which was bulging open, too full to zip. "Typical," she told Liam. "She's always going behind my back. She doesn't trust me."

Liam said, "Oh, now, I'm sure that's not—"

"Darn right I don't trust you," Barbara said. "Who was it who changed my bedroom clock that time?"

"That was months ago!"

"She snuck into my room before she went out and set my clock an hour behind," Barbara told Liam. "I guess she thought I wouldn't notice when I went to bed. I'd wake in the night and look at the clock and think she wasn't due back yet."

Liam said, "Surely, though—"

"Oh, why do you always, always take her side against me?" Barbara demanded.

"When have I taken her side against you?"

"You don't even know what happened! You just jump on in with both feet!"

"All I said was—"

"Do you have a grocery bag?" Kitty asked him. "I've got way too much stuff."

She made it sound as if he were somehow to blame for that. In fact he felt blamed by both of them. He went over to a kitchen cupboard and pulled out a flattened paper bag and handed it to her in silence.

As soon as Kitty left the room, he turned to Barbara and said, "Shall we sit down?"

"I'm really pressed for time," Barbara said. But she followed him into the living room and settled in the rocker. He sat across from her. He laced his fingers together and smiled at her.

"So!" he said. Then, after a pause, "You're looking well."

She was, Saturday clothes or no. She had that fair, clean skin that showed to best advantage without makeup, and her serenely folded hands—the nails cut sensibly short and lacking any sort of polish—struck him as restful. Reassuring. He went on smiling at her, but she had her mind elsewhere. She said, "I'm getting too old for this."

"Pardon?"

"For dealing with teenage girls."

"Well, yes, you *are* a little old," Liam said.

This caused Barbara to give a short laugh, but he was only speaking the truth. (She'd had Kitty at age forty-five.)

"It wasn't so bad with Louise," she said. "Say what you

will about the born-again thing; at least it made her an easy adolescent. And Xanthe I don't even count. Xanthe was such a *good* girl."

Thank heaven for that much, Liam thought, since Xanthe wasn't her own. Wouldn't he have felt guilty if Xanthe had given Barbara any trouble! But she had been so docile—a quiet, obedient three-year-old when Barbara first met her. He'd brought her along to work one morning when his child-care fell through, and the two of them had hit it off at once. Barbara hadn't fussed over her or used that fake, high, cooing voice that other women used or expected Xanthe to rise to any particular level of enthusiasm. She seemed to understand that this child had a low-key nature. And she'd already known that about Liam. She certainly knew *he* was low-key.

So why did she want more than that after they were married? Why did she prod him, and drag him to counseling, and at last, in the end, give up on him?

Women had this element of treachery, Liam had discovered. They entered your life under false pretenses and then they changed the rules. Underneath, Barbara had turned out to be just like all the others.

Take today, for instance. Look at her sitting in his rocking chair. Although she had started out so calm—hands folded in her lap—she grew more restless by the minute. First she picked up an issue of *Philosophy Now* from the floor beside her and examined the cover. Then she set it down and looked around the room, knitting her eyebrows in such a way that Liam felt himself becoming defensive. He sat up straighter. She turned her gaze on him and said, "Liam, I wonder if you might perhaps be a little bit depressed."

"Why on earth would you say that?" Liam asked.

Why did she feel she had the *right* to say it, was what he meant. But she misread the question. She said, "Because you're narrowing your world so. Haven't you noticed? You're taking up a smaller and smaller space. You don't have a separate kitchen anymore or a fireplace or a view from your window. You seem to be . . . retreating."

Luckily, Kitty came into the room just then. She was lugging not just the grocery bag but a pillowcase stuffed with clothing—the pillowcase from Liam's bed, which she hadn't asked permission to take. "Here," she told her mother, and she dropped the pillowcase in Barbara's lap and then bent to pick up her duffel bag.

"What *is* all this?" Barbara asked as she struggled to her feet. "How did you end up with so many belongings?"

"It's not my fault! You're the one who sent me here!"

"Did I tell you to bring your whole closet? Where did all this come from?"

"I had to buy a couple of extra things," Kitty said.

"What? With what money?" Barbara demanded.

Meanwhile they were limping toward the door, hampered by their burdens, yawping at each other like two blue jays. Liam saw them out with a feeling of relief. After they were gone he returned to his chair and sank into it. The silence was so deep it almost echoed. He was alone again.

Monday morning his stitches were removed. A patch of thin gray fuzz hid the scar now. He went to the barber the following day and had his hair cut even shorter than usual, and after that the patch was nearly unnoticeable.

On his palm, the stitches left puckers. They turned the

deepest of the creases there into a sort of ruffle. He wondered if this would be permanent. He sat in his rocker staring down at his palm for minutes on end.

He had too much time to fill; that was the truth of the matter. For a brief while, the fuss of moving in had entertained him—arranging and rearranging his books, scouring three different kitchen stores for the exact type of wall-mounted can opener he was used to in the old place. But that couldn't last forever. And with no summer school now, no papers to grade, no ten-year-old boys in despair over the inconsistencies of *i*-before-*e* . . . well, face it, he was bored. He could sit and read for only so many hours. He could take only so many walks. Of course he could always listen to classical music on his clock radio, but it seemed to him that the station kept playing the same pieces, and most of the pieces sounded like the music they played at the circus. Besides: just sitting, just listening, just staring straight ahead with his hands resting on his kneecaps, was not enough to use up the day.

Nobody called to ask how he was. Not Barbara, not his sister, not any of his daughters. Here he thought he and Kitty had gotten on so well, but he didn't hear a word from her.

The hospital sent him a bill for expenses not covered by his health insurance. They charged him rent for a phone in his room, and he was able to consume quite a large chunk of one morning on a protest call to Accounting.

"Not that I wouldn't have *liked* a phone in my room," he said. "I certainly asked for one. I had no way of getting in touch with my family and letting them know where I was. Everybody was needlessly worried."

The woman at the other end of the line allowed a silence

to develop after each one of his statements. He hoped this meant she was writing down his words, but he suspected she was not. "Hello?" he said. "Are you there?"

Another silence. Then, "Mmhmm."

"Also," he said, "this bill was for three days. For June tenth, eleventh, and twelfth. But I was unconscious on the tenth! How do they think I was able to order a phone when I was unconscious?"

"A visitor could have ordered it," she said after another pause.

"I didn't have any visitors."

"How do you know that, if you were unconscious?"

This last remark came lickety-split, no pause at all, triumphantly. He sighed. He said, "I don't think I had even made it into my room on the tenth. I think I was still in emergency. And meanwhile my family was completely in the dark, wondering what had become of me."

It almost seemed like the truth. He imagined relatives all over town wringing their hands and calling around and checking with the police.

But the woman in Accounting was unimpressed. She told him they would get back to him later. Her tone of voice implied that it wasn't going to be uppermost on anyone's agenda.

At nighttime he slept poorly, no doubt because he wasn't tired. He was bothered by the faint scent of Kitty's shampoo even though he had changed the sheets, and a neighbor's TV was so loud that percussive thumping noises vibrated one wall. When he did finally sleep, he dreamed dreams that exhausted him—complicated narratives that he had to work to keep track of. He dreamed he was a pharmacist advising a customer about her medications, but while he was talking he absentmindedly, unintentionally ate every one of her pills. He dreamed he was leading a policewoman through his apartment—not the woman who had visited in real life but another one, old and crabby—and while they were in the bedroom they heard a sound from the window. "There!" Liam said. "Didn't I tell you?" He was pleased, because in the dream there seemed to be some suspicion that he had made the intruder up. Then he woke, and for an instant he thought that the sound from the window had been real. His heart seemed to stop; he felt suddenly cold, although it was a warm night. But almost immediately, he understood that he had imagined it. The only sounds were the *meep-meep* of tree frogs, the neighbor's TV, the distant rush of traffic on the Beltway. He was surprised that he'd felt such terror. Why should he be afraid? Everybody dies sometime. In fact he was almost *waiting* to die. But evidently his body had other ideas.

His heartbeat returned to normal and the chill faded, and he was left with a feeling of disappointment. Wouldn't you think that that flash of alarm could have jogged his memory?

He had no idea when Cope Development opened for business each day, and so he drove downtown extra early—shortly after eight o'clock. A panel truck occupied the space where he'd parked the last time. He drew up directly behind it, in front of the Mission for Indigent Men. He cut the engine and rolled down his window and prepared himself for a wait.

Within minutes, a woman approached from the other direction, hunting through a red tote as she walked. She brought forth a bunch of keys and climbed the front steps, unlocked the door, and disappeared inside. But no others followed. Maybe this woman was the office manager, or opener, or whatever the term was. The sidewalk remained empty. Liam began to feel deeply, maddeningly bored. His throat developed a hollow ache from holding back his yawns. His face grew sticky with perspiration.

Then around nine o'clock, people started arriving— young men in suits, and women of all ages strolling in twos and threes, talking as they entered the building, laughing and nudging each other. Liam felt a pang of nostalgia for the easy camaraderie of people who worked together.

A man in coveralls walked past Liam's car, climbed into the parked panel truck, and drove away. Immediately afterward, as if by prearrangement, a dingy green Corolla pulled into the vacant space. A woman stepped out from the driver's side: the rememberer. She was wearing another big, folksy skirt, or perhaps the same one, for all Liam knew, and her ringlets were wet-looking now from the heat. She circled behind her car, so close that he could hear the slogging sound of her sandals on the pavement. She opened the front passenger door, and Mr. Cope unfolded himself from his seat and stood upright. He had that old-person knack of remaining cool in sweltering weather. His hatchet face was dry and chalky; his high white collar and close-fitting suit were still crisp.

The rememberer, on the other hand, looked rumpled and uncomfortable. Under the glaring sunlight she was not quite so young as Liam had first assumed. Nor did she seem so professional. She somehow got her purse strap entangled when she tried to close the car door, and as she was guiding Mr. Cope up the front steps she managed to trample on the hem of her own skirt. The elastic waist slid perilously low on one side; she yanked it up again and gave a quick glance around her, luckily not appearing to notice Liam in his car. Then she cupped a hand under Mr. Cope's elbow and shepherded him into the building. The door swung shut behind them.

It wasn't clear to Liam what he had hoped to gain from this sighting. He started his engine and rolled up his window and drove home.

Toward the end of June he phoned Bundy and invited him to supper on a night when Bundy's fiancée had yoga class. He planned a real menu; it gave him something to do. He went to the supermarket for groceries, and he roasted a chicken. It was way too hot for roast chicken, but he didn't know how to cook much of anything else. And Bundy was appreciative, since his fiancée fed him a steady diet of Lean Cuisines.

Liam couldn't quite explain why he and Bundy were friends. It was surely none of *his* doing. But from the day they'd met, at a St. Dyfrig teachers' meeting one September, Bundy had seemed to view Liam with a mixture of fascination and . . . well, *glee* would have to be the word for it. And Liam, almost against his will, found himself playing into that view. Leading Bundy through the apartment this evening, for instance, he flung open the closet door to show off his new tie rack. "A separate little spoke for each tie! And see how it revolves for easy access." Bundy rocked back on his heels, grinning.

When it grew apparent that the apartment's air conditioning couldn't handle the heat of the oven, they moved their meal to the patio. They sat out on the tiny square of concrete in two rotting canvas butterfly chairs left behind by the previous tenant, and they ate from makeshift trays formed by several folded newspaper sections laid across their knees.

Bundy shook his head when he heard about the intruder. He said, "Ah, man. And you're in the county now!" But he showed less sympathy for Liam's memory lapse. "Shoot," he said, "that happens to me just about every weekend. No big deal about *that*."

Then he drifted into St. Dyfrig gossip—the headmaster's latest cockamamie piece of foolishness, the latest dispute with some pigheaded parent. He knew all of Liam's old students and could tell him what most were up to, since he was in charge of athletics for St. Dyfrig's summer program. Brucie Winston had been caught selling drugs, which was something of a dilemma since Brucie's parents had just single-handedly funded the new auditorium. Lewis Bent was failing his make-up math course and there was talk of holding him back next year. Liam had never much liked Brucie Winston, but Lewis was a whole other story. He tsk-ed and said, "Well, that's a shame." He wondered if there were something he should have done differently while Lewis was in his class.

When they'd polished off the dessert (a pint of pistachio ice cream) and it was time for Bundy to go, Liam led him back through the apartment, carelessly leaving the patio door unlocked behind them. Even as he was telling Bundy good night he had an edgy awareness of that unlocked door at his rear. "Sure, you're welcome; any time," he said, almost pushing Bundy out. But it wasn't anxiety that made him hurry back to the patio; it was a sort of magnetic pull, a half-guilty, compelling attraction. All for nothing, as it happened. No one was trying to get in.

That night he dreamed that he woke to a sense of someone standing over his bed. He dreamed that he lay very still, curled on his side, pretending to be asleep. He could hear soft, steady breathing. He could feel a thread-thin blade of cold steel placed lightly against his bare neck. Then the blade was raised in the air to strike the fatal blow.

Who would have guessed that a killer would make that trial move first? Like setting a cleaver against a joint of meat before lifting it to chop, Liam thought. The horror of that image caused his eyes to fly open in the dark. His heart was beating so violently that it rustled his pajamas.

5

There was a parking space in front of the Mission for Indigent Men, but Liam didn't stop there. He drove on past
it, past Cope Development and Curtis Plumbing Supply, and
turned right at the corner and pulled in at a meter halfway up
the next block. When he got out of his car he found he didn't
have any quarters—the only coins the meter accepted—but
he decided to take his chances.

He walked back to Bunker Street, turned left, and slowed
until he was nearly at a standstill. Already, at not even nine
a.m., the sun felt uncomfortably hot on his head and the
back of his neck. He came to a halt near a hydrant and
painstakingly, deliberatively rolled his shirtsleeves up, flatten-
ing each fold with great care. Two men in suits strode past.
He watched after them, but they didn't turn in at Cope
Development.

He studied the graffiti painted across the base of the
hydrant: *BLAST,* in luminous white, with a sloppily drawn

star before and after. He examined the word closely, frowning, as if he were pondering its meaning. Blast. A woman clipped by with a jingling sound of keys or maybe jewelry. She had a purposeful, confident gait. At Cope Development, she pivoted smartly and climbed the steps and disappeared inside.

A green Corolla approached from the other end of the block, stopped just past the mission, and backed into the parking space there.

Liam abandoned the hydrant. He straightened and resumed walking in the direction of Cope Development.

The assistant's unfortunate fashion statements were becoming familiar to him. Even from a distance he recognized the too-long skirt (in some bandanna-type print of red and blue, today) that made her seem to be walking on her knees as she rounded her car, and the sleeveless blouse that rode up and exposed a bulge of bare midriff when she bent to help Ishmael Cope from the passenger seat. Liam was close enough now to hear the inconclusive clucking sound the car door made as she clumsily nudged it almost shut with one hip. He heard the pat-pat of Ishmael Cope's crablike hands checking all his suit pockets before he took hold of the arm she offered.

Liam sped up.

They met in front of the Cope building. The assistant was preparing to inch the old man up the steps. Liam said, "Why! Mr. Cope!"

The two of them turned and peered into his face, wearing almost comically similar expressions of puzzlement and concern.

"Fancy running into you!" Liam said. "It's Liam Penny-well. Remember?"

Ishmael Cope said, "Um . . ."

He turned to his assistant, who instantly flushed all over—a mottled, dark-red flush beginning at the deep V-neck of her blouse and rising to her round cheeks.

"We met at the gala," Liam said. "For juvenile diabetes; remember? We had a long conversation. You suggested I come in sometime and interview for a job."

From their instantaneous reaction—no longer confusion but outright shock—Liam sensed at once that he had made a mistake. Maybe Ishmael Cope didn't have anything to do anymore with hiring employees. Well, of course he wouldn't. Liam cursed his own stupidity. Ishmael Cope said, "A *job*?"

"Why, ah, that is . . ."

"I was going to *hire* someone?"

Ishmael Cope and his assistant exchanged a glance. Clearly a con man, they must be thinking. Or no, perhaps not; for next Mr. Cope said, in a wondering tone, "I promised a man a job!"

So this is what it had come to, was what that glance had meant. A whole new symptom, more advanced than any they'd seen before.

All Liam wanted now was to take back everything he'd said. He had never intended to cause the man distress. In fact, he wasn't sure *what* he'd intended, beyond gaining a few moments of conversation with the assistant. He said, "Oh, no, it wasn't an actual promise. It was more like . . ." He turned to the assistant, hoping she could somehow rescue him. "Maybe I misunderstood," he told her. "I must have. I'm sure I did.

You know how it is at these galas: glasses clinking, music playing, everyone talking at once . . ."

"Oh, sometimes people can't hear themselves think," she said.

That low, clear, level voice—the voice that had murmured "Verity" in Dr. Morrow's waiting room—made Liam feel reassured, although he couldn't say exactly why. He gave her his widest smile. "I'm sorry," he told her, "I don't remember *your* name."

"I wasn't there."

"Oh. Sorry."

He knew he must look like a fool, with all these "sorry"s. He was doing everything wrong. "It's just . . ." he said, "I mistrust my memory so these days; I always act on the assumption that I've met somebody even when I haven't." His laugh came out sounding false, at least to his own ears. "I have the world's worst memory," he told Ishmael Cope.

Which was a stroke of genius, come to think of it. Without planning to, he had arrived at the subject most likely to enlist the man's sympathy.

But Ishmael Cope said, "That must be difficult. And you don't look all that old, either."

"I'm not. I'm sixty."

"Only sixty? Then there's no excuse whatsoever."

This was becoming annoying. Liam glanced toward the assistant. She was sending Mr. Cope a look of amusement. "Now, now," she said indulgently, and then she told Liam, "To hear Mr. C. talk, you'd never know we *all* forget things from time to time."

"The trick is mental exercise," Ishmael Cope said to Liam. "Work crossword puzzles. Solve brainteasers."

"I'll have to try that," Liam said.

He was developing an active dislike for the man. But he gave the assistant another wide smile and said, "I didn't mean to hold you both up."

"About the interview . . ." she said. She glanced uncertainly at Ishmael Cope.

But Liam said, "Oh, no, really, it's not important. It's quite all right. I don't need a job. I don't *want* a job. I was only, you know . . ."

He was edging away as he spoke, backing off in the direction he had just come from. "Good to see you both," he said. "Sorry to . . . Goodbye."

He turned and plunged off blindly.

Idiot.

Traffic was picking up now, and more pedestrians dotted the sidewalk, all bustling toward their offices with briefcases and folded newspapers. He was the only one empty-handed. Everyone else had someplace to get to. He slowed his pace and surveyed each building he passed with an intent, abstracted expression, as if he were hunting a specific address.

What on earth had he expected from that encounter, anyway? Even if things had gone as he'd hoped—if he and the assistant had struck up a separate conversation, if she had admitted outright the true nature of her role—how would that have helped him? She wasn't going to drop everything and come be *his* rememberer. In any event, she couldn't help him retrieve an experience she hadn't been there for. And what good would it have done even if she *could* retrieve it?

He really was losing his mind, he thought.

When he reached his car he found he'd been issued a

parking ticket. Oh, damn. He plucked it from the windshield and frowned at it. Twenty-seven dollars. For nothing.

"Excuse me?" someone called.

He looked up. The assistant was hurrying toward him, pink-faced and out of breath, clutching her purse to her pillowy bosom with both hands. "Excuse me, I just wanted to thank you," she said when she arrived in front of him.

"Thank me for what?" he asked.

"It was kind of you to be so understanding back there. Somebody else might have . . . pushed. Might have pressed him."

"Oh, that's okay," he said, meaninglessly.

"Mr. . . . Pennyworth?"

"Pennywell. Liam," he said.

"Liam. I'm Eunice, Mr. Cope's assistant. Liam, I'm not at liberty to explain but . . . I guess you must have realized that Mr. C. is not in charge of hiring."

"I understand perfectly," he said. "Don't give it a thought."

If he had been the ruthless type, he would have pretended *not* to understand. He would have forced her to spell it out. But she looked so anxious, with her forehead creased and her oversized glasses slipping down her shiny nose; he didn't have the heart to add to her discomfort. He said, "I meant it when I said I didn't need a job. I really don't. Honest."

She gazed at him for such a long moment that he wondered if she had misheard him. And he was sure of it when she told him, finally, "You're a very nice man, Liam."

"No, no, I—"

"Where is it you're employed?" she said.

"Right now? Well, right now, um . . ."

She reached out and laid a hand briefly on his arm. "Forgive me. Please forget I asked that," she said.

"Oh, it's not a *secret*," he said. "I used to teach fifth grade. The school is downsizing at the moment, but that's okay. I might retire anyhow."

She said, "Liam, would you like to get a cup of coffee?"

"Oh!"

"Someplace nearby?"

"I would love to, but—shouldn't you be at work?"

"I'm finished with work," she said.

"You are?"

"Well, at least for . . ." She checked her watch—a big clunky thing on a leather wristband even thicker than her sandal straps. "At least for an hour or so," she said. "I just have to be there for transitions."

"Transitions," Liam repeated.

"Getting Mr. C. from one place to another place. Till ten o'clock he'll be in his office, reading *The Wall Street Journal*."

"I see."

Liam allowed her some time to expand on that topic, but she didn't. Instead she said, "PeeWee's is good."

"Pardon?"

"For coffee. PeeWee's Café."

"Oh, fine," Liam said. "Is that in walking distance?"

"It's right around the corner."

He looked down at the parking ticket he held. Then he turned and jammed it back under the windshield wiper. "Let's go, then," he told her.

He couldn't believe his luck. As they headed up the street he had to keep fighting back a huge grin.

Although now that he had her all to himself, what was he

going to ask? Nothing came to mind. Really he wanted to reach out and touch her—even just touch her skirt, as if she were some sort of talisman. But he dug both hands in his trouser pockets instead, and he was careful not to brush against her as they walked.

"The hiring and firing at Cope is handled by a man named McPherson," Eunice told him. "Unfortunately, I don't know him well."

"Oh, that's all right," Liam said.

"I was hired myself by *Mrs.* Cope."

This was getting more interesting. Liam said, "Why was that?"

"Oh, it's a long story, but my point is, I didn't have many dealings with the Personnel Department."

"How did Mrs. Cope find you?" Liam asked.

"She's friends with my mother."

"Oh."

He waited. Eunice walked beside him in a companionable silence. She had stopped hugging her purse by now. It swung from her shoulder with a faint rattling sound, as if it were full of ping-pong balls.

"The two of them play bridge together," Eunice said. "So . . . you know."

No, he didn't know. He looked at her expectantly.

"I don't suppose *you* play bridge," Eunice said.

"No."

"Oh."

"What?" he asked. "If I did play, you'd get me into a game with Mrs. Cope?"

He was being facetious, but she seemed to give the question serious consideration before she said, "No, I don't guess that's too practical. Well, back to Mr. McPherson, then."

It was on the tip of Liam's tongue to remind her that he wasn't job hunting. Since the job hunt seemed to be his main attraction, however, he kept silent.

This block was even more rundown than Bunker Street. Most of the rowhouses were boarded up, and bits of trash flocked the gutters. The café, when they arrived there, didn't even have a real sign—just *PeeWeEs* scrawled in downward-slanting whitewash across the window, above a pale avocado tree struggling up from a grapefruit-juice tin on the sill. Liam would never have dared to enter such a place by himself, but Eunice yanked open the baggy screen door without hesitation. He followed her into a small front room—clearly a parlor, once, with dramatic black-and-gold wallpaper and a faded, rose-colored linoleum floor stippled to look like shag carpeting. Three mismatched tables all but filled the space. Through a doorway to the rear, Liam heard pots clanking and water running.

"Hello!" Eunice called, and she pulled out the nearest chair and plunked herself down on it. Liam took the seat across from her. His own chair seemed to have come from a classroom—it was that familiar blend of blond wood and tan-painted steel—but Eunice's was part of a dinette set, upholstered in bright-yellow vinyl.

"Do you want anything to eat?" Eunice asked him.

"No thanks," he said—addressing, at the last minute, the large woman in a housecoat who appeared in the rear door-way. "Just coffee, please."

"I'll have coffee and a Tastykake," Eunice told the woman.

"Huh," the woman said, and she vanished again. Eunice smiled after her. Either she was admirably at ease anywhere or she suffered from a total lack of discrimination; Liam couldn't decide which.

He hunched forward in his seat as soon as they were alone. (He had to make the most of this one chance.) Keeping his tone casual, he asked, "Why is it that you're needed only for transitions?"

"Oh, well," Eunice said vaguely. "I'm sort of a . . . facilitator. Sort of, I don't know, a *social* facilitator, maybe you could say."

"You remind Mr. Cope of appointments and such."

"Well, yes."

She picked up an ashtray. Liam hadn't seen an ashtray on a table in years. This one was a triangle of black plastic, with *Flagg Family Crab House, Ocean City, Maryland* stamped in white around the rim. She turned it over and examined the bottom.

"Boy, could *I* ever use reminding," Liam said. "Especially when it comes to names. If I'm, for instance, walking down the street with someone and another person pops up that I know, and I have to all at once make the introductions . . . well, I'm at a loss. Both people's names just fly clean out of my head."

"Have you ever been involved in any community leadership?" Eunice asked him.

"Pardon?"

"Like, had to explain a project or something at a meeting?"

The large woman reappeared just then, scuffing across

the linoleum in rubber flip-flops and carrying a tray. She set down two Styrofoam cups of coffee and a piece of yellow cake wrapped in cellophane.

"Thank you," Liam said. He waited until she was gone before he told Eunice, "No, I don't enjoy public speaking."

"I'm just trying to think what qualities we should stress on your application."

"Oh, well, I—"

"You *have* been speaking to classes, all these years."

"That's not the same, somehow."

"But suppose there was a meeting of people objecting to something. And you were asked to make a speech telling them why they were wrong. I'm thinking you would be good at that!"

When she got going this way, he could understand how he had first taken her for a much younger woman. She was leaning toward him eagerly, holding on to her Styrofoam cup with both hands, oblivious to the bra strap that had slid down her left arm. (Her bra would be one of those no-nonsense white cotton items, circle-stitched, in a super-duper size. He could detect its outline through her blouse.) He shifted his gaze to his coffee. Judging from the strand of bubbles skimming the surface, he wondered if it might be instant. "I'm just not a very public person," he said.

"If we could point up the classroom angle . . . like, stress your persuasive abilities. Every teacher has persuasive abilities!"

"You really think so," he said noncommittally.

Then, "Tell me, Eunice. Have you been working for Mr. Cope long?"

"What? Oh, no. Just a few months."

She sat back and began unwrapping her cake. He seized his advantage. "I like your attitude toward him," he said.

"How do you mean, my attitude?"

"I mean, you're helpful but respectful. You allow him his dignity."

"Well, that's not so hard." She took a bite of her cake.

"Not for you, obviously. You must have a knack for it."

She shrugged. "Want to hear something funny?" she asked when she had swallowed. "My major was biology."

"Biology!"

"But I couldn't find a job in biology. Mostly, I've been unemployed. My parents think I'm a failure."

"Well, they're wrong," he said. He experienced a kind of rush to his head. He had not felt this strongly in years. "Good Lord, you're the diametrical opposite of a failure! If only you knew how you seem from outside, so efficient and discreet!"

Eunice looked surprised.

"At least," he said hastily, "that's how it struck me when I saw you in front of the Cope building."

She said, "Why, thank you, Liam."

"You're welcome."

"I do work really hard at this job. Not everybody appreciates that."

"That's because your purpose is to make it *not* look hard," he said.

"Oh, you're right!"

He took a sip of his coffee and grimaced. Yes, instant, beyond a doubt, and barely lukewarm besides.

"It isn't only names I was talking about," he told her. "When I said I could use reminding, I mean." He shot her a glance. "The fact is, I was hit on the head by a burglar a few weeks ago. Since then I seem to be suffering a bit of amnesia."

"Amnesia!" she said. "You've forgotten your identity?"

"No, no, nothing so extreme as that. It's just that I've forgotten the experience of being hit. I have no recollection of it."

He waited for her to ask, as everyone did, why he would *want* such a recollection, but she just made a tsk-ing sound.

"I guess I should be glad," he told her. "I'm better off forgetting, right? But that's not how I feel about it."

"Well, of course it's not," she said. "You want to know what happened."

"Yes, but there's more to it than that. Even if someone could tell me what happened—even if they told me every detail—I would still feel . . . I don't know . . ."

"You would still feel something was missing," Eunice said.

"Exactly."

"Something you yourself have lived through, and it ought to belong to *you* now, not just to someone who tells you about it. But it doesn't."

"That's it exactly!"

He was grateful to hear it put into words. He felt a sudden flood of affection for her—for the errant bra strap, even, and the headlamp look of her eyes behind her big glasses.

"Eunice," he said consideringly.

She paused in the midst of licking a dab of frosting off one finger.

"Properly speaking," he said, "it should be 'You-*nike*-ee.' That's the way the Greeks would have said it."

" 'You-niss' is bad enough," she told him. "I've always hated my name."

"Oh, it's a fine name. It means 'victorious.' "

She set down her cake. She sat up straighter. "So . . ." she said, "um, tell me, is your . . . wife a teacher too?"

"Wife? I'm not married. The Romans would have said 'You-*nice*-ee.' But I can understand how that wouldn't work in English."

"Liam?" Eunice said. "I really meant it when I said you should apply for a job."

"Oh. Well, actually, since I'm sixty years old—"

"They can't object to that! Age discrimination's illegal."

"Yes, but I meant—"

"Is it the résumé you're worried about? I'll help you. I'm really good at résumés," she said, and she gave a little laugh. "I've certainly had enough practice."

"Well, actually—"

"We could get together and whip one up after I finish work. I could come to your house."

"Apartment," he said without planning to.

"I could come to your apartment."

She would walk into his den and see the patio door where the burglar had slipped through. "Hmm," she would muse aloud. She would turn and examine Liam's face, cocking her head appraisingly. "In my experience," she would say, "a memory that's associated with trauma . . ." Or, "A memory that's imprinted in someone roused from deep sleep . . ."

Oh, don't be absurd. This was just a glorified secretary, working at a made-up job her mother had cadged from a friend.

But even as he was thinking that, Liam was saying, "Well, if you're sure you can spare the time."

"I have all the time in the world! I get off at five o'clock today. Here," she said, and she reached to the floor for her purse and turned it upside down over the table. A wallet and keys and pill bottles and bits of paper fell out. She chose one of the bits of paper—a ruled sheet torn from a memo pad—and thrust it toward him. *Milk, toothpaste, plant food*, he read. "Write down your address," she ordered. "Is it someplace I can find?"

"It's just up Charles near the Beltway."

"Perfect! Write your phone number too. Darn it, where's my pen?"

"I have a pen," he said.

"Hello? Hello?" she shouted.

Liam was startled, until he realized she was calling their waitress. "Can we get our bill?" she asked when the woman appeared.

Without speaking, the woman dug in her housecoat pocket and handed over a chit of paper that seemed as unofficial as Eunice's memo page. Liam said, "Please, let me pay."

"I wouldn't think of it," Eunice said.

"No, really, I insist."

"Liam!" she barked, and she sent him a mock frown. "We'll hear no more about this. You can buy me coffee once you land a job."

Liam looked up at their waitress and found her frowning at him too, but with an expression of utter contempt. He bent meekly over the memo page and wrote down his address.

There was no way on earth that he could work for Cope Development, even if they were misguided enough to offer him a position. And it was nice of Eunice to take an interest, of course; but face it: she was really sort of . . . hapless. People like Eunice just never had quite figured out how to get along in the world. They might be perfectly intelligent, but they were subject to speckles and flushes; their purses resembled wastepaper baskets; they stepped on their own skirts.

Actually, Eunice was the only person he could think of who answered to that description. But still, there was something familiar about her.

He would phone her at Cope Development and cancel their appointment. "I can't work there!" he would say. "I wouldn't fit in. Thanks anyhow."

When he picked up the receiver, though, he realized he didn't know her last name. Admittedly, this was not an insurmountable problem. How many Eunices were they likely to have on their payroll? But he deplored the sound of it—"May I please speak to Eunice?" So unprofessional.

"This is Liam Pennywell calling Mr. Cope's assistant. Eunice, I believe it was."

They would take him for some kind of stalker.

He didn't make the call.

Though a part of him knew full well what a weak excuse that was.

After lunch—a peanut-butter sandwich—he vacuumed his apartment and dusted all the furniture and fixed a pitcher of iced tea. He found himself talking silently to Eunice as he worked. Somehow, he progressed from "The fact is that I'm not the developer type" to "I've had a hard time with this amnesia issue; maybe you can understand." He pictured her nodding sagely, matter-of-factly, as if this syndrome were old news to her. "Let's review this for a moment, shall we?" she might say. Or, "A lot of times, when Mr. C. forgets, I've learned that it helps to . . ." To what? Liam couldn't invent an end for that sentence.

It dawned on him that what he wanted from her was not so much to recover the burglar incident as to make sense of his forgetting it. He wanted her to say, "*Oh*, yes. I've seen this before; it's nothing new. Other people have these holes in their lives."

True, various doctors had said that already, but that was different. Why was it different? He couldn't explain. Something lurked at the edge of his mind but he couldn't quite grab hold of it.

He sat down in his rocker and stayed there, empty-headed, hands loose on his thighs. Long ago when he was young he used to envision old age this way: man in a rocker, idle. He had read somewhere that old people could sit in their chairs and watch their memories roll past like movies, endlessly entertaining; but so far that hadn't happened to him. He was beginning to think it never would.

He was glad he hadn't canceled Eunice's visit.

She showed up just before six o'clock—later than he had expected. He'd started growing a little fidgety. She was carrying a bag of fried chicken from a takeout place. "I thought we could have supper while we worked," she said. "I hope you haven't already fixed us something."

"Why . . . no, I haven't," Liam said.

Fried chicken tended to upset his stomach, but he had to admit it smelled delicious. He took the bag from her and placed it on the table, assuming they would eat later. Eunice, however, made a beeline for his kitchen. "Plates? Silver?" she asked.

"Oh, um, plates are in that cupboard to your left."

She rattled among the cabinets and drawers while Liam drew a wad of paper napkins from the takeout bag. "I brought you some materials describing the company," she called over her shoulder. "Just so you can sound informed about where you're applying."

Liam said, "Ah. The company. Well. I've been thinking. I'm not sure the company and I would be such a very good match."

"Not sure!"

She stopped midway to the table, holding an armful of dishes and silverware.

"I guess at heart I'm still a teacher," he told her.

"Oh, change is always difficult," she said.

He nodded.

"But if you just gave this a try; just tried it to see how you liked it . . ." She set the dishes on the table and began distributing them. "Do you have any soft drinks?"

"No, only iced tea," Liam said. "Or, wait. I think my daughter may have left some Diet Coke."

"I didn't know you had a daughter!" Eunice said. She sounded unduly taken aback, as if she knew everything else about him.

"I have three, in fact," Liam said.

"So you're, what? Divorced? Widowed?"

"Both," Liam said. "Which did you want?"

Eunice said, "Excuse me?" She seemed to be having one of her flushes.

"Iced tea or Diet Coke?"

"Oh! Diet Coke, please."

Liam found a Diet Coke behind the milk and brought it to the table, along with the pitcher of tea for himself. "My refrigerator dispenses ice directly through the door," he told Eunice. "Would you like some for your Coke?"

"No, thanks, I'll just drink from the can."

She was setting out pieces of chicken on a platter. There were biscuits, too, he saw, but no vegetable. He debated fixing a salad but decided against it; too time-consuming. He sat down in his usual place. Eunice took the chair to his left. She smoothed a napkin across her lap and gazed around. "This is a nice apartment," she said.

"Thanks. I don't feel entirely settled yet."

"You've just moved in?"

"A few weeks ago."

He took a drumstick from the platter and put it on his plate. Eunice chose a wing.

"The burglary happened the first night I was here," he told her. "I went to sleep perfectly fine, and I woke up in the hospital."

"That's terrible," Eunice said. "Didn't you want to move out again right away?"

"Well, it was more a matter of . . . I was more concerned about remembering what had happened," Liam said. "I felt as if I had leapt this sort of ditch. This gap of time that I had skipped completely. I hate that feeling! I hate forgetting."

"It's like Mr. C.," Eunice said.

"Ah," Liam said, and he grew very alert.

"You won't breathe a word of this, will you?"

"No, no!"

"What I do for Mr. C. is, like, I'm his external hard drive."

Liam blinked.

"But that is *not to go beyond these walls*," Eunice said. "You have to promise."

"Yes, of course, but—"

"Mrs. C. was just worried to bits, was what she told my mother."

"So . . . excuse me, you're saying—"

"But forget I mentioned it, okay? Let's change the subject."

Liam said, "Okay . . ."

"How can you be both divorced and widowed?" she asked him.

He tried to collect his thoughts. He said, "The divorce was the second wife. The first wife died."

"Oh, I am so, so sorry."

"Well, it was long ago," Liam said. "I never think about her anymore."

Eunice started picking her chicken wing apart with the very tips of her fingers, putting slivers of meat in her mouth while she kept her eyes on his. He didn't want her to ask what Millie had died of. He could see the question forming in her mind, and so he rushed to say, "Two marriages! Sounds pretty bad, right? I'm always embarrassed to tell people."

"My great-grandfather had three marriages," Eunice said.

"Three! Well, I'd never go *that* far. There's something . . . exaggerated about three marriages. Cartoonish. No offense to your great-grandfather."

"This was back in the old days," Eunice said. "His first two wives died in childbirth."

"Oh, then," Liam said.

"How did—?"

"But!" Liam said loudly, slapping both hands on the table. "We don't have a vegetable! What am I thinking? I'm going to make us a salad."

"No, really, I don't need a salad."

"Let's see," he said, and he jumped up and went to the refrigerator. "Lettuce? Tomatoes? Hmm, the lettuce seems a bit . . ."

He returned with a bag of baby carrots. "Did you know there's a store on York Road called Greenish Grocery?" he asked as he sat back down. "I've driven past it. I always picture they'd have brown-edged lettuce, shriveled radishes, broccoli turning yellow . . . Here, help yourself."

Last month, as it happened, had marked the thirty-second anniversary of Millie's death. He wouldn't ordinarily have remembered, but he was writing the date on a check and he happened to notice. June fifth. Thirty-two years; good God. She'd been barely twenty-four when she died. If she were to see him today she would think, Who is that old man?

"I understand these carrots aren't really babies at all," he told Eunice. "They're full-sized but they've been whittled down by machines to make them little."

"That's all right," Eunice said, and she laid the single carrot she'd selected onto her plate. For someone so well padded, she seemed a very dainty eater. "Now, I haven't spoken yet to Mr. McPherson," she said.

"McPherson. Oh. At Cope."

"I thought first you could write him a letter of inquiry, and then I would stop by his office and put in a word of recommendation."

"Well, but—" Liam began.

He was interrupted by the sound of the front door opening. Maybe he was edgier these days than he realized, because his heart gave a sudden thump. Someone called, "Poppy?"

Kitty came staggering in with her duffel bag and a large canvas tote. She still wore her work clothes—the pink polyester tunic she always complained about. Her mascara or whatever it was had blurred so she seemed to have two black eyes. "Oh!" she said when she saw Eunice.

Liam said, "Eunice, this is Kitty, my daughter. Kitty, this is Eunice, um . . ."

"Dunstead," Eunice said. She was sitting almost swaybacked now with her hands folded under her chin. She looked a little bit like a chipmunk. "It's such a thrill to meet you, Kitty!"

"Hi," Kitty said flatly. Then she turned to Liam. "I've reached the end of the line, I tell you. I'm not staying under that woman's roof another minute."

"Well, why not have a piece of chicken," Liam said. "Eunice here was kind enough to bring a—"

"First of all, I am seventeen years old. I am *not a child*. Second, I have always been an extremely reasonable person. Wouldn't you say I'm reasonable?"

"Should I go?" Eunice asked Liam.

She spoke in a low, urgent voice, as if hoping Kitty wouldn't hear. Liam glanced at her. In fact, he did wish all at once that she would go. This was not working out the way he'd imagined; it was getting complicated; he felt frazzled and distracted. But he said, "Oh, no, please don't feel you have to—"

"I think I should," she said, and she rose, or half rose, watching his face.

Liam said, "Well, then, if you're sure."

She stood up all the way and reached for her purse. Kitty was saying, "But *some* people just take this preconception into their heads and then there's no convincing them. 'I know *you*,' they say; 'I don't trust you as far as I can—' "

"Sorry," Liam told Eunice as he followed her toward the door.

"That's all right!" she said. "We can always get together another time. I'll phone you tomorrow, why don't I. Meanwhile, you can be looking through those materials I brought. Did I give you those materials? What'd I do with them?"

She stopped walking to peer down into her purse. "Oh. Here," she said, and she pulled out several sheets of paper folded haphazardly into a wad.

Liam accepted them, but then he said, "Actually, Eunice . . . you know? I really don't think I'll apply there."

She stared up at him. He took another step toward the door, meaning to urge her on, but she held her ground. (He was never going to get rid of her.) She said, "Are you saying that just because Mr. C. forgot he had met you?"

"What? No!"

"Because it means *nothing* that he forgot. Nothing at all."

"Yes, I understand. I just—"

"But we won't go into the particulars," she said, and she slid her eyes in Kitty's direction. "I'll phone you in the morning, okay?"

"Fine," he said.

Fine. He would deal with it in the morning.

"Bye-bye for now, Kitty!" she called.

"Bye."

Liam opened the door for Eunice, but he didn't follow her out. He stood watching her cross the foyer. At the outer door she turned to wave, and he lifted the wad of papers and nodded.

When he went back inside he found Kitty sitting at the table, grasping a chicken breast with both hands and munching away at great speed. She said, "Any chance you'll be going by an ATM any time soon?"

"I hadn't planned to."

"Because I spent my very last dollar on the taxi."

"You came by taxi?"

"What do you think, I carried all this luggage on the bus?"

"I gave it no thought at all, I suppose," he said, and he dropped back down on his chair.

Kitty set her chicken breast on the bare table and wiped her hands on a paper napkin. The napkin turned into a greasy shred. "That woman's younger than Xanthe," she told him.

"Yes, you're probably right."

"She's way too young for *you*."

"For me! Oh, goodness, she's got nothing to do with me!"

Kitty raised her eyebrows. "Think not?" she asked him.

"Good Lord, no! She came to help with my résumé."

"She came because she has this big huge crush on you that sticks out a mile in every direction," Kitty said.

"What!"

Kitty eyed him in silence as she took a carrot from the bag.

"What a notion," Liam said.

He didn't know which was more shocking: the notion itself, or the slow, deep sense of astonished pleasure that began to rise in his chest.

6

Now he saw that Eunice had certain subtle attractions. In looks, for instance, there were qualities that might not be apparent at first glance: the creamy, cushiony softness of her skin, the pale matte silk of her unlipsticked mouth, her clear gray eyes framed by long brown lashes. The dimple in each of her cheeks resembled the precisely drilled dent that forms at the center of a whirlpool. Her nose, which was more round than pointed, added a note of whimsy.

And wasn't her occasional lack of grace a sign of character? Like an absentminded professor, she concentrated on the intangibles. She was too busy with more important matters to notice the merely physical.

She showed a kind of trustfulness, too, that was seldom seen in grownups. The way she had rushed after him on the street, and flung herself into his problems, and thought nothing of coming alone to his apartment . . . In retrospect, Liam found that touching.

It had been years since he had had any sort of romantic life. He'd more or less given up on that side of things, it seemed. But now he remembered the significance that a love affair could lend to the most ordinary moments. The simplest activities could take on extra color and intensity. Days had a purpose to them—an element of suspense, even. He missed that.

He rose too early the following morning, after a restless night. Kitty was still asleep in the den. (That much he had insisted on: he wasn't forfeiting his bedroom a second time.) At first he contented himself with making a great deal of noise over breakfast, but when she hadn't appeared by seven thirty, he tapped lightly on her door. "Kitty?" he called. He opened the door a few inches and peered in. "Shouldn't you be getting up?"

The blanket on the daybed stirred, and Kitty raised her head. "What for?" she asked him.

"For work, of course."

"Work! It's the Fourth of July."

"It is?" he said.

He thought a moment. "Does that mean you have the day off?" he asked.

"Well, *duh!*"

"Oh."

"The plan was, I'd get to sleep as long as I wanted," she said.

"Sorry," he said.

He closed the door.

The Fourth of July! So, well, what about Eunice? Would she call anyhow? And was Kitty going to hang around all morning?

He poured himself another cup of coffee, even though it would give him the jitters. In fact, maybe he had the jitters already, because when the telephone rang, he actually jumped. The coffee sloshed in his cup. He picked up the receiver and said, "Hello?"

"Liam?"

"Oh. Barbara."

"Is Kitty with you?"

"Why, yes."

"You might have thought to tell me," she said. "I got up this morning and looked in her room: no Kitty. And her bed had not been slept in."

"I'm sorry; I thought you knew," he said. "I gathered you two had an argument."

"We did have an argument, and she flounced off to her room and slammed the door. And then I had to go out, and it was past midnight when I got home so I just assumed she was in her bed."

Another time, Liam might have asked what had kept Barbara out so late. (Not that she would necessarily have deigned to answer.) But he wanted to free the telephone line, so he said, "Well, she's here, and she's fine."

"How long is she staying?" Barbara asked.

"She's not staying at all, as far as I know, but why don't you ask *her* about that? I'll have her call when she gets up."

"Liam, you are in no condition to take on a teenage girl," Barbara said.

"God forbid; I wouldn't think of taking—Condition?" he said. "What condition do I have?"

"You're a man. And also you lack experience, since you have never been very involved in your daughters' lives."

"How can you say that?" Liam asked. "I *raised* one of my daughters, entirely by myself."

"You didn't even raise her through toddlerhood. And it was nowhere near by yourself."

A rush of emotions swept through him—a combination of injured feelings and frustration and defeat all too familiar from their marriage. He said, "I have to get off the line. Goodbye."

"Wait! Liam, don't go. Wait a minute. Did she tell you what we argued about?"

"No," he said. "What did you argue about?"

"I have no idea! That's the thing of it. The two of us are just flying apart, and I don't understand why. Oh, we used to get on so well together. Remember what a sweet little girl Kitty was?"

Liam had barely known Kitty as a little girl, to be honest. She'd been one of those last-ditch efforts—a save-the-marriage baby born late in their lives, only she *hadn't* saved the marriage (surprise, surprise), and within the year he'd become a visitor to his own family. And not so frequent a visitor, at that—least frequent of all with Kitty, since she had been so young.

Well. No point dwelling on the past.

He told Barbara, "She's going to be fine; don't worry. This is only a stage they go through."

"Oh, yes, I know," Barbara said on a long sigh. "I know it is. Thanks, Liam. Do have her call me, please."

"I will."

He hung up and looked at his watch. It was almost eight o'clock. Why hadn't he informed Eunice last night that he was an early riser? She could have phoned him an hour ago.

He cleared away his breakfast things and loaded the dish-washer, taking care to be quiet now because if Kitty wasn't leaving for work, he would just as soon she went on sleeping. But while he was sponging the counter, the door to the den opened and she came shambling out, yawning and ruffling her hair. She wore striped pajama bottoms and what looked to him like a bra, although he hoped it was one of those jogging tops instead. It was so difficult to tell, these days. "Now what?" she asked him. "I'm wide awake and it's not but eight in the morning."

"Don't you have any plans?"

"Nope."

"Nothing going on with Damian?"

"Damian's in Rhode Island," she said. "His cousin's getting married."

"Well, your mother would like you to phone her. I hadn't realized you didn't tell her where you would be."

"Wouldn't you think she could figure it out?" Kitty asked. She opened the refrigerator and gazed into it for a long moment. Liam hated it when she did that. He could practically feel the dollars whooshing past her and disappearing. He held his tongue, though, because he wanted to fare better with her than Barbara had. Eventually Kitty reached for a carton of milk and then shut the door. "I really think Mom might be cracking up," she told Liam. "Maybe it's change of life."

"Change of life! Wouldn't she be done with that?"

Kitty shrugged and took a box of cereal from the cupboard.

"I believe menopause hits in the late forties. Or fifties, maybe," Liam said.

"Oh, *menopause;* sure. I'm talking about change of life."

"What?"

An uncertain look crossed Kitty's face. "Do I mean midlife crisis?" she asked.

"Only if you're expecting her to live to a hundred and twenty."

"Well, *I* don't know; I just feel like she's acting crazy. Every little thing I do, it's 'Kitty, stop that,' and 'Kitty, you're grounded,' and 'Kitty, how often must I tell you.' Senile dementia; maybe that's what I mean."

"Do you suppose it has to do with her boyfriend?" Liam asked. "What's-his-name?"

Kitty shrugged again and sat down at the table.

"How is that going, anyway?" Liam asked.

There was only the faintest chance that Kitty would answer, but it never hurt to try. Before she could draw in a breath, though, the doorbell rang. Liam said, "Now, who—?"

He went to the front door and opened it to find Eunice. She stood looking at him with a solemn, oddly dubious expression, holding her purse primly in front of her with both hands. "Why, Eunice!" he said. "Hello!" He was thrown off a bit by her glasses, which he had somehow forgotten—the huge size of them, the smudged lenses.

"Your phone number's unlisted," she said.

"Yes, it is, actually."

"And you didn't write it down for me."

"I didn't?" he said. "Oh!"

"I told the operator I knew you but she still wouldn't give out the number."

"Yes, that's . . . kind of the idea," Liam said. "I apologize. I honestly thought I wrote it down. Freudian slip, I guess."

"Why?" she asked him.

"Why?"

"Why Freudian? You didn't want me to call?"

"No, no . . . It's just that I hate to talk on the phone."

"Oh, I love to talk on the phone!"

She took several steps inside, as if propelled by a gust of enthusiasm. "It's one of my favorite occupations," she said.

She was wearing pants today, wide gauze pants gathered at the waist and gathered at the ankles but ballooning at the hips. He believed that was called the harem style. She would have been better off in a skirt, he felt. But she did have very creamy skin, and the dimples were showing in both her cheeks.

"I forgot it was the Fourth of July," he told her. "I hope you haven't changed any plans."

"I was glad to change my plans," she said. "My parents always throw this lawn party and I'm supposed to be helping them set up."

She gave a little chuckle—a warm, infectious sound—and the dimples deepened. He smiled at her. He said, "Won't you come in and sit down?"

On her way to one of the armchairs, she trilled her fingers at Kitty. "Hi, Kitty!" she said.

"Hi."

"I see I'm interrupting your breakfast."

"Not really," Kitty said. Which was true; she remained hunched over her cereal bowl, shoveling in Honey Nut Cheerios.

Liam said, "Kitty, weren't you going to call your mother?"

"I'll do it in a minute," she said.

"Do it now, please. I promised her you'd call as soon as you were up."

Kitty gave him a look, but she set down her spoon and pushed her chair back. "It's not like it's a national emergency," she said as she went off to the den.

"She didn't leave word where she would be last night," Liam told Eunice. (It seemed a nice, safe, neutral topic.) He settled across from her, in the rocker. "I hadn't realized that till her mother phoned this morning."

"So the two of you get along?" Eunice asked.

"Oh, yes, as well as can be expected. Considering she's an adolescent."

"Her mother is adolescent?"

"What? No, Kitty is. Kitty's the adolescent. I'm sorry; you were asking about her mother?"

"I just meant . . . you know, do you talk with her mother on the phone and all."

"We have to talk on the phone; we've got three daughters," Liam said. "But I should be offering you coffee! It's already made. Would you like a cup?"

"I'd love some," Eunice said. She had a way of drawing back slightly when something pleased her. It gave her a bit of a double chin, which was surprisingly becoming.

She stayed in her chair while Liam rose and went to the kitchen. "Cream? Sugar?" he called.

"Just black."

He could hear Kitty on her cell phone in the den, even through the closed door—the "*Na*-na, *na*-na" of some protest or accusation. To drown her out, he said, "So! Eunice. Tell me about your job."

"There's not a whole lot to tell," she said.

"Well, what exactly would you do in the average day, for instance?"

"Oh, I might go around to different places with Mr. C. Drive him out to check on a project, say. Or we attend a meeting of some sort."

Liam brought her coffee in a cup with a real saucer, part of a matched set that he used so seldom, he'd had to wipe the dust off first. He sat back down in the rocker and said, "You stay with him through the whole meeting?"

"Yes, because I need to take notes. I take separate notes just for him, in a big ring binder that fills up every month or so. And also, well, if he gets a notion to leave, I'm the one who reminds him it's not time yet."

"I see," Liam said. Then he said, "These notes are like regular minutes?"

"No, they've got, you know, tabs that are color-coded."

"Aha!"

Eunice looked startled.

"Different colors for different memories," he suggested.

"Or for different *categories* of memories, really. Like, red is for things that he's already said about certain proposals, so that he won't repeat himself, and then green is for personal information he might want for his conversations. Say somebody at the meeting turned out to have a son who went to school with Mr. C.'s son. That kind of thing."

"Does that actually work?" Liam asked.

"Well, no," she said. "Not very well." She took a gulp of her coffee. "It's just all I could come up with. I'm trying different approaches."

"What else are you thinking of trying?" he asked her.

"I'm not sure." She gazed down into her cup and said, "I'm probably going to get fired."

"Why's that?"

"There are such a *lot* of categories! Life has so many things in it that people need to remember! And Mr. C. is falling farther and farther behind. I'm working as hard as I can, but even so . . . I suppose pretty soon he'll have to retire." She gave Liam a brief, perky smile and said, "So we'd better get busy, right? I won't have an inside track with Cope Development for much longer."

She placed her cup and saucer on the lamp table and bent to rummage through her purse. "First I'll just jot down some of your facts," she said. She brought forth a steno pad and a ballpoint pen.

"I get a notebook all my own!" Liam said in a jokey voice.

"What?"

"A notebook like Mr. Cope's."

She looked at the steno pad and then at Liam. "No, well, Mr. Cope's is more of a binder," she said.

"Yes, I realize that, but . . . I was thinking how nice it would be if you were to keep *my* memories."

"Oh!" she said. She flushed a deep pink and let her pen fall to the floor. Bending down to retrieve it turned her even pinker.

It was possible, Liam thought, that Kitty had been right: Eunice harbored some personal feeling for him. On the other hand, maybe she just reacted this way to life in general.

Kitty chose that moment to emerge from the den. She held her cell phone out at arm's length. "Mom wants to talk to you," she told him. She walked over to him and handed him the phone.

Liam spent a second trying to figure out how such a tiny object could make contact with both his ear and his mouth at the same time. He gave up, finally, and pressed it to his ear. "Hello?" he said.

Barbara said, "Kitty tells me she wants to stay with you all summer."

"She does?"

"Have the two of you not discussed this?"

"No."

Kitty suddenly fell to the floor, surprising him so that he nearly dropped the phone. Kneeling in front of him, she pressed her hands together like someone praying and mouthed a silent *Please please please please.*

"I won't deny that I could use a little help, here," Barbara said. "But I still have a lot of reservations. If we do this, I need to be sure you'll set some limits."

Liam said, "Wait, I—"

"First you'll have to promise me she'll be home by ten on weeknights. Twelve on Fridays and Saturdays. And she is absolutely not allowed one moment alone in the apartment with Damian or any other boy. Is that clear? I've no desire to end up with a pregnant seventeen-year-old."

"Pregnant!" Liam said.

Kitty lowered her hands and gaped at him. Eunice's eyes grew very wide behind her glasses.

"No, of course not," he said hastily. "I'm sure she wouldn't want that either. Merciful heavens!"

"You act as if it's an impossibility, but believe me, these things happen," Barbara told him.

"I'm aware of that," Liam said.

"Okay, Liam. I just hope you know what you're doing."

"But—"

"If she wants to come by for her clothes, I'll be here till late afternoon. Put her on, will you?"

Wordlessly, Liam handed the phone to Kitty. She sprang to her feet and walked off with it, saying, "What. Yes, I hear you. I'm not a *total* dummy."

The den door shut behind her. Liam looked at Eunice.

"Seems all at once I have a long-term visitor," he said.

"She's going to live here?"

"For the summer."

"Well, isn't it nice that she wants to!" Eunice said.

"It's more a case of her *not* wanting to live with her mother, I believe."

"Is her mother a difficult person?" Eunice asked.

"No, not particularly."

"Then why did you two divorce?"

This was beginning to feel like a date, somehow. It might have had to do with the way Eunice leaned forward to ask her questions—so attentive, so receptive. But Liam wasn't sure now that he wanted a date. (At the moment, her head of curls reminded him of a Shirley Temple doll.)

He said, "The divorce was Barbara's idea, not mine. I don't even believe in divorce; I've always felt marriages are meant to be permanent. If it were up to me, we'd still be together."

"What was she unhappy about?" Eunice asked.

"Oh," he said, "I guess she felt I wasn't, um, forthcoming."

Eunice went on looking at him expectantly.

He turned his palms up. What more could he say?

"But you're forthcoming with *me*," she said.

"I am?"

"And you listen so well! You asked all about my job; you

want to know every detail of how I spend my days . . . Men don't usually do that."

"I didn't do it with Barbara, though," Liam said. "She was right. I told her that. I said, 'It's true, I'm not forthcoming at all.' "

This made Eunice blush again, for some reason. She said, "I'll take that as a compliment."

He was still trying to figure out why it should be a compliment when she said, "Maybe your marriage was troubled because of your loss."

"What did I lose?"

"Didn't you say your first wife had died?"

"Oh, yes. But that was a long time before." He slapped his thighs and stood up. "Let me top off your coffee!" he said.

"No, thanks, I'm okay."

He sat down again. He said, "Should we be getting on with my résumé?"

"All right," she said. "Fine." She clicked her pen point. "First, your places of employment."

"Employment. Well. From nineteen seventy-five to nineteen eighty-two, I taught ancient history at the Fremont School."

"The Fremont School? Gosh," Eunice said.

"That was my first job."

"Well, but you're supposed to start with your *last* job," she told him, "and work your way back."

"You're right. Okay: eighty-two till this past spring, I taught at St. Dyfrig."

She wrote it down without comment.

"I taught fifth grade from ninety . . . four? No, three. From ninety-three on, and before that, American history."

He liked this business of proceeding in reverse order. It meant he was listing progressively higher positions instead of lower. (In his opinion, history was definitely higher than fifth grade, and ancient history higher than American.) Eunice took notes in silence. When he stopped speaking, she looked up and said, "Any honors or awards?"

"Miles Elliott Prize in Philosophy, nineteen sixty-nine."

"You were employed in sixty-nine?"

"I was in college."

"Oh. College."

"Philosophy was my major," he said. "Pretty silly, right? Who do you know who's majored in philosophy and actually *works* as a philosopher?"

"How about your professional life? Any awards there?"

"No."

"Let's pass on to your education." She flipped a page of the steno pad. "I have this software program that produces résumés," she told him. "All I have to do is plug in the facts and the program does the rest. My parents gave it to me for Christmas one year. Is your computer Windows or Macintosh?"

"I don't have a computer," he said.

"You don't have a computer. Okay. I'd better write your letter of inquiry, too," she said, and she made another note.

Liam said, "Eunice. Do you really think we should go on with this?"

"What? Why not?"

"I don't have any business experience. I'm a teacher! I don't even know what they're looking for."

Eunice seemed about to offer an argument, but just then Kitty came out of the den. She was wearing shorts now and a

T-shirt that advertised Absolut vodka. "Poppy," she said, "can I borrow your car?"

"My car! What for?"

"I need to get some more of my clothes."

Liam wasn't used to lending out his car. He knew it wasn't *much* of a car, but it was sort of attuned to his ways, he felt. Also, he had a suspicion that there was some kind of insurance complication with teenage drivers.

"Why don't I take you over myself later this afternoon," he said.

"I won't keep it long! I'll have it back before you even miss it."

"Just wait till we're finished here and I'll drive you."

"Geez," Kitty said, and she threw herself into the other armchair. She sat practically on the back of her neck, with her long bare legs stretched out in front of her, and sent him a fierce glare.

"Eunice and I were just discussing my employment," Liam told her.

Kitty went on glaring.

"Eunice thinks I ought to apply at Cope Development, but I was telling her I don't know what I could do there."

"What's Cope Development," Kitty said without a question mark.

"It's a place that develops new properties."

"He would be terrible at that," Kitty told Eunice.

Eunice made a sound between a gasp and a giggle.

"I'm serious," Kitty said. "He's not a good businessman."

"How would *you* know what kind of businessman I am?" Liam asked her. Then he realized that he was undermining his own argument, so he turned back to Eunice and said, "But just in terms of where I'd be comfortable, I don't believe Cope's the right fit. I'm sorry, Eunice."

Eunice said, "Oh."

She looked down at what she'd written. Then she clicked her pen shut. Finally, it seemed, she had heard what he was saying. "I understand," she said gently.

"I'm sorry I put you to so much trouble."

"Oh, that's okay. You've been telling me this all along, haven't you? I guess I've been kind of pushy."

"No, no. Certainly not! You've been wonderful," he said. "I really appreciate your help." He told Kitty, "She's been helping with my résumé. She's got this computer program that . . ."

Kitty was watching him with mild, detached curiosity. Eunice was still gazing down at her steno pad. Her lowered lids gave her a meek and chastened look; all her enthusiasm had left her.

All his had left, too—all his sense of something new in the air, something about to happen.

He said, "But couldn't we go on keeping the notebook anyhow?"

She raised her eyes and said, "Pardon?"

"I mean . . ." he said, and he cleared his throat. "Couldn't we go on keeping in touch?"

"Oh! Of course we could!" she said. "Certainly we could! No matter where you apply you'll need a résumé, right?"

This wasn't what he had meant, but he said, "Right."

He pretended not to hear Kitty's snort of amusement.

7

Early on the fifth of July, Louise phoned and asked Liam if he would babysit. "I know it's short notice," she said, "but my regular sitter has called in sick and I've got a doctor's appointment just around the corner from you. I could drop Jonah off at your place on the way."

"You mean, all by himself?" Liam asked.

"Why, yes."

"But I don't have any toys here. I have nothing to amuse him with."

"We'll bring some with us. Please? Ordinarily I would cancel, but this appointment means a lot to me."

Liam supposed, from her phrasing, that it might be an obstetrician's appointment. He didn't want to seem nosy, though, so all he said was, "Well, okay, I guess."

"Thanks, Dad. I appreciate this."

He wondered why she hadn't asked Barbara, who could pretty much arrange her own schedule in the summertime.

Or why she didn't just take Jonah along with her to the doctor's office. Surely that was allowed, wasn't it? Too bad Kitty had already left for work. He really had no idea what to do with a four-year-old.

They showed up at his door half an hour later—Louise out of breath and rushed-looking, wearing dressier clothes than usual and even a bit of lipstick. Jonah had on a T-shirt and what appeared to be swim trunks, orange Hawaiian-print nylon billowing around his toothpick shins. A knapsack almost bigger than he was loomed on his back. It was obvious from his expression that he would rather be somewhere else. He gazed up at Liam unsmilingly, his eyebrows two worried quirks. "Hi, there," Liam told him.

Jonah didn't answer.

Louise said, "I should be back in an hour or so. There's a snack in Jonah's bag if he gets hungry." She planted a kiss on top of Jonah's head and said, "Bye, sweetheart. Be a good boy."

When the door had slammed shut behind her, there was an uneasy silence.

"So," Liam said finally. He frowned down at Jonah.

Jonah frowned back at him.

"Where's your grandmother?" Liam asked.

Jonah said, "Who?"

"Your Grandma Barbara. Is she working?"

Jonah shrugged. It was an artificial-looking shrug—his sharp little shoulders hitching themselves too high and then staying there too long, as if he had not quite perfected the technique.

"Hard to believe she would have a date so early in the day," Liam mused.

Jonah said, "Deirdre is in *deep, deep trouble.*"

"Who's Deirdre?"

"My sitter. We bet anything she's not sick. We bet she's off with her boyfriend someplace. Her boyfriend's named Chicken Little."

"He's what?"

"Sometimes she brings him to my house to visit. Me and him play soccer together out in the backyard."

"Is that a fact," Liam said.

"Deirdre wears a jewel in her nose, and she's got a chain around her wrist that's really a tattoo."

"This Deirdre sounds like quite a gal," Liam said.

"Me and her are going to the State Fair in the fall."

Was Liam supposed to be correcting Jonah's grammatical errors? It seemed irresponsible just to let them slide past. On the other hand, he didn't want to discourage this sudden chattiness.

"Let's see what's in your knapsack," he said. "I hope you brought something to keep busy with."

"I've got my Bible-stories coloring book."

"Ah."

"And my crayons."

"Well, let's see them."

Jonah struggled out of his knapsack and laid it on the rug. Unzipping it took some doing—everything seemed to be such hard work, at this age—but eventually he brought forth a box of apple juice, a plastic bag of carrot sticks, a pack of crayons, and a coloring book entitled *Bible Tales for Tots*. "I just finished Abraham," he told Liam.

"Abraham!"

Wasn't that the man who'd been willing to slaughter his own son?

"Now I think I'll do Joseph," Jonah said. He started flipping through the coloring book.

"Could I see Abraham?" Liam asked him.

Jonah raised his head and gave him a level stare, as if he didn't quite trust Liam's motives.

"Just a peek?" Liam said.

Jonah turned back several pages to show a picture that had been covered over with jagged swaths of purple, nowhere near inside the lines. From what Liam could make out, it was a benign illustration of a man and a boy walking up a hill. *Abraham obeys God's command to deliver Isaac*, the caption read.

"Thanks," Liam said. "Very nice."

Jonah resumed flipping pages, settling finally on one that read *Joseph had a coat of many colors.* The coat was a sort of bathrobe affair with wide vertical stripes.

"Do they have *your* story? Jonah and the whale?" Liam asked.

Jonah gave another of his effortful shrugs and dumped the pack of crayons out on the carpet. All of them seemed untouched except for the purple, which was worn down to a nubbin. "You're supposed to tell about Joseph while I'm coloring," he said.

"Who, me?"

Jonah nodded vigorously. He selected the purple crayon and started making wild horizontal marks across the coat. There was an extremely high probability that the purple would stray onto the carpet, but Liam was so relieved to have Jonah occupied that he didn't intervene. He sat down in an armchair and said, "Okay. Joseph."

Strange how unconnected he felt to this child. Not that he had anything against him; certainly he wished him well. And it was true there was something fetching about those fragile little ears, and those tiny bare feet in laughably small flip-flops. (The universal appeal of the miniature! Obviously it must serve to perpetuate the species.) But the fact that they were related by blood seemed too much to comprehend. Did other grandparents feel this way? Or maybe it was just that Jonah was growing up in such a different world, with his fundamentalist parents and his *Bible Tales for Tots*.

Liam couldn't for the life of him remember the point of the Joseph story.

Still, he did his best. "Joseph," he said, "had a coat of many colors that was a present from his father, and this made his brothers jealous."

He wondered if the word *jealous* would be familiar to a four-year-old. It seemed doubtful. He tried to guess from Jonah's expression, but Jonah was busily working away, his lower lip caught between his teeth.

"Joseph's brothers were upset," Liam clarified, "because they didn't have any coats of many colors themselves."

"Maybe Joseph could let them borrow his sometimes," Jonah said.

"You would think so, wouldn't you."

"Did he?" Jonah persisted.

"Well, no, I don't believe he did."

Jonah shook his head and paused to peel more paper off his crayon. "That wasn't very sharing of him," he told Liam.

"No, it wasn't," Liam said. "You're right. And also—" He was sneaking a look now at the caption on the facing page.

"Also, he told his brothers about a dream he'd had where all of them were forced to bow down in front of him."

Jonah made a clucking sound of disapproval.

He was coloring Joseph's hair now (another splash of purple), and he seemed engrossed enough that Liam felt he could rise and go off to the kitchen to pour himself a mug of coffee. By the time he returned, Jonah had skipped ahead to *Joseph's brothers sold him into slavery.* Aha. "So Joseph's brothers sold him into slavery," Liam said, settling into his chair again, "and then they went home and told their father he'd been killed."

They had soaked Joseph's coat in an animal's blood to back up their claim, Liam seemed to recall. What a waste of the beautiful coat! he had thought as a child. Now it was no use to anyone! Evidently these things hung on in the memory longer than he would have supposed. He hadn't considered that story in decades. His mother had been quite religious (or, at least, she had turned to her church for support after his father left them), but Liam himself had dropped out of Sunday school as soon as he was old enough to be allowed to stay home on his own.

He tried to read the next caption, but Jonah's arm was obscuring it. As unobtrusively as possible, Liam reached for the newspaper.

Drought. War. Suicide bombers.

At around ten thirty or so, after she had settled Mr. C. in his office, Eunice would be coming to deliver his printed-out résumé. Liam hugged that thought to himself like a package that he was putting off unwrapping. He had something to look forward to, but he didn't want to examine it too closely. He kept it tucked in the back of his consciousness for later.

Of course, eventually he would have to tell her that the résumé was unnecessary. By that time, though, they might know each other well enough to be getting together for other reasons. He wondered if she liked movies. Liam really enjoyed a good movie. He found it restful to watch people's conversations without being expected to join in. But he always felt sort of lonesome if he didn't have someone next to him to nudge in the ribs at the good parts.

Security checks at airports were becoming more and more onerous, he read.

Jonah said, "I'm hungry."

Liam lowered his newspaper. "You want your carrot sticks?" he asked.

"I want something *you* have."

This touched off a faint, nagging echo of annoyance in Liam's mind. He reached back to retrieve a recollection of Xanthe from long, long ago, from her toddler days, always asking for something, always needing. But he forced himself to say, "Sure enough. Let's see what I've got," and he set aside his paper and stood up.

"Celery? Yogurt? Cheese?" he called from the kitchen.

"What kind of cheese?"

"Pepperjack."

"Pepperjack's too prickly."

Liam sighed and closed the refrigerator door. "Raisins?" he asked. "Toast?"

"Raisins would be good."

Liam scooped some raisins from the box and put them in

a cereal bowl. An image came to him of Xanthe standing in
her crib, clutching the bars in tight fat fists. Her hair was plastered to her scalp with sweat and her face was beet-red and
streaming with tears, her mouth a cavernous black rectangle
of misery. He set the bowl on the carpet in front of Jonah and
said, "Here, little guy," and Jonah tossed him a quick glance
before he reached for a handful of raisins.

In Egypt, Joseph became Potiphar's most trusted slave.

"So, Joseph was taken to Egypt, where he had to work
very hard," Liam said.

"Couldn't he run back home?"

"I think it was too far to run."

He wondered what a child was expected to learn from
this story. Was there some sort of moral? He opened out his
newspaper again. Concern was being voiced about missiles in
North Korea. He thought that maybe, if Eunice happened to
be free tonight, he could invite her out for a bite to eat. He
could say it was a thank-you for her help with his résumé.
What could be more natural? Still, he felt a little gut-twinge
of nervousness. Even at his age, the whole rigmarole of dating
seemed intimidating. *Especially* at his age.

He reminded himself that she was just an ordinary, rather
plain young woman, but now her plainness seemed part of
her charm. She was so innocent and guileless, so transparent.
He remembered how she'd taken leave of him yesterday,
after he'd walked her out to the parking lot. She had paused
beside her car door and removed her glasses (just why, he
couldn't say; surely she needed glasses for driving?), and her
face had suddenly seemed so vulnerable that he'd had to sti-
fle an impulse to reach out and cup her head between his
hands. "Bye-bye," she'd told him, lifting her chin. Even that

childish phrase, which he had always found slightly silly, struck him as appealing.

When the doorbell rang, he imagined for an instant that this might be Eunice now. But no, it was Louise, already walking in before he could get out of his chair. "Did you miss me?" she asked Jonah, swooping down on him.

Jonah stumbled to his feet for a hug. "I colored about a hundred pages," he told her.

"Good for you! How was he?" she asked Liam.

"He was fine. Though I don't hold out high hopes for an artistic career."

"Dad!"

"What?"

She cut her eyes toward Jonah, who was busy cramming his crayons back in their box.

"Well, I fail to see what the problem is," Liam told her. "No one's talented at everything."

"Honestly," Louise said, and she dropped into the rocking chair.

Not a word about her doctor's appointment. Should Liam ask? No, that might be seen as intrusive. Instead he said, "Would you like a cup of coffee?"

Louise said, "No, thanks," which may or may not have been significant. (Were pregnant women allowed to drink coffee this month?) She patted her skirt, and Jonah climbed onto her lap and wrapped his arms around her. "What else did you do?" she asked him.

"I ate raisins."

"That's nice." She looked over his head at Liam. "Your wound seems a lot better. I very nearly can't see it."

"Yes, it's pretty well healed," he said. Involuntarily, he

glanced down at his injured palm. It still had a curdled texture, but the skin was a normal color again.

Louise said, "And I assume you've gotten over that little
obsession about your memory."

"I wasn't obsessed!" Liam said.

"You most certainly were. For a while there, everyone
thought you'd gone nuts."

"I just wanted to know what had happened, that's all. You
would too, if you woke up in a hospital without an inkling
why you were there."

She made a little shivering motion with her shoulders and
said, "Let's talk about something else."

"Fine with me," Liam said. "How's Dougall?"

"He's all right."

"Plumbing business going okay?"

"Oh, yes."

Liam liked Dougall well enough—there was nothing *not*
to like—but it was hard to invent any more conversation
about him. He was a genial, oversized man with a pathologi-
cal interest in the workings of inanimate objects, and Liam
had never understood why Louise had selected him for a
husband. Sometimes he thought that she'd been born with a
mental checklist of milestones that she'd sworn to get out of
the way as soon as possible. Grow up, finish school, marry the
first boy she dated, start a family . . . She had been in such a
hurry, and for what? Here she sat, an intelligent young
woman, with no more on her mind than organizing her
church's next bake sale.

Ah, well. Life was a matter of opinion, according to Mar-
cus Aurelius.

"You haven't asked about my doctor's appointment," Louise was saying. "Don't you care why I went?"

Liam said, "Certainly I care."

"You haven't shown the slightest bit of interest."

Oh, it was so tiring sometimes, this business of engaging with other human beings! Liam said, as delicately as possible, "I trust it was nothing life-threatening."

"I'm pregnant again."

"Congratulations."

"Aren't you happy for us?"

"Yes, I'm happy."

"You don't act it."

Liam sat up straighter and gripped his knees. "I'm extremely happy," he said. "I think it will be very nice for Jonah to have a sibling." He glanced at Jonah, who was squatting on the floor to repack his knapsack. "Does he know?" he asked Louise.

Louise said, "Of course he knows. Don't you, Jonah."

"Huh?"

"You know about your new baby brother or sister, don't you?"

Jonah said, "Mmhmm," and zipped his knapsack shut. Louise raised her eyebrows meaningfully at Liam.

"When's your due date?" Liam asked her.

"Early February."

"February!"

People announced these things so far ahead nowadays, it made pregnancies seem to last a couple of years or more.

"If you come up with any good names for girls, let us know," Louise told him. She rose and helped Jonah slip into his knapsack straps. "We're having trouble agreeing on one. A boy is no problem; but any girl's name I like, Dougall thinks it's too froufrou."

"What would it be for a boy?" Liam asked her.

"Madigan, we've decided."

"Ah."

He heaved himself to his feet and followed her toward the door. It was absurd to feel hurt. Madigan had been a very good stepfather. (A very good *father*, Barbara would have amended if she'd been there.) He'd spared Liam the burden of child support, for one thing; the man had been loaded. Liam said, "Nothing biblical this time?"

"We're thinking Jacob for a middle name."

"That's nice."

This reminded him; he said, "Louise, what's the meaning of the Joseph story?"

"Which Joseph story?"

"The coat of many colors, the slavery in Egypt—what are people supposed to learn from it?"

"They're not supposed to learn anything," Louise said. "It's an event that really happened. It's not *made up*; it's not designed for any calculated purpose."

"Oh," he said.

Best not to pursue that.

"Why'd you ask?" she said.

"Just curious." He opened the door for her and then followed her and Jonah into the foyer. "I saw it in Jonah's coloring book and I was wondering."

"You know," Louise said, "you're always welcome to come to church with us on a Sunday."

"Oh, thanks, but—"

"We could pick you up and take you there. We'd be happy to! I'd really love to share my faith with you."

"Thanks anyhow," Liam said. "I guess religion's just not in my nature, sorry to say."

He refrained from telling her that even talking about religion made him wince with embarrassment. Even hearing about it embarrassed him—hearing those toe-curling terms that believers employed, like *share*, in fact, and *my faith*.

But she said, "Oh, Dad, it's in every person's nature! We are every one of us born in sin, and till we let Jesus into our hearts we're condemned throughout eternity."

Well, there was no way he could let *that* pass. He said, "Are you telling me that some little child in Africa is condemned because he's never been to Sunday school? Or some perfectly good Moslem herding camels in Tunisia?"

"You cannot be called *good* until you accept Christ as your personal savior," she said, and her voice echoed off the cinderblocks with a bell-like, clanging tone.

Liam's jaw dropped. "Well," he said, "I guess . . ."

Words failed him for a moment.

"I guess we'll just have to agree to disagree," he said finally.

Words must have failed Louise too, because she just gazed at him for a moment with an expression he couldn't read. Then she turned away and opened the outer door.

Eunice stood on the sidewalk, poised to enter. She took a step backward.

"Oh. Eunice," Liam said.

"Have I come at a bad time?"

"No, no . . ."

Louise gave him a questioning look. Liam said, "Eunice, this is my daughter, Louise, and my grandson, Jonah." He told

Louise, "Eunice is—Why, you've seen her before. You saw her in Dr. Morrow's waiting room."

"I did?" Louise said.

Eunice said, "She did?"

Oops, a slip. Though not too hard to cover up, as it happened. Liam told Eunice, "I realized that only later. I knew you seemed familiar."

Eunice continued to look puzzled, but she held out her hand to Louise and said, "Nice to meet you."

"Nice to meet *you*," Louise said, shaking her hand. "So, do you two have plans for the day?"

"Eunice is just helping me with my résumé," Liam told her.

"Oh," Louise said. "Well, good. You're going to look for a real job! Or at least . . . I mean, surely the zayda job doesn't require a résumé, does it?"

"The . . . ? No, no, no. This would be for something else."

"The very last place on earth I can see him is in a preschool," Louise told Eunice.

"Preschool?" Eunice asked.

"That's what he was talking about the other day."

Liam said, "I know you have to be going, Louise. Bye, Jonah! Good luck with the coloring book."

Jonah hoisted his knapsack higher on his back and said, "Bye." Louise said, "Thanks for watching him, Dad." She seemed to have forgotten their quarrel. She gave him a peck on the cheek, waved to Eunice, and followed Jonah out the door.

"You saw me at Dr. Morrow's?" Eunice asked Liam.

She was still standing on the sidewalk, although he held

the door open invitingly. She had her arms folded across her chest and she seemed planted there.

He said, "Yes, wasn't that a coincidence?"

"I don't recall seeing *you*," she told him.

"You don't? I guess I'm not very memorable."

This made her smile, a little. She unfolded her arms and stepped forward to enter the building.

She was wearing one of her skirts today, and a blouse that showed her cleavage. Her breasts were two full, soft mounds. When she passed him, she gave off a faint scent of vanilla and he had an urge to step closer in order to get a deeper breath of it. He stood back against the door, however, with his hands pressed behind him. There was something bothering the far corners of his mind, something casting a shadow.

"I should have accepted her invitation," he said once they were inside the apartment.

Eunice said, "What?"

"Louise invited me to her church just now and I didn't accept."

He dropped into an armchair, feeling disheartened. Too late, he remembered that he was supposed to seat his guest first, and he started to struggle up again but then Eunice sat down in the rocker.

"I've never been a good father," he said.

"Oh, I'm sure you're a wonderful father!"

"No, a good father would say, 'So what if I'm not religious? This could be our chance to get on a better footing!' But I was so intent on my ... principles. My standards. I blew it."

Eunice said, "Well, anyway. Your grandson is really cute."

"Thanks," he said.

"I didn't picture you being a grandfather."

He wondered what this signified. He said, "I guess it does make me seem awfully old."

"No, it doesn't! You're not old!"

"I must seem pretty old to somebody your age," he said. He waited a beat, and then he said, "How old *are* you, if you don't mind my asking?"

"I'm thirty-eight."

"You are?"

So she wasn't younger than Xanthe after all. He would have to tell Kitty.

When Liam was thirty-eight he already had three children. His second marriage was already behind him, and he'd started to feel his whole life was behind him. But Eunice still seemed so fresh-faced and so . . . unwritten on. She sat very straight-backed, with her bulky sandals placed wide apart, her hands clasped in the valley of paisley skirt between her knees. Her glasses reflected the light in a way that turned them white, giving her a blank, open look.

"You could always change your mind," she told him.

"Excuse me?"

"You could call your daughter on the phone and say you would come to her church after all."

"Well, yes."

"Would she have reached home by now?"

"I doubt it."

"Does she have a cell phone?"

"Look," he said. "I'm not going to call."

Eunice rocked back in her rocker.

"I can't," he said.

"Okay . . ."

"It's difficult to explain."

She went on watching him.

He said, "Did you print up that résumé?"

He couldn't have cared less about the résumé. In fact, the very word was beginning to strike him as annoying. Those pretentious foreign accent marks! For God's sake, didn't some term exist in ordinary English? But Eunice immediately brightened and said, "The résumé!" (She even pronounced it foreignly, with a long *a* in the first syllable.) She bent to dig through her purse, which sat beside her on the floor, and she came up with a crisp sheaf of papers folded in half. "I have to say," she told him, "I'm not entirely satisfied with it."

"Why is that?"

"I couldn't seem to give it any focus. If you're not applying at Cope, I don't know what particular strengths I should be emphasizing—what areas of interest."

He gave a short bark of laughter, and she glanced up from the papers.

"I wouldn't know either," he told her. "Basically, I have no areas of interest."

"Oh, that can't be true," she said.

"It is, though," he said. And then he said, "It really is. Sometimes I think my life is just . . . drying up and hardening, like one of those mouse carcasses you find beneath a radiator."

If Eunice was surprised by this, it was nothing compared to how he himself felt. He seemed to hear his own words as if someone else had spoken them. He cleared his throat and spread his fingers across his knees.

"Well, only on off days, of course," he said.

"I know exactly what you mean," she told him.

"You do?"

"I'm always thinking, Why don't I have any hobbies? Other people do. Other people develop these passions; they collect things or they research things or they birdwatch or they snorkel. They join book groups or they reenact the Civil War. I'm just trying to make it through to bedtime every night."

"Yes," Liam said.

"I don't see myself as a mouse carcass, though, but more like one of those buds that haven't opened. I'm hanging there on the bush all closed up."

"That would make sense," Liam said. "You're younger. You have everything ahead of you."

"Unless I *never* open, and fall off the branch still closed," Eunice said.

Before Liam could make any comment, she said, "Well, enough of that! I sound like some kind of basket case, don't I?"

"No," Liam said.

Then he said, "I turned sixty on my last birthday."

"I know," Eunice said.

"Do you think somebody sixty is too old for somebody thirty-eight?"

When she looked at him now, the light was hitting her glasses at a different angle and he could see directly into her eyes, which were wide and steady and radiant. Her mouth was very serious, almost trembling with seriousness.

She said, "No, I don't think it's too old."

"Me neither," he said.

8

Damian came back from his cousin's wedding with his arm in a cast. He said there'd been a little "contretemps." Liam was so surprised by his wording that he gave Damian a second look. Was there more to him, perhaps, than met the eye? But Damian sat slouched in his usual C shape on the daybed in the den, his good arm tossed carelessly across Kitty's shoulders, long ropes of greasy black hair concealing most of his face. They were listening to a song with very explicit lyrics. All Liam had to hear was a single line and he felt himself growing rigid with embarrassment. In addition, this was, after all, an actual bed they were sitting on, and an unmade bed at that. Liam said, "Wouldn't you two be more comfortable in the living room?" But they just gaped at him, and rightly so; there was no couch in the living room. He'd been noticing that, of late. People couldn't sit close together there.

Liam and Eunice couldn't sit close together either. They

had to occupy separate chairs and smile across at each other like fools.

Although sometimes, as often as possible, Liam would venture to perch on the arm of whichever chair Eunice was inhabiting. He would bring her, say, a Diet Coke and then as if by accident, while talking about nothing much, he would settle on the chair arm and rest one hand on her shoulder. She had soft plump shoulders that exactly, satisfyingly filled the hollows of his palms. Sometimes he would bend to breathe in the scent of her shampoo; sometimes, even, he would bend lower and they would kiss, although it was an inconvenient angle for kissing. She had to crane upward to meet his lips, and if he wasn't careful, he could nick a cheekbone on the sharp-edged frame of her glasses.

He didn't see her nearly as much as he would have liked. She showed up at his apartment at odd hours during the day, and then she came over most evenings, but in the evenings Kitty was usually around and they had to be more circumspect. (What had Liam been thinking, letting Kitty stay with him? Except, of course, that he'd had no way of predicting the turn that his life would take.)

They couldn't go to Eunice's place, because right now she didn't have a place. She was living with her parents. Her father had suffered a stroke in March and she had moved in to help out. Reading between the lines, Liam guessed that this was less of a sacrifice than it seemed. She didn't earn much of a salary at Cope, and she was clearly not the home-making type. Besides which, there was something of the only child in her character—an air of perennial daughterliness, an excessive concern for her parents' good opinion of her. Liam cataloged this trait as he did her others, with scientific interest, without passing judgment. They were still in that stage where the loved one's weaknesses, even, seemed endearing.

Unfortunately, Damian's broken arm was his right arm, immobilized in a right-angle cast from his wrist to above his elbow. Since his car—really his mother's car—had a stick shift, this meant that he couldn't drive. And Kitty couldn't drive either, because it turned out that the extra insurance was way beyond Liam's means. He had honestly thought he'd heard wrong when the agent told him what the premium would be.

This put a real crimp in things. Sometimes, Kitty took the bus to Damian's house directly after work, requiring Liam to pick her up at the end of the evening. Most times, though, Damian's mother dropped Damian off at Liam's, and then it was up to Liam to deliver him back home. (Damian's mother, a widow who seemed much older than her years, refused to drive after dark.) Either way, it seemed Liam was called upon to chauffeur far more than he liked. There were a few blessed occasions when high school friends pitched in, but many of them were off working in Ocean City for the summer, while others were restricted by complicated new laws about driving with peers in the car. Often what happened was that Eunice would volunteer to return Damian on her way home, which was nice of her but it made her leave earlier than Liam wanted her to. And meanwhile, they would have spent the evening with Kitty and Damian; not one minute on their own.

It was no picnic, living with teenagers.

At moments, Liam felt he'd gone back to his teens himself. There was the same lack of privacy, the same guilty secrecy, the same tantalizingly halfway physical relationship.

The same lack of confidence, even, for Eunice alternated between shyness and startling boldness, while Liam himself . . . Well, face it, he was a little out of practice. He had some concerns about looking old, or inadequate, or fat. It had been a long time since anyone had seen him without his clothes on.

Let things proceed at their own leisurely pace, he decided with some relief.

They liked to talk about their first meeting. Their two different first meetings, really. Liam recalled the waiting-room scene; Eunice recalled their coffee at PeeWee's. Liam said, "You seemed so professional. So expert. So *in charge.*"

Eunice said, "You asked me more about myself in one conversation than most men ask in a year."

"You told Ishmael Cope, 'Verity,' and it sounded like a pronouncement handed down from the heavens."

"Even in the midst of a job hunt, you wanted to know about my life."

"How could I not?" he asked, and he meant it. He found her fascinating and funny and complex. She was a perpetual astonishment. He studied her like a language.

For instance: She was chronically late everywhere, but she fantasized that she could outwit herself by keeping her watch set ten minutes ahead.

She acted completely besotted whenever she met a small dog.

Direct sunlight made her sneeze.

Among her most deep-seated fears were spiders, West Nile disease, and choral recitals. (She suffered from the morbid conviction that she might suddenly jump up and start singing along with the soloist.)

In fact she disliked all formal occasions, not only recitals but plays, lectures, symphony concerts, and dining in upscale restaurants. Given a choice, she preferred to stay in, and if they ate out she opted for the humblest café or hamburger joint.

She cared little about food in general—made not so much as a gesture toward cooking, and never seemed to notice what he gave her to eat.

She wasn't used to alcohol and grew charmingly silly after a single glass of wine.

She never wore dresses; just those peasant skirts or balloony slacks.

Nor did she use cosmetics.

She'd had only three serious boyfriends in her entire life—not a one of them, she claimed, worth discussing in any depth.

But her girlfriends, as she called them, numbered in the dozens, reaching all the way back to nursery school, and she was forever rushing off to bachelorette parties or girls' nights out.

She hated spending money, on principle. She drove illogical distances for the cheapest gasoline and she insisted on taking her leftovers home even from McDonald's.

She had a cell-phone plan that gave her one thousand free minutes a month, but the only time she answered it was when it played Mr. Cope's special ring—the "Hallelujah Chorus." The rest of the time, she ignored it.

She was addicted to bad TV—to reality shows and game shows and spill-your-guts talk shows—and confessed to falling asleep every night to the all-night shopping channel. She couldn't understand why Liam didn't own a television set.

She made a habit of leaving love notes for him to find after she left, always signed with a smiley face topped by a curl and a hairbow.

She was refreshingly indifferent to domestic matters. She didn't try to rearrange his furniture, or spruce up his wardrobe, or balance his diet. She thought his tightly made bed was comical. She demonstrated (standing discreetly outside the threshold of his bedroom) the shimmying motion that she imagined he must have to use in order to worm his way between the sheets every night. Liam had to laugh at that.

He laughed a lot, these days.

He knew that many of her traits (her lateness, her overcuteness with the smiley faces and the little dogs) would ordinarily have called forth his most scathing sarcasm, but instead he found himself laughing. And felt, therefore, a bashful sense of pride. He was a better man than he'd realized.

She routinely left stray belongings behind at the end of the evening, sprinkled about like Hansel and Gretel's bread crumbs—an umbrella and a stack of bracelets and her glasses case and once, even, her purse. A homely black cardigan of hers stayed draped over a chair back for days, and whenever he passed it he found an excuse to straighten a sleeve or smooth the fabric before he moved on.

Barbara phoned to ask how things were going with Kitty. It was a good three weeks, by then, since Kitty had moved in. "Very well," Liam said. "No problems whatsoever."

"Is she keeping to her curfew?"

"Of course."

"And you're not leaving her and Damian unchaperoned."

"Certainly not," he said.

Or not any more than he could help, he added privately. He failed to see how anyone could be chaperoned every everlasting minute.

"How about you?" he asked. "Everything going okay?"

"Oh, yes."

"I guess it feels odd to be living on your own," he said. For the first time, it occurred to him that on her own, she could see more of Howie the Hound Dog. He gave a light cough. "Are you managing to keep busy?"

"Oh, yes," she said again.

She was a fine one to complain about other people's unforthcomingness.

It was difficult to tell, from her tone, whether she knew about Eunice. Had Kitty happened to mention her? But he wasn't sure that Kitty and Barbara even kept in touch these days. Of course, Louise could have said something. He definitely sensed that Louise had her suspicions.

One evening toward the end of July, Louise and Jonah dropped in unannounced. She claimed they had been shopping at the mall across the street. Well, obviously they *had* been shopping; Jonah was wearing a new type of combination sneaker and roller skate that he took great pride in showing off. But dropping in was not Louise's usual style. She arrived as Liam was setting the table for supper. He had placed an order for Indian food—Kitty's idea—which hadn't come yet. Eunice was sitting in the living room, reading aloud from the want ads. (Even though they had abandoned the résumé pretext, Eunice made a point of swinging into job-hunting mode whenever Kitty was in earshot.) *"Experienced medical assistant,"* she read. "But really, you wouldn't need *that* much experience if all you had to do was assist somebody." And Kitty and Damian were in the den, where Kitty's radio was shouting something like *I want it I want it I want it.*

When Louise rang the doorbell, Liam assumed it was their food. Then while Jonah was struggling to demonstrate his roller skates on the carpet, the doorbell rang again and it *was* their food, and Liam had to spend several minutes dealing with it. By the time he had spread an array of curry-smelling foil containers across the table, Louise was deep in her interrogations. "You don't like to cook?" she was asking Eunice.

Very clever: the question implied that Eunice played a regular role in this household, which she would have to either confirm or deny. But Eunice was too cagey for that—or maybe just oblivious. "Cook?" she said, looking bewildered. "Who, me?"

"I don't feel Dad gets enough vegetables," Louise told her.

Although, in fact, Louise was never around during Liam's meals and had no inkling what he ate.

Liam said, "There are plenty of vegetables in Indian food, might I point out."

"Listen to this," Eunice said, raising her newspaper. *"Wanted: Driver for my 90-year-old mother. Days only; flexible hours. Must be sober, reliable, punctual and HAVE NO PERSONAL PROBLEMS! OR IF YOU DO, DON'T DISCUSS THEM WITH HER!"*

Liam laughed, but Louise didn't seem to see the humor.

"You could do that," Eunice told him.

"I'll keep it in mind," he said.

Jonah had decided to try his skates on the kitchen linoleum. He was holding on to the sink while his feet slid away from him in opposite directions. "Help!" he called. By now Kitty had emerged from the den, although Damian was still in hiding, and she rescued Jonah by one elbow. "Hey, Louise," she said.

"Hi."

The doorbell rang a third time. Jonah said, "Maybe that will be some better kind of food."

But already the door was opening (a sure sign it was one of Liam's daughters; they never waited to be admitted), and in walked Xanthe. She still had on her social-worker clothes, matronly and staid. "Good grief," she said. "What have you got going here, Dad, some kind of salon?" She gave him a peck on the cheek and then stepped back to study him. "That's healed up nicely," she told him.

For a second, he couldn't think what she was talking about. Oh, yes: the last time she had seen him, he was still in bandages. "What brings you here?" he asked her.

"I came because I've been phoning for days and the line is always busy. I thought you might be dead."

She didn't seem to have lost any sleep over it. She trilled her fingers at her sisters. Then she turned to Eunice, who had lowered her paper.

"Xanthe, meet Eunice," Liam said.

Xanthe cocked her head. "A neighbor?" she asked Eunice.

Eunice said, "Sort of," which was not just cagey, it was an outright lie. (She lived in Roland Park.) She smiled at Xanthe blandly. From where Liam stood, it seemed her glasses were doing that opaque thing they did with reflected light.

Xanthe turned back to Liam and said, "I called several

times last night, and then I called twice this evening. Is something wrong with your phone?"

"It's the Internet," Kitty told her.

"Dad was on the Internet?"

"No, I was," Kitty said. "He doesn't have broadband and so I have to dial up."

"But why are you doing it *here*?"

"I'm living here."

"You're living here?"

"I'm spending the summer."

Xanthe seemed about to say something, but at that moment Damian appeared. He looked a little sheepish, and no wonder. Probably he'd figured out he would be discovered, sooner or later, skulking in the den. "Yo. Jo-Jo," he said to Jonah. He tipped sideways against the wall, jammed his hands in his jeans pockets, and stared defiantly at the others.

Xanthe said, "Damian."

"Hey," he said.

"Hello," she said. She made it sound as if she were correcting him.

Then she turned to Liam and said, "I'll be going now."

"You just got here!"

"Goodbye," she told the room in general.

She walked out.

There was a silence. Liam looked from Louise to Kitty. Louise shrugged. Kitty said, "Well, so anyhow, Lou. Do you have your car?"

"Of course I have my car."

"Could you give me and Damian a ride to Towson Commons?"

"Sure," Louise said.

"And then pick us up when the movie's done?"

"What? No! What kind of life do you think I'm living?"

Adjusting seamlessly, Kitty turned to Liam and said, "Poppy, could *you* pick us up?"

"What time?"

"The movie lets out at eight forty."

"I guess I can do that."

Damian straightened up from the wall and said, "Okay!" and Kitty told Louise, "Let's go, then."

"This minute?" Liam asked. "What about your supper?"

"We're in a hurry. Come on, Jonah."

"I can skate much better outdoors," Jonah told Liam. "Your floors are all wrong."

"You should show me the next time you come," Liam said.

"I'll bring my coloring book, too. Yesterday I did Daniel in the lion's den."

"Oh, good."

"Come *on*, Jonah," Kitty said. "Bye, Poppy. Bye, Eunice."

Then everybody was gone. Louise was the last one out and she let the door slam behind her.

Liam looked at Eunice. Eunice refolded her newspaper and laid it on the coffee table.

"So that was Xanthe," she said in a musing tone.

"You're thinking it's a misnomer, aren't you," Liam said.

"What?"

"Xanthe. It means 'golden.' "

"Well, I'm sure she's very pleasant as a rule," Eunice said.

Liam had been referring to Xanthe's coloring—her brown hair and level dark eyebrows. He was so accustomed to her manner that he hadn't felt the need to comment on it, but now he said, "She was upset on account of Damian, I guess. She thinks he was the one who attacked me."

"Damian?"

"That's what she thinks."

"He wasn't, was he?"

"No, of course not," Liam said.

In a grudging way, he was beginning to like Damian. And he'd seen enough of such boys at St. Dyfrig to know he wasn't bad at heart.

"Maybe it's me," Eunice said.

"Pardon?"

"Maybe Xanthe was upset to find me here."

"Oh, that can't be it. Not at her age."

"If it came as a surprise, it could," Eunice said. "But wouldn't someone have told her? Do she and Kitty not talk?"

"I don't think any of them talk," Liam said. This struck him as odd, all at once. He said, "But I may be mistaken."

"At least I can say now that I've met your entire family," Eunice said.

He didn't know why he felt a momentary impulse to correct her. He wasn't thinking of his sister, surely. Was it Barbara? No, how ridiculous. He said, "So you have." Then he said, "And I've met exactly zero of yours."

Eunice looked unhappy. She said, "Oh. Right."

Although Liam couldn't really work up much interest in her family. It was just her parents, after all—a couple of right-wing Republicans, from the sound of it—and he felt that he was long past the meet-the-parents stage of life. Besides which (here was the real thing), he was uncomfortably aware that he and Eunice's father were members of the same generation, more or less. What a bizarre scene: one gray-haired man playing Daughter's Boyfriend while the other played Stern Dad. Further proof of just how unsuitable this romance really was, at least in the eyes of the outside world.

So he said, "Maybe when your father's a little stronger," and Eunice said, "Yes, maybe when his speech improves." She looked relieved. "Then you could come for a drink," she said. "They've been dying to meet you. We could all sit out on the terrace and have a nice long visit. You would have so much to talk about! Once they got to know you they would love you, I'm just positive."

With every word she uttered, she sounded less convincing. Liam said, "No point rushing though, when he's been so ill."

"Oh, no."

"Plenty of time to meet later."

"Oh, yes."

"How *is* his speech, by the way?"

"It's going well," she said. "Bit by bit, I mean."

"Is he getting any sort of professional help?"

"Oh, yes, every week. I'm the one who takes him, because my mom has her aerobics class then. He sees this cute little girl who talks with a lisp. Can you believe a speech therapist would lisp?"

"Maybe that's why she went into it," Liam said.

"She calls him 'Mithter Dunthtead,' " Eunice said with a giggle. " 'Mithter Thamuel Dunthtead.' "

She looked pretty cute herself, Liam noticed. Laughter always turned her cheeks pink.

He tried to picture the four of them sitting on the terrace. Her parents would ask him where he worked, just making polite conversation, but when he said he didn't work, their expressions would cloud over. Where was he thinking of working, then? Nowhere. And he was twenty-some years older than their daughter, and he'd flubbed up two marriages, and he lived in a rented apartment.

They would exchange glances. Their eyes would narrow in a certain way he knew well.

But things were not as bad as they seemed! he wanted to tell them. He was a better man than he looked!

He did somehow feel, these days, that he was a good man.

She was even less social than Liam, if you didn't count those girlfriends of hers. That was another of her traits. When Liam's old philosophy professor came through town, she claimed Mr. C. had an evening meeting that would keep her from going to dinner with them. When the guidance counselor at St. Dyfrig threw his annual barbecue, she declined on the grounds of the high pollen count.

But one Friday afternoon, Bundy phoned and asked Liam if he felt like going out for a bite to eat. His fiancée had dumped him, he said, and he was tired of sitting home brooding. In view of the circumstances, Liam felt he couldn't refuse, although he had already arranged to spend the evening with Eunice.

"Would you mind if I brought somebody?" he asked.

"Who's that?"

"Oh, just a woman I've gotten to know."

It occurred to him to wonder if demonstrating his new couplehood at that particular moment showed a lack of tact, but Bundy seemed to find the prospect entertaining. "Whoa!" he said. "This I've got to see. Why not? Bring her along."

So Liam called Eunice's cell phone and left a message about the change of plans. He was conscious as he spoke that he was not delivering welcome news; and sure enough, when Eunice called back she sounded less than thrilled.

"I thought we were eating in tonight," she said.

"Well, yes, we were, but Bundy's getting over a breakup."

"You never mentioned any Bundy *before*," she told him accusingly.

"Didn't I? Oh, Bundy and I go way back. He's African American," he added as an enticement.

But still Eunice said, "Maybe I'll skip it. I'm not sure how late Mr. C. will be needing me."

Liam groaned. From time to time, he had the feeling that Ishmael Cope and he were engaged in a sibling rivalry of sorts. He said, "He's got to allow you *some* private life."

"Well, but, and also, Tumbleweed, you said. I don't want to eat at Tumbleweed! It's too fancy. I don't have the right clothes."

"Tumbleweed is not fancy," Liam said. "I'm not even wearing a tie. I doubt Bundy *owns* a tie; he isn't old enough for a—"

But then he saw underneath to what was really bothering her. "Eunice," he said. "Sweetheart. You would look fine, whatever you wore. I'm going to be very proud to introduce you."

"Well, I do have something black," Eunice said. "Black always seems more elegant."

"Black would be perfect," he told her.

They arranged to meet at the restaurant, because Eunice had to stop off at her parents' house to change. Since she and Bundy didn't know each other, Liam made a point of showing up first, and he requested a table in front where he could watch the street for her arrival.

It was true that Tumbleweed wasn't fancy. The lights were fake kerosene lanterns, the decor was Old West (dark, slightly sticky wooden booths and framed Wanted posters), and most of the other diners were Towson University students. Liam couldn't imagine that Eunice would find it intimidating.

Through the front window he saw Bundy striding toward him, a long-legged figure scissoring down the sidewalk in a way that didn't seem particularly heartbroken. A moment later he was settling into the seat opposite Liam. "Where's your lady?" he asked.

"She'll be along."

"See how it works: there's just a limited amount of romance at any one time in the universe. Naomi dumps me; you get lucky. What's her name?"

"Eunice," Liam said.

All at once the name sounded vaguely embarrassing. The *u* sound reminded him of *urine*.

"So!" he said brightly. "Why'd Naomi break it off? Or would you rather not discuss it."

"Not much *to* discuss. I come in yesterday from the gym, she's talking on the phone in this low sexy voice. 'I'm home!' I call, and quick as a flash she says into the phone, 'Fine, let's make that two o'clock. Shampoo and a trim.' In a voice that's totally different, real efficient and bossy, like she'd use with her beautician. Then she slams down the receiver. So after she goes off to the kitchen, I press Redial. Man answers. Says, 'Yo, babe. False alarm?' "

"Plenty of beauticians call people 'babe,'" Liam announced with authority.

"But 'False alarm'? Why'd he say that?"

"Uh, maybe . . ."

"It was her boyfriend, I tell you. The two of them making a fool of me. I tell you, I've been *stupid*. I say to him, 'No, man. It wasn't no false alarm.' Then I go out to the kitchen. 'Naomi, you got some explaining to do.' Know what she says? Says, 'Why you say that?' Says, 'That was just Ron at the beauty shop.'"

"Well. See there?" Liam said. "It was Ron at the beauty shop. And when she hung up in a hurry he assumed she must have some emergency, so when his phone rang again he said, 'False alarm?'"

"How'd he know it was Naomi?" Bundy asked him.

"He had caller ID, of course."

"Right. What's a place of business want with caller ID?"

"It seems to me that caller ID would be very useful in business," Liam said. He considered for a moment. "Interesting," he said. "If not for modern technology—caller ID and Redial—you would still be a happy man."

Bundy snorted. "I'd still be a blind man," he told Liam. He accepted a menu from their waitress. Then he gave her a second look; she was young and blond and her waist narrowed in as gracefully as the stems on their water goblets. "How are *you* this fine evening?" he asked her.

"I'm good, thanks," the waitress said. "Will a third party be joining you?"

Liam said, "Yes, she ought to be—"

Then here Eunice was, all at once, rushing in out of breath

and saying, "I'm sorry, I'm so sorry, I knew I'd never get away in time!"

True to her word, she was wearing black. Or her blouse, at least, was black—plain black cotton with big white buttons like Necco wafers. Around her neck hung a rope of jaw-breaker-sized red beads that gave her a sweetly clownish air, and lacy silver earrings shaped like upside-down Christmas trees dangled a good three inches below her earlobes.

"Am I all right?" she asked Liam. He had risen as far as the booth would allow, and so had Bundy.

Liam said, "Yes, you look very—" but already she was hurtling on. She said, "It's Mr. C.'s fault I'm late. He told me he had to go to the restroom and of course I couldn't go with him so I said, 'Fine, I'll wait out front,' and then he never came back so I said to this man going in, not even one of ours, I don't know *who* he was, I said, 'Excuse me, if you see an elderly gentleman could you please—' Well, not to bore you with all the details but by the time I got home I had about two minutes to make it to the restaurant and so I had to change clothes in one split second, which is why I'm wearing what I'm wearing. I mean, I know I shouldn't be wearing—"

"Eunice, this is my friend Bundy Braithwaite," Liam said. "Eunice Dunstead."

"How you doing," Bundy said, still half standing. He wore a distinctly startled expression, it seemed to Liam.

Eunice said, "I wouldn't ordinarily combine this blouse with this skirt."

"Won't you have a seat?" Liam asked her.

"My mother always tells me," Eunice said, sitting down next to him, "she says, 'Eunice, a person's top half should

never, ever be darker than the bottom half. It looks Mafioso,'
she says. And yet here I am—"

"It can if the two halves share some little bit of color in
common," Bundy said.

Eunice stopped speaking.

"Your skirt's got squiggles of black," he told her.

"Oh."

"Case closed."

Bundy was looking amused now, which Liam didn't mind
in the least. She *was* amusing; she was charmingly amusing,
and she was letting her soft bare arm rest lightly against his
own.

"Shall we order a bottle of wine?" he asked. He had an
urge to celebrate, all at once.

But it emerged that Bundy didn't want wine. He wanted
hard liquor. "I am a man who's been shafted," he told Eunice
after they'd placed their drink orders. "I don't know if Liam
mentioned."

"He did say something about that."

"So mere wine will just not cut it. My fiancée has dumped
me flat. She claims I don't trust her."

Liam hadn't heard this part. He said, "You just now
admitted you don't trust her."

"I think these earrings are a little too much," Eunice said.

Liam looked at them. He said, "They're fine."

"I can take them off, if you like."

"They're *fine*."

"Are you listening to this, or not?" Bundy asked Eunice.
"I'm telling how my *heart* was ripped out."

Eunice said, "Oh, excuse me." She straightened her back

and folded her hands and looked at him obediently, like a child in a classroom.

"I come in from the gym yesterday," Bundy began all over again, "I hear Naomi on the phone with her boyfriend. Most definitely it was her boyfriend. I could just tell, you know? By her voice. But when I mention something to that effect, she says no, it was her beautician. Right. Then she says well, okay, she only told me it was her beautician because she knew I would be jealous of anybody else. Fact is, she says, it was a guy from work. They were just discussing work. I say, 'Oh, right.' She says, 'See what I mean? You don't trust me! You don't give me credit! You never, ever talk to me; you sit watching your dumb sports shows on TV, and then when I meet a man who will have a real conversation, you get all bent out of shape!' "

"Maybe you're well rid of her," Eunice told him.

"Say what?"

"Why do you even care? You want to watch TV; she wants to do something else; let her do it! Let her go off with her beautician!"

"He's not her beautician."

"Let her go off with whoever! Maybe every day she's been thinking, What are we together for? Don't I deserve something better than this? Someone who understands me? And meanwhile, *you* could be with some woman who enjoys watching sports on TV."

"Huh," Bundy said. He rocked back in his seat.

Liam was trying to figure out whether this applied to him in any way. Should he, for instance, buy a television set?

Eunice said, "But I don't mean to interfere."

"No, no . . ." Bundy said. Then he said, "Huh," again.

Their waitress arrived with their drinks. She set a Scotch in front of Bundy, and he took hold of it immediately but he waited until their wine had been poured before he raised his glass to Liam and Eunice.

"Cheers," he said. And then, "So. Eunice. How did you meet our boy, here?"

"Well," Eunice said. From her declarative tone of voice, and the important way she resettled herself in her seat, it was clear that she was about to embark on a serious narrative. "One day about a month ago," she said, "I am walking down the street with my employer. My employer is Ishmael Cope? Of Cope Development? I take notes for him at meetings and such. And we are just walking down the street when up comes Liam out of nowhere and stops to say hello to him."

"Liam knows Ishmael Cope?" Bundy asked.

"Just a nodding acquaintance," Liam told him.

"They'd met at this charity ball for diabetes," Eunice said.

"Liam went to a charity ball?"

"Yes, and so . . . wait, I'm telling you what happened. Liam stops to talk to him but Mr. C. is a little . . . like, absentminded these days but Liam is just so considerate with him, just so sweet and diplomatic and considerate—"

"*Liam?*" Bundy said. "You're talking about our boy *Liam?*"

Liam was starting to feel annoyed with Bundy, and maybe Eunice was too because she said, very firmly, "Yes, Liam. I guess you don't know him well. Liam is just this . . . very thoughtful kind of person, not your usual kind of person at all. He is not like any other man I've ever known. There's something different about him."

"*That* I'll agree with," Bundy said.

Liam wished Bundy didn't seem to be enjoying this so much. But Eunice smiled at him, and a dimple dented her cheek as if someone had poked her gently with an index finger. "It was love at first sight," she told him. Then she turned to Liam. "For me it was, at least."

Liam said, "For me too." And he saw now that that was the truth.

Through drinks, through soup, through their entrées (steaks for Eunice and Bundy, rockfish for Liam), Liam was mostly silent, listening to the other two and taking secret pleasure in the warmth of Eunice's thigh pressed against his. Bundy returned to his breakup; Eunice made appropriate murmuring sounds. She tsk-tsk-ed and shook her head, and one of her Christmas-tree earrings landed on her plate with a clatter.

It wasn't that Liam didn't know her shortcomings. He saw the same woman Bundy must see: plump and frizzy-haired and bespectacled, dumpily dressed, bizarrely jeweled, too young for him and too earnest. But all these qualities he found lovable. And he pitied poor Bundy, who would have to go home alone.

Although he too, as it happened, went home alone that evening. (Eunice had promised to get back to the house in time to help her father to bed.) Even so, Liam left the restaurant feeling unspeakably lucky.

As he was crossing the street to his car, he was very nearly knocked down by some halfwit driver turning without stopping, and his reaction—his thudding heart and cold sweat and flash of anger—made him realize how much, nowadays, he did not want to die, and how dearly he valued his life.

Then he went to Eddie's grocery store.

He went to the Charles Street branch of Eddie's on a Monday afternoon. He needed milk. Milk was all he got, and so he assumed he would be through the checkout line in a matter of minutes. Except, wouldn't you know, the woman in front of him turned out to have some trouble with her account. She wanted to use her house charge but she couldn't remember her number. "I shouldn't have to remember my number," she said. She had the leathery, harsh voice of a longtime smoker, and her pale dyed flippy hair and girlish A-line skirt spelled out Country Club to Liam. (He had a prejudice against country clubs.) She said, "The Roland *Park* Eddie's doesn't ask my number."

"I don't know why not," the cashier told her. "In both stores, your number is how we access your account."

"Access" as a verb; good God. The world was going to hell in a handbasket. But then Liam was brought up short by what the woman said next.

She said, "Well, perhaps they do ask, but I just tell them, 'Look it up. You know my name: Mrs. Samuel Dunstead.' "

Liam gazed fixedly at his carton of milk while the manager was called, the computer consulted, the account number finally punched in. He watched the woman sign her receipt, and then he cleared his throat and said, "Mrs. Dunstead?"

She was putting on her sunglasses. She turned to look at him, the glasses lowered halfway from the top of her head where they had been perched.

"I'm Liam Pennywell," he told her.

She settled her glasses on her nose and continued to look

at him; or at least he assumed she did. (The lenses were too dark for him to be sure.)

"The man who's been seeing your daughter," he said.

"Seeing . . . Eunice?"

"Right. I happened to overhear your name and I thought I'd—"

"Seeing, as in . . . ?"

"Seeing as in, um, dating," he said.

"That's not possible," she told him. "Eunice is married."

"What?"

"I don't know what you're trying to pull here, mister," she said, "but my daughter's a happily married woman and she has been for quite some time."

Then she spun around and seized her grocery bag and stalked off.

The cashier turned her eyes to Liam as if she were watching a tennis match, but Liam just stared her down and so eventually she reached for his milk and scanned it without any comment.

9

He could think of several possibilities.

First, this might have been a different Mrs. Dunstead.

(But a different Mrs. *Samuel* Dunstead? With a daughter named Eunice?)

Or maybe the woman had Alzheimer's. An unusual, reverse kind of Alzheimer's where instead of forgetting what had happened, she remembered what had not happened.

Or maybe she was just plain crazy. Driven frantic with worry over her daughter's lack of a husband, she had hallucinated a husband and perhaps even, who knows, a houseful of children to boot.

Or maybe Eunice was married.

He drove home and put the milk in the refrigerator and folded the grocery bag neatly and stowed it in the cabinet. He sat down in the rocking chair with his hands cupping his knees. In a minute he would phone her. But not yet.

He thought of the clues that had failed to alert him: the fact that her cell phone was the only way he could reach her; never her home phone. The fact that he always had to leave a message for her to call him back and that she alone, therefore, determined when they would talk. He thought of how she preferred to see him at his apartment or someplace out of the way where she was certain not to run into anyone she knew. How she found a dozen reasons to end their evenings early. How she was all but unavailable on weekends. How she hadn't introduced him to her parents or to any of her friends.

If he'd read this in some Ask Amy column, he would have thought the writer was a fool.

But her open, guileless face! Her childlike unself-consciousness, her wide gray eyes magnified by her enormous glasses! She seemed not merely innocent but completely untouched by life, unused. You could tell at a glance, somehow, that she'd never had a baby. And his daughters, who always claimed they could sense if a person was married—had they mentioned any warning bells when they met Eunice? No.

But then he remembered her reluctance to go to movies with him. Always she gave some excuse: the movie might be too violent, or too depressing, or too foreign. And the few times she did go, she wouldn't hold hands. She was chary about showing affection anywhere out in the world, in fact. In private she was so cuddly and confiding, but in public she moved subtly away from him if he ventured to drape an arm across her shoulder.

He must have *decided* not to know.

The kitchen telephone rang and he stood up and went over to look at it. *DUNSTEAD E L.* For a moment, he considered not answering. Then he lifted the receiver and said, "Hello."

"Do you hate me?" she asked.

His heart sank.

"So it's true," he said.

"I can explain, Liam! I can explain! I was *planning* to explain, but it never seemed . . . My mother just now phoned and left this distraught-sounding message. She said, 'Eunice, such a strange man in the grocery store; he claimed you and he were dating.' She said, 'You aren't, are you? How could you be dating?' I don't know what I'm going to tell her. Can I come over and discuss this?"

"What's to discuss?" he asked. "You're either married or you're not."

Against all evidence, he noticed, he seemed to be waiting for her to say that she was not. She hadn't actually stated in so many words that she was, after all. He still had a shred of hope. But she just asked, "Will you be home for the next little bit?"

"Don't you have to work?"

"I don't care about work!" she said. "I'll be there in twenty minutes."

He hung up and went back to his rocking chair and sat down. He placed his hands on his knees again. He thought, What will I get up in the morning for, if I don't have Eunice?

This was how little time it took, evidently, to grow accustomed to being with somebody.

She'd been planning to tell him for weeks, she said. For as long as she had known him, really. She just hadn't found the right moment. She had never meant to deceive him. She said all this while she was still out in the entranceway. He opened his front door and she fell on his neck, her face wet with tears, circlets of damp hair plastered to her cheeks, wailing, "I'm so sorry, I'm so sorry, I'm so sorry! Please say you don't hate me!"

He disentangled himself with some difficulty and led her to one of the armchairs. She collapsed in it and buried her face and rocked back and forth, sobbing. After a few moments of standing by in silence, Liam went to sit in the other armchair. For a while he studied the only exposed part of her—her two cupped hands—and then he thought to ask, "Why is it you don't wear a wedding ring?"

She straightened and swiped at her nose with the back of her wrist. "I'm subject to eczema," she said in a clogged voice.

"Ah."

"And plus, my fingers are fat. Rings don't really look good on me."

Liam adjusted the crease on one trouser leg. He said, "So this is an . . . ongoing marriage. Current, I mean."

She nodded.

"And do you have children?"

"Oh! No!" She looked shocked. "Neither of us wanted them."

He supposed that was some slight comfort.

"Also, we haven't been getting along too well," she added after a moment. "Cross my heart, Liam: it's not as if you're breaking up this perfect couple."

Liam resisted the urge to lash out with some cutting remark. ("What are you going to say next: 'My husband doesn't understand me'?")

"We didn't get along from the start, now that I think about it," she said. "It was almost an *arranged* marriage, really. His mom and my mom played tennis together and I guess they got to talking one day and decided they ought to match up their two loser children."

She sent Liam a glance, perhaps expecting him to interrupt and tell her, as he usually did, that she was not a loser. But he said nothing. She lowered her gaze again. She was twisting the hem of her skirt as if it were a dishrag.

"At least, we looked to *them* like losers," she said. "I was thirty-two years old at the time and still not married and had never yet held a job in my chosen field. I was selling clothes in this dress shop that belonged to a friend of my mom's, but I could tell she was about to let me go."

Liam wondered how Eunice would have managed without her mother's network of friends.

"And he was thirty-four and not married either and his whole world was his work. He worked at a lab down at Hopkins; he still does. Another biology major. I suppose they thought that meant we had something in common, I mean something besides being losers."

She sent Liam another glance, but still he didn't interrupt.

"I knew from day one it was a mistake," she said. "Or underneath, I knew. I must have known. I looked at him as a fallback. Someone I just settled for. Maybe that's why I didn't change my name when we got married. He said after the wedding, he said, 'Now you're Mrs. Simmons.' I said, 'What? I'm not Mrs. Simmons!' Besides, think about it: Eunice Simmons. It would have had that weird hiss between the two *s* sounds."

They seemed to be getting off the subject, here. Liam said, "Eunice. You told me you'd had only three boyfriends in your entire life."

"Well? And I did! I promise!"

"You didn't say a word about a husband."

"Yes, I realize that," she said. "But when you and I met, there wasn't any reason to tell you about my husband. We were discussing a job application. And then you were so . . . just so nice to me, so interested in my work and asking me questions. My husband isn't interested at all. He never asks me questions. My husband is sort of negative, if you want the honest truth."

Each time she said "my husband," it struck Liam like a physical blow. He felt himself actually wincing.

"He has this sad-sack kind of attitude that drags me down," she said. She swiped at her nose again and then opened her purse and started digging through it, eventually coming up with a tissue. "He's very pessimistic, very broody. He's not good for my mental health. I see that now. And then when you came along . . . Well, I think I was looking for someone and I didn't even know it! Isn't it amazing how that works?"

Liam didn't trust himself to answer.

Eunice lifted her glasses slightly and blotted her lids with the tissue. Her lenses were so fogged that he wondered how she could see through them.

(Ordinarily, this would have made him smile. Now it caused his chest to hurt.)

He said, "All right, through some unfortunate oversight you didn't tell me you were married. But how about what you *did* tell me? Do you really live at home with your parents?"

"No."

"No! Where, then?"

She folded her tissue into a square. "In an apartment at the St. Paul Arms," she said.

"An apartment with your husband."

"Yes."

"So every night, you've gone home to your husband after you've left me."

She raised her eyes to Liam's. "He's usually not there, though," she said. "Lots of times he spends the night at the lab. We barely see each other, I promise."

"Still, you told me this whole long story about moving back home with your parents. You *invented* it. And I believed it! So your father didn't have a stroke?"

"Of course he had a stroke! You think I would make something like that up?"

"I really have no idea," he said.

"He had a very serious stroke, and he's still recovering. But I'm not living there; I just go over to help out."

"And when you come to my place, you tell your husband you're with your parents."

"Right."

"And you tell your parents you're with your husband."

She nodded.

"It's like that bigamist movie," Liam said. "Didn't Alec Guinness play a bigamist, once?"

"I don't know what you're talking about," she said. She wrinkled her eyebrows, struck by a new thought. "Maybe what I'll tell Mom is, you're someone from work I had coffee with once and you must have somehow gotten the wrong idea."

Liam decided to pretend he hadn't heard this. He said, "How about last Saturday, when you went on that all-day retreat with Cope Development? Was there really a retreat?"

"*Yes*, there was a retreat! They have four retreats a year! Why would I tell you they did if they didn't?"

"And the speech troubles? The therapist who lisps? That was just a fiendishly creative lie to keep me from meeting your parents?"

"No, it was not a lie!" she said indignantly. "There *is* a speech therapist. She does lisp. I'm not . . . devious, Liam!"

"You're not devious," he repeated slowly.

"Not in the way you're thinking. Not concocting stories out of whole cloth. It was only that I felt so attracted to you, right off, and I thought about what it would be like to start over with the right person, do it *right* this time, but I knew you wouldn't give me a second glance if you found out I was married. You said as much, right at the start. You as much as told me you wouldn't. You said you didn't believe in divorce."

"I did?"

"You said you thought marriage should be permanent. You said divorce was a sin."

All at once he was the one at fault, somehow. He said, "How could I have said that? I'm divorced myself."

"Well, I'm only quoting what you told me. So what was I to do—announce that I was married?"

"You could have. Yes."

"And lose my one last chance at happiness?"

He pressed his fingers to his temples. He said, "I can't possibly have said divorce was a sin, Eunice. You must have misunderstood. But I do take marriage seriously. Even though mine didn't work out, I always tried to behave . . . honorably. And now I find I've been seeing another man's wife! Can you imagine how that makes me feel? It's what happened when I was a boy—an outsider coming along and wrecking my parents' marriage. How could I justify doing the same thing myself?"

"Oh, *justify*," Eunice said. "All those righteous words. But this is your only life, Liam! Don't you think you deserve to spend it with the person you love?"

Her cell phone rang—the "Hallelujah Chorus," slightly muffled by her purse. She ignored it. She was gazing at Liam imploringly, sitting forward in her chair and clutching the square of tissue.

"You'd better answer that," he told her.

"It's only Mr. C.," she said.

"Well, *answer* it, Eunice. You don't want to lose your job."

She reached into her purse, but she kept her eyes on Liam's face. No doubt she considered him heartless for thinking of her job at such a moment. But it wasn't really her job he was thinking of. He was just seizing the opportunity to slip out of their conversation.

Because how could he argue with her? It *was* his only life. Didn't he deserve to spend it with the person he loved?

He didn't walk her to her car. He went with her to the door, but when she raised her face for a kiss he drew back. She said, "Liam? Should I come over this evening?"

"I don't think so," he said.

The refusal gave him a perverse sense of satisfaction. A part of him, he was interested to observe, did in fact hate her. But only a part, so when she asked, "You're not ever going to let me come again? We're never again going to see each other?" he said, "I just need some time to think, Eunice."

Then he hated her all the more when he saw the look of relief that passed across her face. He felt a sudden urge to tell her that now he *had* thought, and they were finished. If people couldn't trust each other, what was the point in their being together?

He kept himself in check, however, and he closed the door on her gently instead of slamming it.

He was familiar with those flashes of hatred. (He'd been married two times, after all.) He knew enough not to act on them.

But once he was resettled in his chair, he sank into a deep, bitter anger. He started with the memory of that scene with Mrs. Dunstead—so humiliating, so grimace-producing. What she must have thought! He went back over Eunice's lies, each of which humiliated him further because he couldn't believe he had been so willfully blind for so long. And he reflected upon the fact that in some ways she really was, as she said herself, a loser. In *many* ways she was a loser. She was naive and literal-minded and she couldn't keep a job for the life of her and besides, who would have trouble finding work in *biology*, for Lord's sake? She wore sandals that looked like dugouts. She was subject to blushes and rashes. Only a friendless, aging man with not enough to do would have talked himself into loving her.

Had he really been that desperate?

And then the worst of all: he had encroached upon a marriage. He wasn't so very different from Esther Jo Baddingley, the aptly named Other Woman who had torn his family apart.

Louise's church would probably say that he was not in the least different—that a sin was a sin, no matter what, even when it was unwitting. But Liam, of course, knew better. On that score, he was guilt-free.

Or very nearly guilt-free.

Or he *should* have been guilt-free.

He dropped his head into his hands.

Kitty came home from work with a paper bag full of tomatoes. She said one of the dentists lived out in Greenspring Valley and all of his tomatoes had ripened at the same time. "So can we make some kind of pasta dish for supper?" she asked Liam. "Something Italian, and Damian can come eat with us?"

"Certainly," Liam said, not moving.

Those times when Eunice had drawn away from him as Kitty entered the room, it wasn't for Kitty's sake at all. She had been thinking of herself. Her reputation. She hadn't wanted a witness.

"Hello?" Kitty said.

Then, "What are you just sitting there for?"

"No reason."

"Are you all right?"

"I'm fine."

He got to his feet and went to the kitchen, followed by Kitty with her bag. "Let's see," he said, opening a cabinet.

"Egg noodles, but just a handful. Angel-hair pasta, another handful. Well, maybe we could combine them. I do have oregano. No garlic, though. I think we'd have to have garlic for anything Italian."

"I'll ask Damian to bring some from his mom's," Kitty said.

"Okay."

He bent to take a pot from a cupboard. It felt unusually heavy. He seemed to be moving through mud. His arms and legs weighed a ton.

Kitty started setting the tomatoes out on the counter. "Some of these look past their sell-by date," she told him.

"All the better to make a sauce with! Easier to squash!"

His voice had a fake cheeriness to it, but Kitty didn't seem to notice.

She went off to change out of her work clothes, and the instant she was gone, the kitchen telephone rang. *DUN-STEAD E L.* He began hunting for the olive oil. The telephone went on ringing. "Aren't you going to get that?" Kitty called from the den.

"No."

He worried she would come get it herself, but then he heard her talking to Damian on her cell phone. He could always tell when it was Damian because she spoke in such a low voice that it sounded like humming.

The kitchen phone fell silent in the middle of a ring, giving a final broken-off peep that struck him as pathetic.

He wondered if Eunice cooked supper for her husband. It stood to reason that she must, at least if the husband ever emerged from his lab, and yet Liam couldn't picture it. He

couldn't picture her shopping for groceries, either, or vacu-
uming, or ironing. When he tried to, the husband material-
ized in the background. He was a shadowy figure in a
sleeveless undershirt, muscular and sullen, something on the
order of Marlon Brando in *A Streetcar Named Desire*.

Negative, Eunice had called the husband. What had she
meant by that? Liam seemed unable to stop himself from
parsing every word of the afternoon's conversation. *He's not
good for my mental health* was a strike against her—one of
those New Age remarks that only the young and self-centered
would make. Oh, definitely he was better off without her.

Or else not.

If he had known from the very beginning that she was
married, he wouldn't be in this predicament. It would have
been so easy to turn off his feelings before they got started;
he did it all the time, everyone did, without even thinking
about it.

(A memory came to him of Janice Elmer at St. Dyfrig,
whose husband was away with the National Guard. She had
asked Liam once if he liked Chinese food, and he had said, "I
don't like *any* food"—a reaction so emphatic that he realized
it was his instinctive defense against the possibility, probably
imagined, of some compromising invitation.)

Now, though, it was too late to turn off his feelings for
Eunice. Now that he was so used to her.

He put the tomatoes in the pot to simmer, and he added
the empty bag to his grocery bag full of newspapers, which
he carried out to the recycling bin. The sun had begun to sink
and the air outside was cooler than inside, with a bit of a
breeze stirring the pines above the walkway. He saw some-

one ahead of him carrying an empty cardboard box—a heavyset man in a Hawaiian shirt. "Why, hello there!" the man said, stopping to let him catch up.

"Hi," Liam said.

"How's it been going?"

"Uh, fine."

"You don't remember me, do you. Bob Hunstler? The folks who called 911?"

"Oh! Sorry," Liam said. He shifted his bag to one side and shook hands.

"I guess you saw where they caught your guy," Mr. Hunstler said.

"They did?"

"It was in last Saturday's paper. Did you miss it? Guy right here in the complex."

"In *this* complex?" Liam asked. He looked around him.

"Well, not actually living here. But his mother does. Mrs. Twill? In Building D? We *know* the woman, by sight at least. Just as nice as she can be. It's not her fault she's got a deadbeat son, now, is it."

"No, I suppose not," Liam said.

"They caught him over in B, making off with a sound system. Seems every time he came to visit his mom, he'd just nip by someone's apartment on the way out and pick himself up a little something to take home."

"Is that right," Liam said. "I haven't heard a thing from the police."

"Well, maybe since the fellow in B caught him redhanded, they figure there's no need to bring in any others."

Mr. Hunstler resumed walking, swinging the cardboard

box at his side, but Liam slowed to a stop. "Good seeing you," he called.

"Oh, weren't you headed to the bin?"

"I'm going to check for that paper."

Mr. Hunstler raised his arm in half of a wave and plodded on.

Back in the apartment, Liam dumped his bag upside down in a chair. Saturday, August fifth. Aha. He found the police news listed in the Maryland section. *Man Nabbed in County Burglaries;* that would have to be it. A paragraph barely an inch and a half long, without a photo.

> *The arrest of Lamont Edward Twill, 24, is expected to bring to a halt a recent rash of break-ins in Baltimore County. Mr. Twill was tackled by a resident of the Windy Pines development, where he was seen loading stolen electronic equipment into his panel truck.*
>
> *A search of his Lutherville lodgings revealed a number of items reported missing from homes in the Towson and Timonium areas over the past several months.*

"Your tomatoes are popping," Kitty said, coming into the room.

"Turn them down, then."

"What are all these papers?"

He held the Maryland section out to her. "My burglar," he told her.

"Really?"

She took the newspaper from him and read where he pointed. "Well, what do you know," she said. Then she handed the paper back to him and wandered off toward the stove. "I thought you were going to wait for garlic before you started cooking these," she called a moment later.

"I'll add it when it comes."

"It won't do much good at *that* stage."

Liam didn't bother answering. He was reading the news item over again. He wished they'd included a photograph. Maybe some random detail would have struck a spark in his brain. Just a glimpse of a mustache, say, or a birthmark or a scar, and he would think, Wait! Haven't I seen that somewhere before?

The familiar strain of trying to remember what wasn't there brought him back to Eunice—the original Eunice; Eunice as he had first fantasized her when he'd imagined that she might rescue him.

And she had rescued him, really.

He refolded the newspaper and dropped it on top of the others.

It turned out that combining egg noodles with angel-hair pasta wasn't such a good idea. Or at least, the two should have been cooked in separate pots. The noodles still showed some resistance in the middle, while the angel hair was over-done. Liam and Kitty plowed through theirs regardless, but Damian, Liam noticed, forked up each strand of angel hair one by one and left the noodles behind. Even though Liam's policy was never to apologize for his cooking, he did say, "Maybe the noodles should have been given a few more minutes."

"Naw, they're *great*!" Damian told him.

Liam felt touched. So did Kitty, evidently, because she reached over and gave Damian a tender pat on the wrist.

Liam averted his eyes.

Damian was very interested in the news of the arrest. He thought Liam should go inventory the stolen goods. "You might find something there that you didn't even know you were missing," he said.

"In that case, why bother getting it back?" Liam asked him.

"Because six months from now you might suddenly think, Hey, didn't I used to own a what's-it? And then you'll be sorry you didn't go check when you had the chance."

"Well, it's not as if these things are sitting on public display somewhere," Liam said.

He wished Xanthe could hear their conversation. She'd been so sure the intruder was Damian! He remembered how she'd flounced off in a huff when she found out Damian was visiting. She hadn't been back since, in fact. But here Damian sat, blithely unaware that anyone would dream of suspecting him. He was proposing now that Liam attend the lineup.

"Lineup? What lineup?" Liam asked him. "Why would they have a lineup? You've been watching too much TV."

"They ought to at least offer to let you meet the guy. Don't you want to see who it was? Don't you want to, like, confront him?"

"Oh, I'm not much of a one for confrontation," Liam said. "I *would* be, maybe, if I thought it would bring my memory back—"

He stopped himself, because he knew everybody felt he was making too much of the memory issue. He said, "But as far as meeting him just to see who he is . . . well, what's the point? It's not as if he singled me out. This was like those accidents you read about in the paper: an overpass collapses and a man driving underneath is instantly killed. He stayed in his lane, obeyed the lights, checked his rearview mirror, observed the speed limit, and *still* he was killed. These things just happen."

"That guy didn't just happen to hit you on the head," Damian said.

"Actually, he *did* just happen to, because I just happened to be there. No sense going up to him now and asking why."

Damian knotted his brow, clearly baffled. He might have continued arguing, but just then the kitchen telephone rang. Liam stayed seated. Kitty said, "Want me to answer that?"

"Never mind," Liam said.

"That's okay, I'm finished." She stood up and went to lift the receiver. "Hello?" she said. "Hi. Sure, just a sec. It's Eunice, Dad."

"I'm eating," Liam told her. And to prove it, he reached for the tomato sauce and ladled a spoonful onto his empty plate.

After a pause, Kitty said, "Eunice? Can he call you back later? Okay. Bye."

She returned to the table and sat down. Neither she nor Damian spoke.

"I think you were right about the garlic," Liam said. "I should have added it at the start. I can't even taste that it's there."

He picked up the Parmesan cheese and sprinkled it on his sauce. Out of nowhere, a memory came to him of a spaghetti dinner he'd eaten with Eunice the week before, in a dingy little café in the mall across the street. The waitress had started out by introducing herself. "Hi," she'd said. "I'm Debbie, and I'll be your server tonight." It was a practice that always made Liam roll his eyes, but Eunice seemed quite taken with it. All during their supper she had happily employed the woman's name. "Debbie, could we have more bread?" and, "That was delicious, Debbie." At the time, Liam had felt a bit irritated with her. Now, though, it struck him as funny. An actual bubble of laughter escaped him, and he ducked his head lower to hide it and busied himself with his meal.

10

Liam's father lived off Harford Road, in a neighborhood of unassuming little cottages from the 1940s with drab clapboard siding, squat front porches, and carefully kept plots of grass. Liam could have found the place in his sleep, and not only because it was a straight shot out Northern Parkway. He had been traveling there since his teens. In fact, it was the first address he'd ever driven to, the first day he had his license. He'd asked permission to borrow the family car and then made his escape (was how he thought of it), gripping the steering wheel with both hands and constantly checking the rearview mirror as his driver's ed instructor had taught him, but the faint tingle down his spine had come less from new-driver nerves than from the knowledge that he was betraying his mother. She would have been so distressed if she had known where he was going. She was, in general, a woman easily distressed. "That hurts my feelings" was her most characteristic remark. Also, "I just don't seem to have any appetite," as she pushed her plate away sadly after Liam had done something to disappoint her. He had disappointed her often, although he had tried his best not to.

The scenery hadn't changed much in all these years. Even the flowers in the yards had a dated look—ball-shaped clumps of blue or white on bushes pruned into balls themselves. There was an abundance of lawn ornaments—plaster gnomes and fawns and families of ducks, birdbaths, windmills, reflective aluminum gazing globes, wooden cutouts of girls in sunbonnets bending over the flower beds with their wooden watering cans. Liam's father's yard had a miniature pony cart planted with red geraniums and hitched to a plaster pony.

Liam parked behind his father's great long barge of a Chevy and walked up to the porch. He hadn't phoned ahead. He never did. In his youth he had been aiming for an offhand, happenstance effect, and by now it was a tradition. Anyhow, the couple always seemed to be at home. Bard Pennywell had retired long ago from Sure-Tee Insurance, and Esther Jo had been asked to leave back when they got married.

It was Esther Jo who answered the doorbell. "Liam!" she said. They had never developed the habit of kissing when they met. For Liam as a teenager, she had seemed too dangerous, too obviously sexy for him to risk it. By now she was a puffy, pigeon-shaped woman in her early seventies, wearing a pinafore apron and cloth mules, but if you knew to look for the clues—the finger waves pressed into her faded blond hair, the eyebrows plucked to unsteady threads—you could still detect the office glamour girl she had once been.

"I hope I haven't come at a bad time," Liam told her.

"No, no, not at all. Your dad was just—Bard? It's Liam! Your dad was just mowing the grass out back. Not that we have much to mow, these days. Hasn't it been dry! I've forgotten what rain feels like, almost."

She was leading Liam into the living room, which always struck him as an oddly girlish place. A row of stuffed animals lined the brocade love seat, and the dark wooden bookcase held an array of dolls in old-fashioned dresses, with crinolines and pantaloons peeking out from under their hems.

Liam settled in an armchair, but he stood again when his father entered the room. "Well, hi there, stranger!" his father said. He wore a crisply ironed shirt and a striped tie; he wasn't the kind of man who dressed casually even to mow the lawn. Unlike Liam, he had thinned and shrunk as he aged, and the top of his head was completely bald, his hair no more than two tufts of white bracketing a narrow, deeply wrinkled face.

As they shook hands, Liam said, "I just thought I'd stop by and see how you were doing."

"We're doing fine! Not bad at all! This is a nice surprise, son." Bard lowered himself onto the love seat, reaching behind him without looking to move aside a teddy bear in a cheerleader costume. "How've you been? How're the girls?"

"Everyone's fine," Liam said, sitting back down. "They send their love."

Or they would have, he reasoned, if they had known he was coming here. There was almost no contact between the two parts of Liam's family.

"I'm just going to fetch some iced tea," Esther Jo said. She had her arms folded tightly under her bosom, as if she felt the need to warm herself. "You two sit right where you are. Don't get up! Just sit right here and have a nice talk. I'm going to leave you to it."

She left the room, her mules making whispery sounds on the floorboards.

"I'd have thought you'd be at work now," Liam's father said, glancing at his watch. It was shortly before noon, Liam knew without checking. "Is summer school finished already?"

"I'm not doing that this year," Liam said.

"Ah. Needed a break, did you."

"Well . . . and I've been busy moving."

"Moving! Where to?"

"A smaller place, up near the Beltway. Remind me to give you the phone number."

His father nodded. "*We* should move," he said. "Get shed of all this yard work. But, I don't know, your stepmother loves her house so."

Since Liam could never quite connect Esther Jo with the term "stepmother," he experienced a little blank spell before he said, "Oh. Well, that's understandable."

"She says, 'Where would I put all my pretty things? Where would my sister stay when she visits?' "

"It's not as if an apartment couldn't have a guestroom," Liam said.

"No, but, *you* know."

"In fact, I've got Kitty staying with me at this very moment."

"Do you now!" His father smoothed the point of his tie.

Really the two of them had nothing to say to each other. Why did Liam have to learn this all over again on every visit?

They tried, though. Both of them tried. His father said, "How *is* Kitty, by the way?"

"She's fine," Liam said. "She's working this summer in a dentist's office."

"Thinking of being a dental hygienist, is she."

"Why, no. It's just a summer job, is all. Filing charts."

His father cleared his throat. "And your sister?" he asked.

"She's fine too."

Liam found himself listening for some sound from the kitchen, wondering when Esther Jo would be coming back to rescue them. "I actually haven't seen Julia in a while," he said.

"Me neither," his father said, and he gave a dry cough of a laugh, although his face remained unsmiling. (He hadn't seen Julia in forty-some years, and even then it was just because he'd shown up uninvited at her high school graduation.) He shifted in his seat slightly, as if he regretted his little joke, and smoothed his tie again.

"I've been laid off at St. Dyfrig," Liam said.

At least it was a conversational topic.

"Laid off!"

"They're folding their two fifth grades into one class next year."

"But you've been there forever!"

"Just about," Liam said.

"Don't you have seniority?"

"Oh, well, I don't know. That's not how it works there."

"How *does* it work?"

"I don't know, I told you," Liam said. He looked gratefully toward the kitchen, from where he heard the clink of ice cubes approaching.

"Real brewed tea!" Esther Jo announced, appearing with a tray. "I have to say I've just never held with instant. Seems to me instant has a sort of dusty taste." She set the tray on the coffee table and distributed a tall glass to each of them. In the interim, she had put on lipstick. Her shiny, cherry-red lips reminded Liam of the days when she and his father were first together, when she had been movie-star pretty in her buxom sweater sets and her tightly packed straight skirts with the kick pleats.

Wasn't it amazing, he thought, that even a species as supposedly evolved as the human race was still so subject to biology. And now here they sat—his ancient father shriveled to a husk, the femme fatale's swollen feet stuffed into calico mules.

"Liam's lost his job," Bard told Esther Jo.

"Oh, no, Liam!" Esther Jo said.

Liam said, "Yep."

"What are you going to *do*?" she asked.

"Well, I'm thinking that over."

"You just know somebody's going to snatch you up in half a second," she told him. "How about one of the public schools? They're dying for good teachers in the public schools."

"I'm not certified, though," Liam said.

"Well, *something*'s going to come along, I'm sure of it. You know what?" she said, setting down her glass. "I should tell your fortune."

"Oh, yes, hon, good idea," Bard told her. "You haven't done that in a long time."

"Not for me, at any rate," Liam said.

He remembered her telling his fortune when he'd been applying to graduate schools. She had said he would go to a place that was good for him professionally but not personally.

What was *that* all about? you'd have to ask, but never mind; at least if she told his fortune now it would give them something to fill the silence with. He said, "Would you be willing?"

"Well, if I still know how," she said. "Seems like the older all our friends get, the less they wonder about. I can't think when was the last time . . . Betty Adler, maybe. Was it Betty?" she asked Bard. "Betty was wanting to know if she should move to New Mexico to be near her married daughter. Here, let me skootch this footstool around."

She slid the footstool over in front of Liam and settled on it, slanting her knees decorously to one side. This close, she gave off a faint scent of roses. "Show me your hands," she commanded, and Liam held his hands out to her obediently. She took hold of them both at the base of his fingers and bent them slightly backward to flatten them. Her own fingers were chilled and dampish from her iced-tea glass. She said, "Now, first what I like to do is—oh!"

She was staring at his left palm—the gnarly line of his scar.

"What *happened*?" she asked him.

"I had a little accident."

She made a clucking sound, looking dazed. "Well, this just skews everything every which way," she said. "I never ran into such a thing before."

"It's only a scar," Liam told her. For some reason, he felt it was important to carry through with this now. "I don't see why it would make any difference."

"But am I supposed to treat it like a brand-new line, or what? And how do I read what's underneath it? I can't *tell* what's underneath it! I mean, your left hand is your whole entire past! I wonder if one of my books deals with this."

"If it's my past, why do we care?" Liam asked. "We just want to know about my future."

"Oh, you can't read one without the other," Esther Jo told him. "They're intermingled. They bounce off of each other. That's what the amateurs fail to understand."

She released his hands with a dismissive little pat that gave Liam a sense of rejection, absurdly enough.

"Let's see if I can explain this," she said. "You know how farmers can predict what kind of winter they'll have by looking at the acorns and berries? Those acorns and berries are the way they are because of what has gone before—how much rainfall there's been and et cetera, et cetera. A whole lot depends on the weather that's already happened. And the farmers know that."

She gave a quick, self-confirming nod.

"Well, just the same way, a real fortune-teller—and I'm not one to brag, but I *am* a real fortune-teller; I've just always had the gift, somehow—a real fortune-teller knows that your future depends on your past. It keeps shifting about; it's not carved in stone. It keeps bouncing off whatever happened earlier. So, no, I can't do a thing without seeing what's in your left palm."

And she sat back on her footstool with an annoyingly smug expression and laced her fingers around her knees.

Liam said, "Couldn't you at least give it a try?"

She shook her head vigorously.

"You know what they say," she told him. " 'Those who forget the past tend to regret the future.' "

"What?"

Bard said, "Aw, now, hon. Seems to me you might this once make an exception."

"It's not a matter of choice," she told him.

He said, "At least it would help us to pass the time, look at it that way."

"Pass the time!" she said. She stared at him. "Have I not just told you I'm a real fortune-teller?"

"Oh, well, *real;* ha-ha . . ."

"Do you not know I've been reading people's futures since I was seven?"

"The boy was only wondering where to find a job, Esther Jo."

Liam said, "Oh, no, it's not important." Now he felt foolish, as if he were, in fact, a "boy" begging for crumbs of wisdom. "I was just curious," he said. "I know it doesn't mean anything."

"Doesn't mean anything!" Esther Jo echoed.

"Or, rather . . . of course it means something, but . . ."

How had things reached such a state? But it wasn't *his* fault. He honestly didn't think he should be shouldering the blame for this. He looked across at his father, who seemed unperturbed.

"Well, silly me, right?" Esther Jo said. "Silly me to think you-all would take it seriously."

She jumped up from the footstool, more spryly than you would expect from a woman her age, and stalked back to her chair and flung herself into it. "I don't know why I bothered," she told the ceiling.

"Oh, princess," Bard said mildly. "Can't we just have a nice visit? Drink your tea."

"I'm not thirsty," she said, still addressing the ceiling.

"Come on, hon. Be nice."

She didn't answer, but she picked up her glass and took a sip, finally.

Liam said, "Well, anyhow, I should be running along. I just wanted to pop in and say hello."

Bard looked relieved. "We appreciate that," he said. "Always good to see you, son."

He and Liam stood up, but Esther Jo stayed seated, gazing down into her glass. Liam said, "Thank you for the tea, Esther Jo."

"You're welcome, I'm sure," she murmured, still not raising her eyes.

Bard clapped him on the shoulder and told him, "I'll see you out."

Ordinarily Liam would have protested, but he allowed it this time. As they descended the porch steps, he said, "I didn't mean to hurt her feelings."

Bard said, "*Oh*, well," and looked off toward the pony cart as if he had never noticed it before. Liam felt disappointed; he'd been hoping (he saw now) for his father to say something significant, give some clue about his life.

They reached the curb, and Liam slowed and turned. He said, "By the way, I've been . . . going out with someone lately."

"Have you now," Bard said, finally focusing on him.

"I just met her this summer."

"Good for you, son. It's not right being on your own."

"Except, now I find out she's married."

There was a pause. His father looked at him with an unreadable expression.

"When we met, I had no idea," Liam said.

"She didn't tell you?"

"Not a word."

His father sighed and then bent to pluck a weed.

"That's hard," he said when he'd straightened.

"I never would have gotten involved if I had known," Liam told him. "There's no way I would intentionally break up somebody's marriage."

"Ah, well, you can't always pick and choose these things," his father said.

"I guess the thing to do is to end it," Liam said.

His father gazed off toward a neighbor's garden gnome. Eventually he said, "Now, I don't know as I would agree with that, son. When you get to be my age, you start realizing that you'd better grab whatever happiness comes your way, in this world."

Liam said, "Well, if *that's* your reasoning, then why not say the same to . . . oh, a child molester, for instance? 'Go for it,' you'd tell him. 'Whatever makes you happy.' "

"Liam! Good Lord above!"

"Well? What's the difference?"

"There's a ton of difference! A child molester's ruining somebody's life!"

This time the pause stretched on for a very long time. Liam made no attempt to end it.

"You are surely not saying that Esther Jo and I ruined your mother's life," Bard said.

Liam didn't answer. To be honest, he didn't know what he was saying. This conversation wasn't one he'd planned on having.

"Or *your* life," Bard said.

"No, of course not," Liam said finally.

"So! What do you call this little thing?" Bard asked. He was looking at Liam's car.

"I call it a Geo Prizm," Liam said. He took his keys from his pocket.

"I prefer something a bit more substantial, myself," Bard said. "Especially on the Beltway. They drive like maniacs on the Beltway! And not a cop in sight. I wish you kids would stop acting like I walked out on you or something."

The change of topic was so sudden that Liam almost missed it. He was about to step around to the driver's side when he stopped short and said, "Pardon?"

"I didn't *desert*, you know. I did play fair and square. I leveled with your mother and asked her for a divorce. I sent her money every month as regular as clockwork, and I tried to stay in touch with you and Julia. You think I had it easy? It was hell, there, for a while. And everybody looking at me like I was the villain—some bad guy in a dime novel. I was no villain. I just couldn't bear to go to my grave knowing I'd wasted my life. I just wanted my share of happiness. Can't you understand how I felt?"

Liam didn't know how to answer that.

"Nothing wrong with *you* getting a share of happiness too," Bard said. Then he winced, as if he had embarrassed himself. He raised a hand in a kind of salute and turned and started back up the walk, and Liam got into his car.

Damn, he'd forgotten to leave his new telephone number. Well, he could do that some other time. They seldom talked on the phone anyhow. The unspoken assumption was that the number was for dire emergencies, most likely involving

Bard's health. Of course, by now even Esther Jo—once the scandalously younger woman—was a candidate for such emergencies; but Liam could more easily imagine that it would be she making the fateful phone call one morning, notifying him that she couldn't wake his father. And that would be the end of the grand, heroic love story that had rocked the little Pennywell household and the Sure-Tee Insurance Company.

He stopped for a light on Northern Parkway and watched a young mother crossing in front of him with her baby in a carrier on her chest—an arrangement that always struck him as boastful. Here I am! Look at what I've got! The baby leaned forward like a figurehead, and perhaps to balance his weight the mother leaned backward, which gave her a cocky, strutting gait. You would think she had invented parenthood. Liam supposed that he must once have felt that way himself, although he couldn't remember it. He did remember collecting Millie and the newborn Xanthe from the hospital and marveling at how only two of them had walked in but three of them were leaving.

And now Xanthe was in her mid-thirties and mad at him about something.

We live such tangled, fraught lives, he thought, but in the end we die like all the other animals and we're buried in the ground and after a few more years we might as well not have existed.

This should have depressed him, but instead it made him feel better. The light turned green and he started driving again.

11

Eunice said that her husband made a hobby of being miserable.

She said he was the kind of man who took bad weather personally.

The kind who asked, "Why me, God?" when his assistant was hit by a car.

And he was always railing against other people's grammatical errors.

"He has a thing about dangling modifiers," she told Liam. "You know what a dangling modifier is?"

"Of course."

"Well, I didn't. Like 'At the age of eight, my mother died.' They drive him crazy."

"Oh, I agree," Liam said. "And, 'Walking on the beach, a shark appeared.' "

"What? Last spring he kept a day-to-day tally of all the dangling modifiers in the *Baltimore Sun*, and at the end of a month he sent the list to the editor. But it was never published."

"Such a surprise," Liam murmured.

"So the next month I kept a tally of my own, in one of those little appointment books that come in the mail for free. Every single day I wrote either 'Added' or 'Subtracted.' 'Added' meant my husband had added something positive to my life that day. 'Subtracted' meant he'd been a negative. His 'Added' rating was twelve percent. Pretty pathetic! But you know what he did when I showed him? He just pointed out the mistakes in my method of computation."

Liam massaged his forehead with his fingertips.

"Well, it was a month with thirty-one days in it," Eunice said. "Anybody would have had trouble."

Liam made no comment.

"He completely ignored the real issue, which was that I'm not happy with him."

"Yes, but still," Liam said, "you are *with* him."

"I can leave, though, Liam! I don't have to stay. Why don't you ask me to leave him?"

"Why don't I go out in the street and ask a stranger for his billfold."

"What?"

"You're somebody else's wife, remember? You're already committed."

"I can undo the commitment! People undo them all the time. You undid yours."

"That was just between me and Barbara. There wasn't any third party stealing one of us away."

"Look," Eunice said. "All I have to do is go through a little spell of legal this-and-that and then you and I can be together, aboveboard. Don't you *want* to marry me?"

They were traveling in circles, Liam thought. They were like hamsters on an exercise wheel. Day after day they hashed all this out—Eunice showing up puffy-eyed at six a.m., or telephoning in an urgent whisper from Ishmael Cope's office, or arriving straight from work already talking as Liam opened the door to her. How about if this very minute she went to live on her own? she asked. *Then* would it be all right for them to marry? And what sort of interval would he require? A month? Six months? A year?

"But still," he said, "the fact would remain that you were married when I met you."

"Well, what can I do about *that*, Liam? I can't un-ring the bell!"

"My point exactly."

"You're impossible!"

"The *situation* is impossible."

They argued so long sometimes that the apartment grew dark without their noticing, and they neglected to turn on the lights until Kitty walked in and said, "Oh! I didn't know anybody was here." Then they would hasten to greet her, using their most everyday voices.

It was Liam's own fault that this was dragging on. He knew that. He could have said, "Eunice, enough. We have to stop seeing each other." But he kept procrastinating. He told himself that first they needed to talk this over. They had to get squared away. They didn't want to leave any loose threads trailing.

Pathetic.

At the end of their conversations he generally had a headache, and his voice was fogged and elderly-sounding from overuse. But really there *was* no end to their conversations. The two of them just went on and on until they'd worn themselves out, or till Eunice broke down in tears, or till Kitty interrupted them. Nothing was ever resolved. The week crawled past, the weekend came, another week began. Everything remained the same as the day he'd found out she was married.

What did this remind him of? The final months with Millie, he realized—their repetitive, pointless wrangling during the period just before she died. Now he could see that she must have been severely depressed, but all he knew then was that she seemed dissatisfied with every facet of their life together. She would carp and complain in a monotone, going over and over the same old things, while the baby fussed in the background and, yes, the light in the apartment slowly faded, unnoticed. "You always . . ." Millie said, and "You never . . ." and "Why can't you ever . . . ?" And Liam had defended himself against each charge in turn, like someone hurrying to plug this leak, that leak, with new leaks eternally springing up elsewhere. Then often he would give up and leave—just walk out, feeling bruised and damaged, and not come back until he was sure that she had gone to bed.

Although Eunice and Millie were not the least bit similar. Eunice had more energy; she was more . . . defined, Liam supposed you could say. Yet somehow she gave him that same feeling that he was the person responsible. She had that same way of looking to him to straighten out her life.

As if he were capable of straightening out anybody's life, even his own!

He said, "Eunice. Sweetheart. I'm trying to do the right thing, here." But what *was* the right thing? Was it possible, in fact, that he was being too rigid, too moralistic, too narrow-minded? That the greater good was to make the very most of their time here on earth? Yes! Why not? And he felt a flood of joyous recklessness, which Eunice must have guessed because she sprang up and crossed the room to throw herself in his lap and wrap her arms around his neck. Her skin was warm and fragrant, and her breasts were squashed alluringly against his chest.

Did she sit like this in her husband's lap?

Her husband's name was Norman. He drove a Prius, from the first year Priuses were manufactured. He had a twin sister, Eunice said, who was developmentally disabled.

Liam set Eunice gently aside and stood up. "You should go," he told her.

Louise phoned on Friday morning and asked if he could watch Jonah. "My sitter has up and eloped," she said, "without a word of notice."

"Did she marry Chicken Little?" Liam asked.

"How do you know about Chicken Little?"

"Oh, I have my sources."

"I could strangle her," Louise told him. "Tomorrow's Homecoming Day at our church and I promised I'd help decorate. Dougall says just take Jonah along, but that way I'd be more of a hindrance than a help."

"Sure, bring him here," Liam said.

"Thanks, Dad."

In fact, he welcomed the diversion. It would be something to think about besides Eunice. He felt the two of them had spent this past couple of weeks in some cramped and airless basement.

Louise was beginning to look noticeably pregnant. Thin as she was, she had no place to hide a baby, Liam supposed. She wore a short skirt and a skimpy tank top, and her collarbones stuck out so far you could almost wrap your fingers around them. Behind her, Jonah trailed listlessly with an armful of picture books. "Hi there, Jonah," Liam said.

"Hi."

"Are we going to be coloring again?"

Jonah just gave him a look.

"*Someone* got up on the wrong side of bed today," Louise murmured.

"Well, never mind; we'll be fine," Liam said. "Should I give him lunch? How long will you be gone?"

"Just till noon or so, I hope. It depends how many others turn up. We're in charge of decorating the Communing Room; that's where they're feeding the Homecomers."

Communing Room, Homecomers . . . It was almost a foreign language. But Liam was determined to avoid any appearance of disapproval. "Is this like Homecoming Day in high school?" he asked in his most courteous tone. "People coming back who've graduated or moved?"

"There's nothing *high-schoolish* about it, Dad!"

"No, I just meant—"

"This is for sinners who've come to see the error of their ways. Which is a far cry from graduating, believe me."

"Yes, of course," Liam said.

"I don't know why you have to try and pick a quarrel about these things."

"It must be my contrary nature," Liam said meekly. He followed her to the door. "Did you bring any snacks?" he thought to ask. "I don't have all that much around that Jonah will eat."

"He's got Goldfish in his knapsack."

"Oh, good."

He saw her out and then returned to the living room. Jonah was still standing there, holding his armful of books. They studied each other in silence. "Well," Liam said finally. "Here we are, I guess."

Jonah heaved a deep sigh. He said, "I don't think Deirdre's going to take me to the State Fair now."

"Why not? She could still do that."

"She got married."

"Married people go to the fair."

"But my mom won't ever speak to her again."

"That's just talk," Liam said. "You know how your mom talks."

"I didn't really like Chicken Little anyway," Jonah said confidingly.

"You didn't?"

"He cheats at soccer."

"How can you cheat at soccer?" Liam asked.

Jonah gave one of his shrugs. "I don't know; he just does," he said. "It's very inappropriate."

"Well, tell you what: let's read some of those books you've brought. What did you bring?"

Jonah held the pile out. Dr. Seuss, Liam saw, and another Dr. Seuss, and a Little Bear book . . . He said, "Good! You choose which one we'll start with."

Before they could sit down, he had to help Jonah out of

his knapsack. Then they settled in an armchair, Jonah squinched tightly into the few remaining inches on Liam's right side. Jonah was wearing gym shoes today, incongruously large red high-tops. They stuck straight out in front of him, and the left one kept knocking into Liam's right knee. He really should buy a sofa, Liam thought for the hundredth time. The image of Eunice came to mind, and he had a sudden hollow feeling.

He was going to be one of those men who die alone among stacks of yellowed newspapers and the dried-out rinds of sandwiches moldering on plates.

He opened the first book on Jonah's pile and started reading aloud. *The Cat in the Hat*, it was. He knew it well. His daughters used to complain that he read too fast and so he made a point of taking his time, enunciating each word and adding plenty of expression. Jonah listened without reacting. His small head gave off a heated smell, like fresh-baked bread or warm honey.

Hop on Pop. Green Eggs and Ham. Father Bear Comes Home, which Jonah interrupted halfway through to announce that he had to pee. "Go ahead; I'll wait," Liam said. He was glad of the respite. Reading with expression was making his throat ache.

When Jonah came out of the bathroom he didn't return to the armchair but went instead to his knapsack, which was lying on the floor. He pulled out a plastic bag of Goldfish crackers and sat down on the carpet to eat them, selecting each cracker one by one as if some were better than others. It wasn't clear whether he'd tired of Little Bear or was merely taking a break. Liam marked their page, just in case. He said, "Would you like to work on your coloring a while?"

"I'm done with coloring," Jonah said.

"You finished the book?"

"I stopped liking it."

"Oh."

Jonah turned the bag upside down, emptying the rest of the Goldfish onto the carpet along with a shower of orange dust. "You know Noah?" he asked Liam.

"Noah in the Bible?"

Jonah nodded.

"I know Noah."

"He made about a hundred animals die," Jonah said.

"He did?"

"He left them to drown. He only took two of things."

"Oh. Right."

"He took two giraffes and let all the rest drown."

"Well, he didn't have a whole lot of room, bear in mind."

"Where'd he buy gas?" Noah asked.

"Excuse me?"

"Where'd he buy gas for his boat if he was the only guy in the world?"

"He didn't need gas," Liam said. "It wasn't that kind of boat."

"Was it a sailboat, then?"

"Why, yes, I guess it was," Liam said. Although he had never noticed sails in the pictures, come to think of it. "Actually," he said, "I guess he didn't need sails either, because he wasn't going anywhere."

"Not going anywhere!"

"There was nowhere *to* go. He was just trying to stay afloat. He was just bobbing up and down, so he didn't need a compass, or a rudder, or a sextant . . ."

"What's a sextant?"

"I believe it's something that figures out directions by the stars. But Noah didn't need to figure out directions, because the whole world was underwater and so it made no difference."

"Huh," Jonah said. He seemed to have lost interest. He licked the tip of one finger and started picking up the crumbs from the carpet.

Liam thought of pointing out that this was only a sort of fairy tale, but he didn't want Louise any madder at him than she already was.

Eunice said that sometimes, she wondered if Mr. C.'s memory trouble could be contagious.

"For instance," she said. "We've just now been to a retirement party for the receptionist. Their receptionist's retiring. Mr. C. takes a handful of nuts from a bowl and starts to eat them, but then he stops. 'These nuts are *ransomed*,' he says. I say, 'What?' 'They're ransomed. Take them away.' 'Oh,' I said. 'You mean—' But then I couldn't think of the word. I could not think of the word. I knew it wasn't 'ransomed,' but I couldn't think what it *should* be."

They were standing in the kitchen alcove, where Liam had gone to fetch the ice water she'd requested the instant she arrived. (Outside it was hot and humid, a typical August afternoon as heavy as mud.) He held a glass beneath the dispenser in the refrigerator door, and Eunice stepped up behind him and wrapped her arms around him and laid her cheek against his back.

"It's like I slipped into Mr. C.'s world for a minute," she said. Her breath was warm and moist against Liam's left shoulder.

He filled the glass with water and turned to face her. Instead of taking the glass from him, she unbuttoned the top button of his shirt. He said, "Your water."

"It's like I saw what it must feel like to be him," she said. "How . . . evaporating and blurry and scary."

"Let's go to the living room," he told her.

He was trying to back away from her, but he was trapped against the refrigerator. Eunice unbuttoned the rest of his buttons, focusing on them intently and not looking up at his face. "Let's not," she said. "Let's go to the bedroom."

"We can't do that," he told her.

"There's no place to sit in the living room."

"There are two very comfortable armchairs."

"Let's go to bed," she said.

Her fingertips were delicate points of warmth against his skin. She dropped her hands to his belt and undid his buckle.

"We should sit down," Liam said. He moved to one side of her.

"We should *lie* down," Eunice told him.

He started toward the living room, still holding the glass of water, but when she followed him he slowed to a stop and let her press herself to his back and hug him once again. He felt confused by the combination of her tight embrace and his loosened waistband. His shirttails had worked themselves free of their own accord, and he thought how good it would feel to be free of *all* his clothes. He wanted to put the water glass someplace but he didn't want to separate from her long enough to do that.

Then the front door burst open and someone caroled, "Knock knock!"

In walked Barbara, lugging a blue vinyl suitcase.

Liam jerked away from Eunice and clutched his shirtfront together with his free hand.

Barbara said, "Oh, excuse me," but not in a particularly apologetic tone. She seemed amused, more than anything. She set down the suitcase to push back a lock of hair that had fallen over her forehead.

Liam said, "What are you doing here?"

"You did leave your door unlocked," Barbara pointed out.

"That doesn't mean you should walk on in!"

"Well, I said, 'Knock knock.' Didn't I?" Barbara asked Eunice. "I don't believe we've met."

Liam said, "This is . . . a friend of mine, Eunice Dunstead. She was just helping me with my résumé."

"I'm Barbara," Barbara told Eunice.

Eunice said, "I have to go." Her cheeks were splotched with patches of red. She snatched up her purse from the rocking chair and rushed toward the door. Barbara moved aside to let her pass, gazing after her thoughtfully. Liam seized her moment of inattention to put down the water glass and buckle his belt.

"Sorry," Barbara told him once the door had slammed shut.

"Honestly, Barbara."

"I'm *sorry!*"

"What are you here for?" he asked.

"I brought Kitty's beach things."

"Beach?"

Casually, as if his mind were on something else, he let a

hand drift to his shirtfront again and he felt for each button and buttoned it. Barbara tilted her head to watch.

"She's spending a few days in Ocean City with Damian's aunt and uncle," she said. "Didn't she clear this with you?"

"Um . . ."

"Liam, are you not keeping track of Kitty's comings and goings? Because if that's the case, she shouldn't be in your care."

"I'm keeping track! I just forgot," he said.

"Really."

Eunice would be traveling farther away every second, in tears and no doubt despairing of him, reflecting on how cowardly he was and how unchivalrous and disloyal. But Barbara, for once, seemed in no hurry to leave. She went over to the rocking chair and sat down, plucking at her T-shirt where it was clinging to her stomach. Her outfit today was singularly unattractive. The T-shirt was stretched and smudged with grass stains, and her loose khaki shorts revealed her wide white thighs, pressed even wider against the chair seat.

As if she guessed what he was thinking, she said, "I look a mess. I've been cleaning."

He said nothing. He sat in the armchair furthest from her, perching on the very edge of it to suggest that he had things to do.

"So," she said. "Tell me about this Eunice person. How long have you known her?"

"What's it to you?" Liam demanded.

It felt so good to speak this way—to say what he wanted, for once, without worrying about Barbara's opinion of him— that he did it again. "What's it *to* you, Barbara? What business is it of yours?"

Barbara rocked back in her chair and said, "My, my!"

"I don't ask you about Howie, do I?"

"Who?"

"Howie the Hound Dog. Howie the Food Phobe."

"Are you referring to Howard Neal?"

"Right," Liam said, risking it.

"Goodness, Liam, where'd you dig *him* up from?"

He scowled at her.

"Gosh, I haven't thought of Howard in . . ." She shook her head, looking amused again. "Well. So Miss Eunice is off-limits. Fine. Forget I asked."

Liam said, "You and I *are* divorced, after all. I do have a private life."

"You're always going on about your private life," Barbara said, "but have you ever considered this, Liam: You're the only Baltimorean I know who leaves his front door unlocked. Even though you've had a burglary! You leave it completely unlocked, but then any time someone walks in you complain that they're intruding. 'Tut-tut!' you say. 'I'm veddy, veddy private and special. I vant to be alone!' "—this last uttered in a bad Greta Garbo accent. "We're damned if we do and damned if we don't. Here's solitary sad old Liam, only God help anybody who tries to step in and get close."

"Well, maybe if they knocked first—"

"And I suppose this poor Eunice person is just like all the rest of us," Barbara said. "All those benighted females who broke their hearts over you. She imagines she'll be the one who finally warms you up."

"Barbara! She is not *poor*! She is not 'this poor Eunice person'! Jesus, Barbara! What gives you the *right*?"

Barbara looked startled. She said, "Well, pardon me."

"Isn't it time for you to leave?"

"Fine," she said. "Okay." She rose to her feet. "I only meant—"

"I don't care what you meant. Just leave."

"All right, Liam, I'm leaving. Have Kitty call me, please, will you?"

"Okay," he said.

Already he was feeling sheepish about his outburst, but he refused to apologize. He stood up and followed Barbara to the door. "Goodbye," he told her.

"Bye, Liam."

He didn't see her out to the parking lot.

He thought of Eunice: how staunch she had been and how forthright. She had not said, "Pleased to meet you," when she and Barbara were introduced. She had not stuck around and made small talk. "I have to go," she had said, and she had gone. While he himself, longing though he was to run after her, had cravenly sat down with Barbara and held a meaningless conversation. He was so concerned about appearances, about what Barbara thought of him, that he had failed to show the most basic human kindness.

The fact was that Eunice was a much better person than he was.

Everyone knew the St. Paul Arms. It was a shabby gray apartment building a couple of blocks from the Hopkins campus, home to graduate students and instructors and lower-level university staff. From his old place, Liam could have walked there in a matter of minutes. Even from his new place it was not that much of a drive, but this afternoon it seemed to take forever. Every stoplight changed to red just before he reached it; every car ahead of him was trying to make a left turn in the face of oncoming traffic. Liam chafed all over with frustration. He drummed his fingers on the steering wheel as he waited for an elderly pedestrian to inch, inch through a crosswalk.

It had not been all that long, really, since Eunice had rushed out his door. He had hopes originally of waylaying her in front of her building, intercepting her before she got inside. As the minutes passed, though, he saw that this was unrealistic. All right: he would just stride on into her apartment and state his case. If the husband happened to be there, fine. It wouldn't change a thing.

The car radio was playing a Chopin étude that tinkled on endlessly, going nowhere. He switched it off.

There weren't any parking spots in front of her building and so he turned into a side street and parked there. Then he walked back up St. Paul and pulled open the heavy wooden door of the St. Paul Arms.

Drat, an intercom. A locked glass inner door blocking his way and one of those damn fool intercom arrangements where you had to locate a resident's special code and punch it in. He searched for Dunstead, realizing to his dismay that he'd forgotten what the husband's last name was; but he was in luck: *Dunstead/Simmons*, he found. Oh, yes: the hiss between the two *s* sounds. He stabbed in the code.

First he heard a dial tone and then Eunice's overloud "Yes?"

"It's me," he said.

No response.

"It's Liam," he tried again.

"What do you want?"

"I want to come up."

In the silence that followed, he frowned down at the collection of footprinted takeout menus that paved the vestibule floor. Finally, a buzzer sounded. He seized the handle of the glass door as if it were about to vanish.

She lived in 4B, the list in the vestibule had said. The elevator looked unreliable and he decided to take the stairs. Evidently a lot of other people had made the same choice; the marble treads were worn down in the middle like old soap bars. Above the second floor, the marble gave way to threadbare plum-colored carpet. Now he regretted spurning the elevator, because he was growing short of breath. He didn't want to arrive puffing and panting.

Probably the husband was a jogger or something. For sure he was younger and fitter.

On the fourth floor, one door was open and Eunice stood there waiting—a good sign, he thought. But when he reached her, he found her expression set in stone, and she didn't step back to let him in. "What do you want?" she said again.

"Are you by yourself?"

An infinitesimal adjustment to the angle of her head meant yes, he surmised.

"We need to talk," he said.

"Don't bother; I already know I'm only a 'friend.' "

"I apologize for that," he said. He glanced around. The hall was empty, but people could be listening from behind their doors, and she was making no effort to keep her voice down. "Could I come in?" he asked.

She hesitated and then stepped back, just a grudging few inches. He sidled past her to find himself in a long, narrow corridor with dark floorboards, a braided oval rug, and a claw-footed drop-leaf table littered with junk mail.

"I am extremely sorry," he told her.

She lifted her chin. From the spiked and separated look of her lashes, he could tell she must have been crying, but her face was composed.

He said, "Please say you forgive me. I hated to let you walk out like that."

"Well, get used to it," she said. "You can't have things both ways, Liam. You can't ask me to stay with my husband and then not let me walk out on you."

"You're absolutely right," he said. "Please, do you think we could sit somewhere?"

She released an exasperated puff of a breath, but then she turned to lead him down the corridor.

If he hadn't known better, he would have said that her living room belonged to an old lady. It was over-furnished with piecrust tables, satin-striped love seats, bowlegged needlepoint chairs, and faded little rugs. Her mother's doing, he supposed. Or *both* mothers' doing—the two women rendezvousing here with their truckloads of family detritus, arranging everything just so for their helpless offspring. Even the pictures on the wall looked like hand-me-downs: crackled seascapes and mountainscapes and a full-length portrait of a woman in a bell-skirted dress from the 1950s, not long enough ago to be of interest.

He settled on one of the love seats, which was as hard as a park bench and so slippery that he had to brace his feet to keep from sliding off. He was hoping for Eunice to sit beside him, but she chose a chair instead. So much for all her complaints about his lack of couches.

"She's moving in with you, isn't she," she said.

"What?"

"Barbara. She's moving in."

"Good grief! What a thought. *No*, she's not moving in. For Lord's sake, Eunice!"

"I saw that suitcase! That powder-blue suitcase."

"That was Kitty's suitcase," Liam said.

"It was an old person's suitcase; you can't fool me. Only an old person would have a powder-blue suitcase. It was Barbara's. I bet she's got a whole matching set stashed away in her attic."

The notion of Barbara as an "old person" brought Liam up short.

"She's moving in with you and picking up where she left off," Eunice said. "Because that's how married people *are;* they go on being involved for all time even if they're divorced."

"Eunice, you're not listening. Barbara was bringing Kitty her beach things; Kitty's going to Ocean City. I can't help what kind of suitcase she put them in! And anyhow," he said, stopped by a thought. "What do you mean, that's how married people are? You're the one who's married, might I point out."

Eunice sat back slightly in her chair. "Well, you're right," she said after a pause. "But, I don't know. Somehow I don't *feel* married. I feel like everyone's married but me."

Both of them were quiet for a moment.

"I feel like I'm always the outsider," she said. "The 'friend' who's 'helping with the résumé.' "

She indicated the quotation marks with two pairs of curled fingers.

"I already told you I was sorry about that," Liam said. "It was very wrong of me. Barbara just caught me by surprise, is what happened. I was afraid of what she might think."

"You were afraid because you still love her."

"No, no—"

"Well, why aren't you sweeping me off my feet, then, and carrying me away? Why aren't you saying, 'Barbara be damned! You're the woman I love, and life is too short to go through it without you!' "

"Barbara be damned," Liam said. "You're the woman I love, and life is too short to go through it without you."

She stared at him.

A key rattled in the front door, and someone called out, "Euny?"

The man who appeared in the entranceway was lanky and fair-skinned, wearing jeans and a short-sleeved plaid shirt and carrying a plastic grocery bag. His blond hair was very fine and too long, overlapping his ears in an orphanish way, and his pale, thin mustache was too long too, so that you couldn't help picturing how the individual wisps would grow unpleasantly moist whenever he ate.

Eunice jumped up but then just stood there, awkwardly. "Norman, this is Liam," she said. "We're just . . . working on Liam's résumé."

"Oh, hi," Norman told Liam.

Liam rose and shook Norman's hand, which seemed to be all bones.

"Don't let me interrupt," Norman said. "I'm going to go ahead and start dinner. Will you be eating with us, Liam?"

Liam said, "No, I—" at the same time that Eunice said, "No, he's—"

"I should be getting along. Thanks anyway," Liam said.

"Too bad," Norman said. "It's tagine tonight!" and he held up his grocery bag.

"Norman's going through a Middle East phase right now," Eunice told Liam. Her cheeks were flushed, and she didn't quite meet either man's eyes.

"You do the cooking?" Liam asked Norman.

"Yes, well, Eunice is not much of a hand in the kitchen. How about you, Liam? Do you cook?"

"Not really," Liam said. The way Norman kept using his first name made him feel he was being interviewed. He said, "I take more of a canned-soup approach."

"Well, I can understand that. I used to be the same way. Progresso lentil; that was our major food group, once! Just ask Eunice. But some of the people in my lab, they're from these different countries and they're always bringing in their native dishes. I started asking for their recipes. I do like Middle Eastern the best. It's not just a phase," he said with an oddly boyish glance of defiance in Eunice's direction. "Middle Eastern really is a very sophisticated cuisine."

Demonstrating, he opened the grocery bag and stuck his head inside and drew a deep breath. "Saffron!" he said, reemerging. "Sumac! I tried to find pomegranates, but it must not be the season. I'm thinking I might use dried cranberries instead."

"That's an idea," Liam said.

He was edging toward the front hall now. This meant getting past Norman, who stood obliviously in his path and asked, "Do *you* know when pomegranate season is, Liam?"

"Um, not offhand . . ."

"Pomegranates fascinate me," Norman said. (Eunice raised

her eyes to the ceiling.) "When you think about it, they're kind of an odd choice for people to eat. They're really nothing but seeds! Some of the Middle Easterners I know, they chew the seeds right up. You can hear the crunch. But me, I like to bite down on them just partway so I can get the juicy part off without breaking into the hulls. I don't like that bitter taste, you know? And those rough little bitter bits that stick in your teeth. Then I spit the seeds out when no one is looking."

"Norman, for heaven's sake, let him get home to his supper," Eunice said.

"Oh," Norman said. "Sorry." He switched the grocery bag to his left hand so he could shake hands again with Liam. "It was good to meet you, Liam," he said.

"Good to meet *you*," Liam told him.

He was conscious, as he started toward the hall, of Eunice following close behind, but he didn't look in her direction even when they were out of Norman's sight. At the door he said, in a loud, carrying voice, "Well, thanks for your help!"

"Liam," she whispered.

He reached for the doorknob.

"Liam, did you mean what you said?"

"We'll have to talk!" he told her enthusiastically.

From the rear of the apartment he could hear the clanging of pots now, and Norman's tuneless whistling.

"See you soon!" he said.

And he stepped out into the hall and closed the door behind him.

Heading up North Charles, he drove so badly that it was a wonder he didn't have an accident. Cars seemed to come out of nowhere; he failed to start moving again whole moments after lights turned green; his acceleration was jerky and erratic. But it wasn't because he had anything particular on his mind. He had nothing on his mind. He was trying to keep his mind empty.

His plan was to get to his apartment and just, oh, collapse. Stare into space a long while. He envisioned his apartment as a haven of solitude. But when he walked into his living room, he found Kitty kneeling on the carpet. She was unpacking the blue vinyl suitcase, setting stacks of clothing in a half circle around her. "I know I had more swimsuits than *these*," she said, not looking up.

He crossed the room without answering.

"Hello?" she said.

"How many could you possibly need?" he asked. The question was automatic, like a line assigned to him in a play—the uncomprehending-male question he knew she expected of him.

"Well," she said. She sat back on her heels and started ticking off her fingers. "There's my sunbathing suit, for starters. That's a minimum-coverage bikini with no straps to leave a tan line. And then my *backup* sunbathing suit, the exact same cut, to wear if the first one gets wet. Then my old-lady suit; ha! For when Damian's aunt and uncle are with us . . ."

He sank into an armchair and let her babble on until she said, again, "Hello?"

He looked at her.

"Did you hear what I just told you? I won't be staying for supper."

"Okay."

He wasn't hungry for supper himself, but when he checked his watch he found it was after six. He rose heavily and went to the kitchen alcove to fix himself whatever was easiest. In the refrigerator he found half an onion, a nearly empty carton of milk, and a saucepan containing the dregs of the tomato soup he'd heated for lunch. ("Progresso lentil; that was our major food group once," he heard Norman say.) He definitely didn't want soup. In the cupboard he found a box of Cheerios, already opened. He shook a cupful or so into a bowl. Then he added milk, got himself a spoon, and sat down at the table.

Kitty was trying on a beach robe striped in hot pink and lime green. "Does this make me look like a watermelon?" she asked him.

He forgot to answer.

"Poppy?"

"Not at all," he said.

He took a spoonful of Cheerios and chewed dutifully. If Kitty said anything further, he couldn't hear it over the crunching sound.

He'd forgotten how he disliked cold cereal. It had something to do with the disjunction between the crispy dry bits and the cold wet milk. They didn't meld, or something. They stayed too separate in his mouth. He took another spoonful, and he started considering pomegranates. He knew what Norman had meant about trying to eat the juicy part without biting into the seeds. The few times he'd eaten pomegranates himself, he had done the same thing, and Norman's description brought back vividly the tart taste behind the sweetness, and the sensation of little hard pieces of seed lodging in his molars. Yes, exactly; he knew exactly.

He could almost *be* Norman; he knew so exactly how Norman felt.

Kitty said, "Is this one better?"

She was modeling another beach robe, a short blue terrycloth affair that wouldn't protect her nearly as well from the sun. Before he could tell her so, though, there was a knock on the door.

Kitty called, "Come in?"

Instead of coming in, whoever it was knocked again.

Kitty heaved a put-upon sigh and went over to open the door. Liam took another spoonful of cereal. "Oh," he heard her say. "Hi." He twisted in his chair to see Eunice walk in, hugging a gray nylon duffel bag. It was a large bag but it couldn't have been very full, because it flopped loosely over her arms, empty in the middle and bulging only slightly at either end.

He set his spoon down and stood up. He said, "Eunice?"

"Barbara be damned," she told him in a hard bright voice. "Norman be damned. *Everyone* be damned."

"Eunice, no."

"What?"

"No," he said. "We can't do it. Go away."

"What?"

Kitty was staring from one of them to the other.

"I'm sorry, but I mean it," he told Eunice.

He could see her start to believe him. The animation drained gradually from her face until all her features sagged. She stood motionless, flat-footed, her clunky sandals turned outward in a ducklike fashion, her arms full of withered gray nylon.

Then she turned and left.

Liam sat back down on his chair.

Kitty seemed about to say something, but in the end she just gave a little shake of her shoulders, like a shiver, and tightened the sash of her beach robe.

12

L iam's rocking chair, where he had so fondly imagined himself whiling away his old age, was not really all that comfortable. The slats seemed to hit his back wrong. And the smaller of the armchairs was *too* small, too short in the seat for his thighs. But the larger armchair was fine. He could sit in the larger armchair for days.

And he did.

He watched how the sun changed the color of the pines as it moved across the sky, turning the needles from black to green, sending dusty slants of light through the branches. There was a moment every afternoon when the line of shade coincided precisely with the line of the parking-lot curb out front. Liam waited for that moment. If it happened to pass without his noticing, he felt cheated.

He told himself that the shine would soon enough have worn off, if he and Eunice had stayed together. He would have started correcting her grammar, and she would have begun to notice his age and his irritability. He would ask why she had to stomp so heavily when she walked, and she would say he never *used* to mind the way she walked.

Oh, and anyhow, the world was full of people whose lives were meaningless. There were men who spent their entire careers picking up litter from city streets, or fitting the same bolt into the same bolt-hole over and over and over. There were men in prison, men in mental wards, men confined to hospital beds who could move only one little finger.

But even so . . .

He remembered an art project he had read about someplace where you wrote your deepest, darkest secrets on postcards and mailed them in to be read by the public. He thought that his own postcard would say, *I am not especially unhappy, but I don't see any particular reason to go on living.*

One morning as he was sitting there he heard a knock, and he sprang up to answer even though he knew he shouldn't. But he opened the door to find a stranger, a lipsticked woman with wildly bushy red hair and brass earrings the size of coasters. She stood with one hip slung out, holding a can of Diet Pepsi. "Hi," she said.

"Hi."

"I'm Bootsie Twill. Can I come in?"

"Well . . ."

"You're Liam, right?"

"Well, yes . . ."

"I'm Lamont's mom. The guy they arrested?"

"Oh," Liam said.

He stepped back a pace, and she walked in. She took a

swig from her can and looked around the living room. "You get way more light than I do," she said. "Which direction is this place facing?"

"Um, north?"

"Maybe I should lose my window treatments," she said. She crossed the room to plunk herself down in the chair he had just vacated. She was wearing pedal pushers in a geometric red-and-yellow print, and when she set her right ankle on her left knee the hems rode up to expose gleaming, bronzed shins.

This was not the plump little Jack-and-the-Beanstalk widow Liam had envisioned when he heard of her son's arrest.

"What can I do for you, Mrs. Twill?" he asked, settling in the rocking chair.

"Bootsie," she said. She took another swig of soda. "Lamont is out on bail," she said. "He wants to have a jury trial. He's going to plead not guilty."

Liam wondered how that could possibly work. But then, what did he know about such things? He tried to look sympathetic.

"I figured I would ask you if you'd be a character witness," she told him.

"Character witness!"

"Right."

"Mrs. Twill—"

"Bootsie."

"Bootsie, your son assaulted me, did you know that? He knocked me out with a blow to the head and he bit me in the palm."

"Yes, but, see, he didn't take anything, now, did he. He did not take one thing of yours. He was probably, like, overcome with remorse when he saw what he'd done, and he left."

Liam rocked back in his chair and stared at her. He considered the possibility that this was all a joke—some sort of *Candid Camera* situation set up by, maybe, Bundy or someone.

"Don't you think?" she prodded him.

"No," he said levelly. "I think I made a noise and the neighbors heard and he got scared and ran away."

"Oh, why are you so *judgmental?*"

He chose not to answer that.

"Hey," she said. "I realize you've got reason to be mad at him, but you don't know his whole story. This is a good, kind, good-hearted, kindhearted boy we're talking about. Only he's the product of a broken home and his father was a shithead and in school he had dyslexia which gave him low self-esteem. Plus I think he might be bipolar, or whatchamacallit, ADD. So okay, all I'm asking is a second chance for him, right? If you could tell the jury how he broke into your apartment but then had remorseful thoughts—"

"Look. Mrs. Twill."

"Bootsie."

"I was *unconscious*," Liam said. "Your son knocked me unconscious; are you hearing me? I don't have the slightest idea what thoughts he may have had because I was out cold. I don't even know what he looked like. I don't even remember hearing him break in. I've completely lost all memory of it."

"Okay, fine, but it might come back to you, maybe. I mean if you were to see him. So here's what we could do: I could take you to visit him. Or bring him to your place, if you want.

Sure! Whatever's most convenient for *you*; you get to call the shots, absolutely. And he could tell you how he was overcome with remorse and such, which would be interesting for you to hear; you haven't heard his side of it. And then meanwhile you would be looking at him and you might think, Hey! *Now* I remember! Seeing him would, like, bring it all back to your mind, you know?"

Liam did know. It was the sort of scenario he had fantasized when he had been so distressed about his amnesia. But at some point, he seemed to have stopped caring about that; he couldn't say just when. If the memory of his attack were handed to him today, he would just ask, Is that *it*?

Where's the rest? Where's everything else I've forgotten: my childhood and my youth, my first marriage and my second marriage and the growing up of my daughters?

Why, he'd had amnesia all along.

"And here's another thing," Mrs. Twill was saying. "If you were just to look into his face, then even if it didn't remind you, you'd understand what a nice kid he is. Just a kid! Real shy and clumsy, always nicks himself shaving. That would tell you about his character. It might even help you get over this. I mean, I know you must feel spooked these days. I bet every time a floorboard creaks, your heart beats faster, am I right?"

She was wrong. Every time a floorboard creaked, he just cleared his throat or rattled his newspaper—covered the sound up in some way, as he had always covered suspicious sounds up even before the break-in.

All along, it seemed, he had experienced only the most glancing relationship with his own life. He had dodged the tough issues, avoided the conflicts, gracefully skirted adventure.

He let Mrs. Twill leave her telephone number because that was the easiest way to get rid of her, and then he showed her out.

When he sat back down in his armchair (unpleasantly warm now from Mrs. Twill's bony rear end), he found he had lost the thread of his thoughts. He felt restless and distracted. He wondered if he should take a walk. Or go grocery shopping, maybe? He was nearly out of orange juice. He rehearsed the preparations in his mind: make a list, collect his recyclable bags . . .

He saw Mrs. Twill as she had looked when he'd opened the door—her who-cares posture, her garish lipstick, her unfamiliar, unwelcome, un-Eunice face.

"Oh, Liam," he heard Eunice say again. O *Liam*, he saw in her round schoolgirl script, for she had a habit of spelling *oh* without the *h*, which had lent her little smiley-face notes an unexpectedly poetic tone. *(O I wish Mr. C. didn't have that budget meeting tomorrow . . .)*

Sometimes, without his say-so, the most specific memories of Eunice would suddenly swim up. Her refusal to drive on major highways, for instance, because she feared what she called the "peer pressure" of the drivers behind her on entrance ramps. Her tendency to talk about any subject that was on her mind, regardless of her audience, so that she was perfectly capable of asking the mailman what gift she should bring to a baby shower. And the way she had of biting her lower lip when she was concentrating on something—her two small, pearly front teeth recalling the teeth of an old-fashioned bisque doll that one of his daughters had owned.

Or the harder memories, from after he'd learned she was married. "But what about our only *life?*" he heard her say, and it was almost a melody, a plaintive little clear-voiced song hanging in the air of the room.

Why was it that he had known so many sad women?

His mother, to begin with—abandoned by her husband, perennially in poor health, no solace remaining to her but her children, as she was forever pointing out to them. "If *you* two left me, I don't know how I'd bear it," she said. And then what did Liam do? He left her. He accepted a partial scholarship to a college in the Midwest, although the University of Maryland had offered a scholarship too, and a full one at that. How could he? all her church friends asked. Thank the good Lord for Julia; daughters were always a comfort; but wouldn't you think Liam could stay in the same geographical area, at least? When his mother was so alone, so unfortunate, such a victim of circumstance! A saint, in fact. (As she said so often: "I just seem to put myself last, even though everyone tells me I shouldn't. I know they must be right, but I'm just made that way, I guess.")

Liam offered no defense. There really wasn't any defense. He reminded himself, very sensibly, that somebody would always be saying *something* disapproving. No point letting it get to him.

Funny, it used to be so simple to sum his mother up, but now that he looked back he seemed to be ambushed by complexities. He saw again the frightened look in her eyes when she was going through her last illness, and her tiny, curled hands. It struck him that life in general was heartbreaking—a word he didn't toss off lightly.

His girlfriends had been sad types as well, not that he had

consciously chosen them for their sadness. Sooner or later, it seemed, every girl he dated ended up revealing some secret sorrow—an alcoholic father or a mentally ill mother or, at the very least, an outcast childhood.

Well, who knows. It could be that the whole world was that way.

Millie, though: Millie was his golden girl. She was tall and slender, with a veil of straight blond hair and a beautiful pale face. Her eyes were deep-set and startlingly light in color, the lids luminous as eggshells, and she had a floating, sashaying style of walking.

Millie, he thought now, forgive me. I'd forgotten how much I loved you.

His first glimpse of her had been at a friend's apartment. She was playing the cello in an impromptu, very inept and cobbled-together string quartet, which was making her laugh. She laughed with her hair tossed back, her body loose and relaxed, her knees spread open to accommodate her instrument. This was misleading, as it turned out. Millie was not an open-kneed kind of person. She wasn't even a cellist; she was a harpist. Liam learned later that she'd gone a few months earlier to pick up a skirt from the cleaner's, but the cleaner had closed for lunch hour and so she'd stepped into the music store next door and bought herself a cello instead. That was Millie for you: whimsical. Fey. A sort of water maiden. Liam had fallen head over heels. He had pursued her single-mindedly until she agreed to marry him, less than six months after they met.

Had he been too insistent? Had she harbored some mis-givings? He hadn't thought so at the time, but now he was less sure. At the start of their marriage, he had believed she was content. (Though always, now that he looked back, rather muted, a bit remote.) It was true she was not an *enjoyer.* She seemed to find sex something of a trial, and she deplored the excessive notice that other people—even Liam, back then—paid to food and drink. In fact she soon became a strict vegetarian, which made her even more pallid and translucent-looking.

But the major change dated from her pregnancy. This was an unplanned pregnancy, admittedly, but not the end of the world. They were both in agreement on that. When she started sleeping too much and grew even more disconnected from everyday life, well, it was only to be expected, wasn't that so? But then she didn't change back again after the baby was born.

Or maybe she'd been that way all along, and Liam had just lacked the wisdom to perceive it.

Like being dragged down by the ankles into a swamp, that was how his life began to feel. Millie was already submerged and he was struggling to support the weight of her.

Of course the university psychologist was consulted, but Millie said he didn't know what he was talking about and so that had come to nothing. And then for a brief time, her doctor had conjectured that she might be suffering from a silent form of appendicitis—some chronic, low-grade infection that would explain her constant tiredness and lack of zest. Both of them (Millie too, it saddened Liam now to recall) had been almost giddy with relief. Oh, then! Just something medical! Something curable with surgery!

But that theory had been discounted, by and by, and she

had returned to dreary hopelessness, barely slogging through the days. Often Liam would come home in the evening to find her still in her bathrobe, the baby straggly-haired and fretful, the apartment smelling of soiled diapers, the sink piled high with unwashed dishes. Oh, Lord, just go ahead and *die*! he'd thought more than once. Not meaning it, of course.

Could it be that underneath, he had guessed ahead of time that she might take those pills? And had done nothing to prevent it?

No, he didn't think so.

But he had to admit he had blamed her for her unhappiness. He had felt a kind of superiority; he had wondered why she didn't just pull herself together, for God's sake.

The old woman from the apartment next door stepped out into the hall as he came home one evening. She said, "Mr. Pennywell, that baby has been crying since morning. Every now and then it gets quiet but then it starts crying again. Since eight o'clock in the morning and its voice has gone all croaky. Twice I rang your bell but nobody answered, and your wife has got the door locked."

"Well, thanks," he said, not feeling thankful in the least. Interfering old biddy. He couldn't be expected to do everything! He let himself into the apartment and then he thought, Since eight o'clock in the morning?

He had left for his carrel in the library shortly after seven. Millie had been a humped shape beneath the afghan on the living-room couch. She often got out of bed at night when she couldn't sleep and watched old movies on TV. He had switched the TV off and left without trying to wake her.

Eight o'clock in the morning, he thought, and he stood

frozen, not even breathing, hearing the great, hollow, echoing silence beneath the baby's hoarse sobs.

People said, trying to be helpful, "It's only natural to feel angry." But Liam shrugged them off.

"I'm not in the least angry," he said. "Why would you think I was angry?"

Instead he was very brisk and efficient. He devoted the first few weeks to finding childcare, juggling work and a baby. He did love his daughter; or he felt attached to her, at least; or at least he felt deeply concerned for her welfare. Still, his favorite daydream from that time was the vision of himself sitting alone in an empty room for hours and hours and hours, uninterrupted, undisturbed, unneeded by a single human being.

But, "I'm doing fine!" he told friends. "Never better!"

He saw the adjustment in their expressions, a sort of clicking over from solicitous to shocked to carefully neutral. "Well, good for you," they said.

They said, "It's wonderful you're able to get on with your life this way. Put it all behind you! Very healthy."

He and Xanthe moved back to Baltimore in the fall. It was an admission of defeat; he was learning just how much rearing a toddler could take out of you. He rented an apartment not far from where his mother and his sister lived, and he started teaching at the Fremont School—a comedown, no doubt about it. At his university he'd held an instructor's position and he was starting his dissertation. At the Fremont School he taught history, not even his field, only peripherally related to the philosophers he loved so much. But it was a very prestigious school, and without any education credits he felt lucky to have been hired.

He put Xanthe in a daycare center that seemed to be closed more often than it was open; it observed holidays he didn't even know existed, which meant he was always scrambling to find sitters. He relied heavily upon his mother, inadequate though she was, and a few older black women provided by an agency. Xanthe endured these patchy arrangements without objecting—in fact, without reacting in any way whatsoever. She was a stolid child, solemn-faced and watchful and very obviously motherless. Somehow she gave off a visible aura of motherlessness. Her lack of a mother was so pathetically apparent that women took one look at her and turned into crazy people. They brought Liam muffins and cookies and giant country hams. They stood at his door smiling dazzlingly, offering to tidy his place a bit and wondering if his daughter had any particular food preferences. Xanthe ate barely any food at all. He didn't know how she stayed so chubby, as little as she ate.

These women had extra circus tickets and free passes to Disney movies. They knew of a special spray that would ease the tangles out of little girls' hair. They loved, loved, loved having picnics on Cow Hill.

Liam himself hated picnics. He hated the two spots of dampness that always developed on the seat of his trousers even in the driest weather. He seemed to be a magnet for mosquitoes. And it took so much effort to rise to these women's high pitch. They were all of them, every last one of them, full of gaiety and enthusiasm. He sat by their checkered tablecloths feeling like a *puddle* of a man, sunken and speechless, next to his speechless child.

Barbara, on the other hand, had required nothing of him. He got to know her when he started eating lunch in the school library in order to avoid the other teachers, two of whom were Picnic Ladies. Of course eating in the library was not allowed, but his lunch was unobtrusive—a slice of cheese, a piece of fruit—and Barbara pretended not to notice. At the time she was in her early thirties, a friendly, pleasant-faced woman a couple of years older than he, not someone he gave any special thought to. Generally she left him to his own devices, or they would have, at most, a brief conversation about some book he'd slipped at random from a shelf. She wasn't at all like the others.

Through his first year there and half of his second, he plodded along in his comfortable, undemanding routine. Fall semester, spring semester, fall semester again. Young students who were likable enough, by and large, and who occasionally showed a spark of interest in his lessons. Lunches in the library, with Barbara stopping by his table to exchange a few words or occasionally settling for a moment onto the chair beside his. She knew the bare facts of his life by now, and he knew *her* facts, such as they were. She lived alone on the third floor of an old house on Roland Avenue. She had a father in a nursing home. She found her job very congenial.

One day, as she was showing him a new book about the city-state of Carthage, he kissed her. She kissed him back. They were level-headed adults; they didn't make a big to-do about it. He certainly didn't feel that tremulous elation that he'd felt in the early days with Millie, but neither did he want to. He appreciated Barbara's cheerfulness. He liked her self-reliance.

Oh, but probably he *should* have made a to-do. He must have been a terrible husband. (Well, obviously he had been, if you considered how it all ended.) When he thought back to how Barbara used to dance at the students' proms—throwing her whole heart into "Surf City" and "Dr. Octopus"—he asked himself how he could have been so blind. She must have wanted so much, underneath! And he had given her so little.

All this dwelling on the past was Eunice's fault. If not for her—or the loss of her—he wouldn't be thinking about such things.

In the most unforeseen way, Eunice really had turned out to be his rememberer.

Kitty came back from Ocean City with skin the color of caramel, except for the bridge of her nose, which was pink and peeling. She walked in with her bag slung over her shoulder, leaving the door wide open behind her. "Poppy!" she said. "Hi there!"

It was Sunday morning, and Liam was fixing scrambled eggs for breakfast. It took him a moment to register her presence.

"Can you give Damian a ride?" she asked him.

"Where to?"

"His mom's, in a while. Otherwise he'd have to go right now with his aunt and uncle."

"I guess so."

She threw her bag on a chair and spun around to return

to the door. "It's okay!" she called in a piercing voice. So much noise, all of a sudden! Liam felt a bit dazed.

When she came back, she had Damian with her. He was carrying a knapsack and he was as white-skinned as when he'd left. "At least *someone* heeds the warnings," Liam told him.

Damian said, "Huh?"

"The dermatologists' warnings."

Damian looked blank.

"He lay out as much as I did," Kitty said, "but the sun doesn't affect him."

Liam said, "Really." This seemed a bit creepy, as if Damian were some sort of vampire, but he put the thought out of his mind. "Anybody want breakfast?" he asked.

"Breakfast!" Kitty said. "It's almost eleven."

"I got a late start."

"*I'll* say you did."

"It is the weekend, after all."

"And you look like a homeless person. Are you growing a beard or something?"

"It's the weekend!" he said again. He rubbed his chin.

Damian said, "I could go for some breakfast."

"You ate breakfast hours ago," Kitty told him.

"That's why I could eat again."

"Not now, Damian; we've got to talk."

Liam was puzzled (hadn't they had the whole beach trip to talk?), but then he realized he was the one she planned to talk to. She stepped up to face him and said, "Poppy, I've been thinking."

He braced himself.

"I'm thinking I should stay here for the school year," she said.

"What! Stay with *me*?"

"Right."

He felt a confusing mixture of reactions to this proposal. How about his privacy, how about his nice solitary life? But also, he was conscious of an odd sense of relief. He set down his spatula. "There's not enough room, though," he said. "There's only my study."

"You're not using your study!"

"I haven't been able to, might I point out."

"What would you be doing there?"

He couldn't come up with an answer. He said, "Oh, well, let's talk about this later. We've got plenty of time to discuss it."

"No, we don't. Summer's almost over."

"It is?"

"School begins in two weeks."

"It does?"

Last Thursday, a woman had phoned from a place called Bet Ha-Midrash and told him she had heard he might be interested in a job there. "A job," he'd said, caught off guard.

"A job as zayda in our three-year-olds' class."

"Oh," he'd said. "Okay . . ."

"Would you like to send us your application?"

"Okay . . ."

But somehow he'd been assuming he had weeks and weeks yet to do that, and in fact he hadn't given it any further thought. "It's August," he said now, disbelievingly.

"It's *late* August," Kitty told him.

"Isn't that always the way?" Liam asked Damian. "Summer just flies right by."

And Eunice had been merely a summer romance, if you didn't know the whole story.

Damian had seated himself at the table, and he was biting into a piece of toast—Liam's toast, as it happened. He might not have realized Liam was addressing him. Kitty said, "Summer didn't fly by for *me*. I was buried alive in a dentist's office."

"Well, I'll have to think this over," Liam said, stalling for time. He dished his eggs onto a plate. "Of course it will depend on what your mother says."

"She's going to say no," Kitty told him.

"So in that case you can't do it, can you."

"But if you talked to her—"

"I told you I would."

"When?"

"Oh . . . I'll call her this afternoon."

"No, not on the phone! It's too easy for her to say no, on the phone. We should go visit her in person."

Liam studied her suspiciously.

"I want her to realize we're serious," Kitty said. "You and me should drive over there right this very minute and lay out all our reasons."

"What *are* our reasons?"

"We don't get in each other's hair, for one thing."

Liam said, "If by that you mean that I'm more lax, then your mother is going to say that you should be with *her*. And she would be right."

Oops, he had sent Kitty into her prayerful-maiden pose. Plop onto the floor, hands clasped to her breast. Damian stopped chewing and stared at her. "Please, please, please," she said. "Have I given you any trouble this summer? Have I violated my curfew by one single eentsy minute? I'm begging you, Poppy. Have mercy. All I could think of at the beach was, School's about to start and I'm going to have to go back home and deal with Mom again. It's not fair! I should get to live with you a while. I've never lived with you, not when I was old enough to know it. In my whole entire life all I've had is this little bit of summer—July and part of August. Xanthe and Louise had *lots* more time than that. And it's only for a year, you know. After this I'll be in college. You'll never have another chance at me!"

Liam laughed.

It seemed ages since he had laughed.

"Well," he said, "let's see what your mother says."

Kitty clambered to her feet and smoothed her clothes down.

Damian asked, "Have we got any marmalade?"

It was proof of how serious Kitty was about all this that she wouldn't let Damian come with them to Barbara's. "You would just complicate things," she told him. "We'll drop you off at your mom's house on the way."

Damian said, "Thanks a lot!" but Kitty paid no attention; she'd already moved on to Liam.

"I hope you're planning to shave," she told him.

"Well, I could do that, I guess. Once I've had my breakfast."

"And how about what you're wearing?"

"How about it?"

"You're not planning to go *out* in those clothes, are you?"

He glanced down at them—a perfectly respectable T-shirt and a pair of pants that he always referred to as his gardening pants, although he didn't garden. "What's wrong with them?" he asked. "It's not as if I'm appearing in public."

"Mom will think you look . . . not reliable."

"Fine, I'll change. Just let me finish my breakfast, will you?"

Kitty backed off then, but he was conscious of her hovering at the edges of his vision, fidgeting and flouncing about and picking things up and putting them down. Damian, meanwhile, had assumed a horizontal position in an armchair with the sports section from the *Sun*. Every now and then he read out a baseball score to Kitty, but she didn't seem to be listening.

As Liam was shaving, it occurred to him to wonder why he had said yes to her. He didn't want this child living with him permanently! For one thing, he was tired to death of all these fruity-smelling shampoos and conditioners crowding the rim of his bathtub. And the carpet in the den had not been visible since she'd moved in there.

But when he emerged, presentably dressed, he found she had washed and dried the breakfast dishes and cleaned up the kitchen. He was touched by the earnestness of the gesture even though he knew it wouldn't likely be repeated.

It was an overcast day, but pleasant enough that people were out and about on their Sunday pursuits—tooling down the bike lane along North Charles, jogging, walking, spilling forth from various churches. On the street where Damian's mother lived, two teenage boys were tossing a football back and forth, and Damian exited the backseat with barely a "Thanks" and went to join them. "I'll let you know how it goes!" Kitty called after him.

Damian lifted an arm in acknowledgment, but he didn't turn around. It was his broken arm—the cast gray with dirt by now and scribbled over with graffiti. Evidently it didn't hinder him, though, because when one of the boys sent the football his way he caught it easily.

"On Tuesday they're cutting his cast down so it's not covering his elbow anymore," Kitty told Liam, "and then he can drive again. You won't have to chauffeur me around after that. See how it's all working out for me to live with you?"

"Just don't get your hopes up," Liam warned her. "I'm not sure your mother's going to go for this."

"Oh, why are you always so *negative*? Why do you always expect the worst?"

He left the question unanswered.

In Barbara's neighborhood—*his* neighborhood, once upon a time, green and manicured and shaded by old trees—the central fishpond was surrounded by children feeding bread crumbs to the ducks. Strollers and tricycles dotted the grass, and blankets were spread here and there for babies to sit on. Liam drove slowly, for safety's sake. He braked to let a small group cross in front of him, two couples shepherding a little girl and a taller boy who might have been her brother. "It *was* the same turtle we saw last time; I know it was," the little girl was saying, and Liam wondered if it was the same turtle he and his daughters used to see. Louise always tried to pet it; she would lean so far over the edge of the pond, reaching a hand toward the water, that Liam had felt the need to grab hold of her overall straps in case she fell in. And once

Xanthe actually *had* fallen in, when the girls went ice skating on a winter afternoon. The pond wasn't deep enough to be dangerous, but the water had been cruelly cold. She had arrived home in tears, Liam remembered, and Louise had been crying too, in sympathy.

He turned onto Barbara's street and parked in front of their old house, which was a modest white clapboard Colonial, not half as large or imposing as most of the others. When she and Madigan married there had been some talk of their buying a place in Guilford, but she hadn't wanted to leave her neighbors. Secretly, Liam had been glad of that. He would have felt even more rejected, more *ousted*, if she had moved somewhere he couldn't picture in his mind's eye when he thought about her.

He was just stepping out from behind the wheel when Kitty said, "Oh, shoot."

"What is it?"

"Xanthe's here."

He looked around him. "She is?" he said. "How do you know?"

"That's her car in front of us."

"That's *Xanthe's* car?"

It was one of those new sharp-edged, boxy things, pale blue. The last he'd known, Xanthe drove a red Jetta. But Kitty said, "Yup."

"What happened to the Jetta?"

"She traded it in."

"Is that a fact," Liam said. He tried to remember how long it had been since he and Xanthe had seen each other.

"This is the last thing we need," Kitty said as they started up the front walk.

"Why's that?"

"She's mad at me, I don't know what for. It would be just like her to take Mom's side against me out of spite."

"She's mad at me too," Liam said.

"Great."

If Xanthe was including Kitty in this snit of hers, then it must be true that Damian was the reason. Someone ought to inform her that an entirely different person had been arrested for the break-in. Liam started to say as much to Kitty, but he stopped himself. Kitty probably had no inkling of Xanthe's suspicions.

They were already at the front door when Kitty said, "Wait, I think I hear them out back," at the same time that Liam, too, heard voices coming from the rear of the house. They turned to take the path that led through the side yard. When they emerged from under the magnolia tree, they found Barbara and Xanthe eating lunch at the wrought-iron table on the patio. Nearby, Jonah was squatting on the flagstones to draw lopsided little circles with a stick of chalk. He was the first to spot them. "Hi, Kitty. Hi, Poppy," he said, standing up.

"Hi, Jonah."

Liam hadn't realized before that Jonah called him Poppy.

Barbara said, "Well, look who's here!" but Xanthe, after the briefest glance, took on a flat-faced expression and resumed buttering a roll.

"You didn't use sunblock, did you?" Barbara asked Kitty. "When I told you and told you! Where are your *brains*? You're fried to a crisp."

"Oh, why, thank you for inquiring, Mother dear," Kitty said. "I had a perfectly lovely trip."

Unruffled, Barbara turned to Liam. "I've got Jonah for the weekend," she said, "because Louise and Dougall are off with their church on a Marriage Renewal Retreat."

Liam had a number of questions about this—did their marriage *need* renewing? should he be worried?—but before he could ask, Barbara rose, saying, "Let me bring out some more plates. You two sit down."

"No plate for me, thanks. I just finished breakfast," Liam said.

But Barbara was already heading toward the back door, and Kitty was making violent shooing motions in his direction. "Go with her!" she mouthed.

Dutifully, Liam set off after Barbara. (It was a relief, anyhow, to leave the chilly atmosphere surrounding Xanthe.) He held the screen door open, and Barbara said, "Oh, thanks."

As they entered the house, she told him, "I don't think that child has the least little grain of sense. Just wait till she gets melanoma! Then she'll be sorry."

"Ah, well, *we* grew up without sunblock."

"That's different," she said, illogically.

Liam loved Barbara's kitchen. It had never once been remodeled, as far as he knew. At some point a dishwasher had been fitted in next to the sink, but the general look of it dated from the 1930s. The worn linoleum floor bore traces of a Mondrian-style pattern, and the refrigerator had rounded corners, and the cupboards had been repainted so many times that the doors wouldn't quite close anymore. Even the plants on the windowsill seemed old-fashioned: a yellowed philodendron wandering up to the curtain rod and down again, and a prickly, stunted cactus in a ceramic pot shaped like a burro. He could have just sunk onto one of the red wooden chairs and stayed there forever, feeling peaceful and at home.

But here came Kitty to remind him of his mission. She let the screen door slam behind her and she gave him a conspiratorial glance but then wandered over to the sink, ho hum, and turned the faucet on for no apparent reason.

"By the way," Liam said. He was speaking to Barbara's back; she was reaching into the dish cupboard. She wore white linen slacks that made her look crisper than usual and more authoritative. He said, "I've been thinking."

It wasn't clear if she had heard him over the sound of running water. She set two plates on the counter and opened the silverware drawer.

"I've been wondering if Kitty should stay on with me during the school year," he said.

Assuming sole responsibility for the question—*I've* been wondering—was meant as a gesture of gallantry, but Kitty spoiled the effect by shutting off the water decisively and spinning around to say, "Please, Mom?"

Barbara turned to Liam. "Excuse me?" she said.

"She would stay on at my place," Liam said, "just for her senior year, I mean. After that she'd be leaving for college."

"What, Liam: are you saying you'd be willing to monitor her homework, and drive car pool to lacrosse games, and pick her up from swimming practice? Are you going to meet with her college advisor and make sure she gets her allergy shots?"

This sounded like more of a commitment than he had realized, actually. He sent an uncertain glance toward Kitty. She took a step forward, but instead of going into the prayerful-maiden act he half expected, she flung a hand in his direction, palm up, and said, "*Someone* ought to keep a watch. Just look at him!"

Liam blinked.

Barbara examined him more closely. She said, "Yes, what's wrong with you?"

"What do you mean, what's wrong with me?"

"You seem . . . thinner."

He had the impression that she had been about to say something else, something less complimentary.

"I'm fine," he told her.

He scowled at Kitty. He'd be damned if he would say a single word further on her behalf.

Kitty gazed blandly back at him.

Barbara said, "Kitty, would you take these things to the patio, please?"

"But—"

"Go on," Barbara said, and she handed Kitty the plates with a cluster of silverware laid on top.

Kitty accepted them, but as she backed out the screen door her eyes were fixed beseechingly on Liam.

He refused to give her the slightest sign of encouragement.

"It's not for my sake at all," he told Barbara as soon as they were alone. "She's trying to put one over on you."

"Yes, yes . . . Liam, I don't want to be intrusive, but I'm wondering if your life can *accommodate* a teenager."

"Well, maybe it can't," Liam said. What the hell.

"You wouldn't be able to have a person spend the night with you if Kitty were there; you realize that."

"Spend the night?"

"If I had known you were involved with someone, I never would have let Kitty come stay with you in the first place."

"I'm not involved with anyone," he said.

"You're not?"

"No."

"Well, the other day it seemed—"

"Not anymore," he said.

"I see," she said. Then she said, "I'm sorry to hear that."

Something in the tone of her voice—so delicate, so tactful—implied that she assumed the breakup was not his own choice. Her face became kind and sorrowful, as if he'd just announced a bereavement.

"But!" he told her. "As for Kitty! You know, you might have a point. I would probably make a terrible father over the long term."

Barbara gave a short laugh.

"What," he said.

"Oh, nothing."

"What's so amusing?"

"It's just," she said, "how you never argue with people's poor opinions of you. They can say the most negative things—that you're clueless, that you're unfeeling—and you say, 'Yes, well, maybe you're right.' If I were you, I'd be devastated!"

"Really?" Liam asked. He was intrigued. "Yes, well, maybe you're . . . Or, rather . . . Would you be devastated even if you truly did agree with them?"

"Especially if I agreed with them!" she said. "Are you telling me that you do agree? You believe you're a bad person?"

"Oh, not bad in the sense of evil," Liam said. "But face it: I haven't exactly covered myself in glory. I just . . . don't seem to have the hang of things, somehow. It's as if I've never been entirely present in my own life."

She was silent, gazing at him again with that too-kind expression.

He said, "Do you remember a show on TV that Dean Martin used to host? It must have been back in the seventies; Millie liked to watch it. I can't think now what it was called."

"The Dean Martin Show?" Barbara suggested.

"Yes, maybe; and he had this running joke about his drinking, remember? Always going on about his drunken binges. And so one night one of the guests was reminiscing about a party they'd been to and Dean Martin asked, 'Did I have a good time?' "

Barbara smiled faintly, looking not all that amused.

"Did he have a good time," Liam said. "Ha!"

"What's your point, Liam?"

"I might ask you the same question," he told her.

"You might ask what my point is?"

"I might ask if I'd had a good time."

Barbara wrinkled her forehead.

"Oh," Liam said, "never mind."

It was a relief to give up, finally. It was a relief to turn away from her and see Kitty approaching—matter-of-fact, straight-forward Kitty yanking open the screen door and saying, "Did you decide?"

"We were just discussing Dean Martin," Barbara told her drily.

"Who? But what about *me?*"

"Well," Barbara said. She reflected a moment. Then she

said—out of the blue, it seemed to Liam—"I suppose we could give it a try."

Kitty said, "Hot dog!"

"Just conditionally, understand."

"I understand!"

"But if I hear one word about your bending the rules, missy, or giving your father any trouble—"

"I know, I know," Kitty said, and she was off, racing toward the front stairs, presumably to go pack.

Barbara looked over at Liam. "I meant that about the rules," she told him.

He nodded. Privately, though, he felt blindsided. What had he gotten himself into?

As if she guessed his thoughts, Barbara smiled and gave him a tap on the wrist. "Come and have some lunch," she said.

He forgot to remind her that he wasn't hungry. He followed her back through the kitchen and out the screen door.

On the patio, Jonah had abandoned his chalk and was sitting on the very edge of the chair next to Xanthe. "We saw an *animal*!" he shouted. "You've got an animal in your backyard, Gran! It was either a fox or an anteater."

"Oh, I hope it was an anteater," Barbara said. "I haven't had one of those before."

"It had a long nose or a long tail, one or the other. Where's Kitty? I have to tell Kitty."

"She'll be here in a minute, sweets. She's packing."

Liam pulled up a chair and sat down next to Jonah. He was directly opposite Xanthe, but Xanthe refused to look at him. "Packing for what?" she asked Barbara.

"She's going to stay on with your dad."

"Huh?"

"She's staying on during the school year. *If* she behaves herself."

Then Xanthe did look at him, openmouthed. She turned back to Barbara and said, "She's going to *live* with him?"

"Why, yes," Barbara said, but now she sounded doubtful.

"I cannot believe this," Xanthe told Liam.

Liam said, "Pardon?"

"First you let her stay there all summer. You say, 'Okay, Kitty, whatever you like. By all means, Kitty. Whatever your heart desires, Kitty.' Little Miss Princess Kitty lolling about with her deadbeat boyfriend."

Liam said, "Yes? And?"

"When you never let *me* live with you!" Xanthe cried. "And I was just a child! And you were all I had! I was *way* younger than Kitty is when you and Barbara split up. You left me behind with a woman who wasn't even related to me and off you went, forever!"

Liam felt stunned.

He said, "Is that what you've been mad about?"

Barbara said, "Oh, Xanthe, I *feel* related. I've always felt you were truly my daughter; you must know I have."

"This is not about you, Barbara," Xanthe said in a gentler tone. "I have no quarrel with you. But *him*—" And she turned back to Liam.

"I thought I was doing you a favor," Liam said.

"Yeah, right."

"You had your two little sisters there, and you seemed so happy, finally, and Barbara was so loving and openhearted and warm."

"Why, thank you, Liam," Barbara said.

He stopped in mid-breath and glanced at her. She was looking almost bashful. But he needed to concentrate on Xanthe, and so he turned back. He said, "Epictetus says—"

"Oh, not him again!" Xanthe exploded. "*Damn* Epictetus!" And she jumped up and began to stack her dishes.

Liam gave her a moment, and then he started over. In his quietest and most pacifying voice, he said, "Epictetus says that everything has two handles, one by which it can be borne and one by which it cannot. If your brother sins against you, he says, don't take hold of it by the wrong he did you but by the fact that he's your brother. That's how it can be borne."

Xanthe made a *tssh!* sound and clanked her bread plate onto her dinner plate.

"I'm trying to say I'm sorry, Xanthe," he said. "I didn't know. I honestly didn't realize. Can't you find it in your heart to forgive me?"

She snatched up her silverware.

In desperation, he pushed his chair back and slid forward until he was kneeling on the patio. He could feel the unevenness of the flagstones through the fabric of his trousers; he could feel the ache of misery filling his throat. Xanthe froze, gaping at him, still holding her dishes. "Please," he said, clasping his hands in front of him. "I can't bear to know I made such a bad mistake. I can't endure it. I'm begging you, Xanthe."

Jonah said, "Poppy?"

Xanthe set her dishes down and took a grip on his arm. "For God's sake, Dad, get up," she told him. "What on earth! You're making a fool of yourself!" She pulled him to a standing position and then bent to brush off his knees.

"Goodness, Liam," Barbara said mildly. She plucked a leaf from his trousers. All around him, it seemed, there was a flutter of pats and murmurs. "What will you think of next?" Xanthe asked, but she was guiding him back to his chair as she spoke.

He sank onto the chair feeling exhausted, like a child who had been through a crying spell. He looked sideways at Jonah and forced himself to smile.

"So," he said. "Shall we have some lunch?"

Wide-eyed, Jonah pushed a bowl of potato salad a few inches closer to him.

"Thank you," Liam said. He ladled a spoonful onto his plate.

The two women returned to their seats, but then they just sat watching him.

"What?" Liam asked them.

They didn't answer.

He chose a deviled egg from a platter and set it on his plate. He reached for a tuna-salad sandwich that had been cut in a dainty triangle.

It occurred to him that here he was, finally, dining with a couple of Picnic Ladies after all.

At the window end of the Threes' room stood a long wooden table that was known as the Texture Table. Every morning as the children came in they headed for the Texture Table first to see what activity had been set up for them. Sometimes they found dishpans of water, and cups and pitchers for pouring. Sometimes they found sand. Often there were canisters of modeling clay, or bins of dried beans and pasta, or plastic shapes, or fingerpaints. Fingerpaints were Liam's least favorite. He was supposed to monitor the Texture Table while Miss Sarah peeled the newer arrivals away from their mothers, and on fingerpaint days he spent all his time stopping the little boys from laying tiny red and blue handprints up and down the little girls' dresses, and across the seats of the miniature chairs, and in each other's hair. It was Liam's opinion that fingerpaints ought to be abolished.

Miss Sarah, however, believed that fingerpainting expanded the soul. Miss Sarah was full of such theories.

(*Overly* full, if you asked Liam.) She seemed about twelve years old, and she wore jeans to work, and her round, freckled face generally bore a smudge of ink or chalk or felt-tip pen. She told Liam that fingerpainting was especially beneficial for children who were too fastidious—too "uptight," as she put it. Most of the uptight ones were girls. They would tug at Liam's sleeve with tears in their eyes, with looks of outrage on their faces, and say, "Zayda, see what Joshua did?"

Then Liam would have to assure them that the paints would wash out, after which he would steer Joshua (or Nathan, or Ben) by the shoulders to the other end of the table. "Here, try the tractor," he would say. "Run the tractor through this puddle of purple and you can make purple tread marks."

He never knew ahead of time what the Texture Table would hold, because his hours were eight till three and the next day's table was not set up until late in the afternoon, after the cleaning staff had come through. So every morning when he arrived, he approached the table feeling mildly curious. After all, it might be a real surprise—something they hadn't encountered before, a donation from a parent or a local business. Once it was a huge supply of bubble wrap. The children had immediately grasped the possibilities. They had set to work popping, popping bubbles with their little pincer fingers, snap-snap-snap all up and down the table. Even Liam popped a few. There was something very satisfying about it, he found. Then Joshua and his best friend, Danny, conceived a plan to roll up the sheets of wrap and wring them out like dishcloths, popping dozens of bubbles at once, and from there they moved on to setting the rolls on the floor and stamping on them with both feet. "You're hurting our ears!" the little girls cried, covering their ears with their hands. "Zayda, make them stop!"

Liam was baffled by the children's unquestioning trust in him. From the first day of school, it was "I have to pee, Zayda," and "Zayda, will you fix my ponytail?" No doubt at this age they would trust nearly anyone, but Miss Sarah said it also helped that he didn't act all fake-chirpy with them. "You talk in a normal grumbly voice," she said. "Kids like it when grownups don't try too hard."

Though she herself clearly found Liam a bit lacking.

On Halloween the Texture Table bore pumpkins with their tops cut off, and the children reached in up to their elbows and scooped out fistfuls of seeds and fibers. Then they drew faces on the pumpkins with black markers, because knives, of course, were not allowed.

At Thanksgiving they had gourds of all shapes and colors and sizes, some smooth and some pebbly and warty. (But there wasn't a lot you could do with gourds, it soon emerged.)

For Hanukkah they made menorahs out of a special clay that could be baked in a regular oven. These were just humped glazed bands with nine holes for candles—nothing fancy. Liam incised the children's names on the bottoms of their creations, and then while they were having Sharing Time he carried the menorahs in a cardboard box to the kitchen where he and Miss LaSheena, the cook, laid them one by one in the preheated oven. The clumsy little objects—streaky and misshapen, their holes obviously drilled by very small fingers—seemed to give off some of the chil- dren's own fervor and energy. Liam turned over an especially garish purple-and-green affair with five extra holes. *Joshua*, he read. He might have known.

It came as news to him that small children maintained such a firm social structure. They played consistent roles in their dealings with each other; they held fierce notions of justice; they formed alliances and ad hoc committees and little vigilante groups. Lunches were parodies of grownups' dinner parties, just with different conversational topics. Danny held forth at length on spaghetti's resemblance to earthworms, and some of the little girls said, "Eww!" and pushed their plates away, but then Hannah—first clearing her throat importantly—delivered a discourse on a chocolate-covered ant she'd once eaten, while shy little Jake watched everybody admiringly from the sidelines.

At nap time they spread their sleeping bags in rows—Hello Kitty, Batman, Star Wars sleeping bags—and instantaneously conked out, as if done in by the passions of the morning. It was Liam's job to watch over them while Miss Sarah took her break in the teachers' lounge. He sat at her desk and surveyed their little flung-down bodies and listened to the silence, which had that ringing quality that comes after too much noise. He could almost hear the noise still: "That's not fair!" and "Can I have a turn?" and Miss Sarah reading A. A. Milne aloud: *"James, James, Morrison, Morrison, Weatherby George Dupree . . ."*

And the *chink!* of Eunice's earring as it dropped onto her dinner plate.

He had lost his last chance at love; he knew that. He was nearly sixty-one years old, and he looked around at his current life—the classroom hung with Big Bird posters, his

anonymous apartment, his limited circle of acquaintances—
and knew this was how it would be all the way till the end.

*King John was not a good man, he had his little ways, and
sometimes no one spoke to him for days and days and days.*

It seemed to be expected each Christmas that he should buy
Jonah a gift. This year he settled on a jigsaw puzzle showing
a mother and baby giraffe. He believed Jonah had a special
fondness for giraffes. The grownups in the family no longer
exchanged gifts; or maybe they did exchange gifts but they
didn't tell Liam about it, which was fine with him. Louise
and Dougall brought Jonah by on Christmas Eve afternoon,
and Liam served instant cocoa with the kind of marshmal-
lows that he knew Jonah preferred—the miniatures rather
than the big, puffy ones.

Jonah seemed very big compared with the three-year-olds
Liam saw daily. (He was nearly five by now.) He wore a
Spider-Man jacket that he refused to take off. Louise said it
was an early Christmas present. "We're trying to spread out
the deluge," she said. "His other grandparents go *way* over-
board."

"Well, in that case maybe he could open my present early
too," Liam said.

"Can I?" Jonah asked, and Louise said, "Why not."

She was sitting in an armchair while Dougall, a tubby,
soft, blond boy of a man, was squeezed into the rocker. Liam
always had the impulse to avert his eyes from Dougall out of
kindness; he seemed so uncomfortable in his own body.

Jonah really liked his present. Or at least, he said he did.
He said, "Giraffes are my favorite animals, next to elephants."

"Oh," Liam said. "I didn't know about the elephants."

"Go ahead and give him *his* present," Louise told Jonah.

"I have a present?" Liam asked.

"He's old enough now to learn that giving goes both ways," Louise said.

"I made it myself," Jonah told him. He was pulling it from his jacket pocket—a small flat rectangle wrapped in red tissue. "Why don't I just unwrap it for you," he said.

"That would be very helpful," Liam said.

Jonah was so eager that he flung bits of tissue everywhere. Eventually he uncovered a bookmark decorated with pressed leaves. "See," he said, placing it on Liam's knee, "first you glue the leaves to the paper and then the teacher sticks this clear stuff over the top of them with her hot shiny metal thinga-majig."

"That's called an iron," Louise said, clutching her hair. "I'm mortified."

"I'll use it right away," Liam told Jonah.

"Do you like it?"

"I not only like it; I need it."

Jonah looked pleased. "I told you," he said to his mother.

"He insisted it was you who should get that," Louise told Liam. "I believe it was originally supposed to be a parent gift."

"Well, too bad," Liam said merrily. "It's mine now."

Jonah grinned.

"Where's Kitty?" Dougall asked Liam. (His first utterance since "Hi.")

"Um, she's at Damian's, I believe."

Louise said, "What do you mean, you *believe?*"

"Well, actually I know. But she's due home any second. She said she'd be here for your visit."

She had promised to help with the entertaining, Liam remembered wistfully. (He sometimes found Dougall a bit difficult to converse with.)

"That girl is running hog wild," Louise told him.

"Oh, no, no; by and large she's been very responsible. This is just the exception that proves the rule."

"You know, I've never understood that phrase," Louise said thoughtfully. "How could an exception prove the rule?"

"Yes, I see your point. Or 'honored in the breach rather than in the observance.' "

"What?"

"That's another one that seems to contradict itself."

Louise said, "When I was—"

"Or 'arbitrary,' " Liam said. "Ever notice how 'arbitrary' has two diametrically opposite meanings?"

He was beginning to find entertaining easier than he had envisioned.

"When I was Kitty's age," Louise persevered, "I wasn't allowed to go out on Christmas Eve. Mom said it was a family holiday and we had to all be together."

"Oh, I can't imagine that," Liam said. "Your mother never made a big to-do over Christmas."

"She most certainly did. She made a *huge* to-do."

"Then how about the time she gave away the tree?" Liam asked.

"She what?"

"Have you forgotten? Myrtle Ames across the street came by in a tizzy one Christmas morning because her son had suddenly decided to visit and she didn't have a tree. Your mom said, 'Take ours; we've already had the use of it.' I was in the side yard collecting firewood and all at once I saw your mom and Myrtle, carrying off our Christmas tree."

"I don't remember a thing about it."

"It still had all its decorations on," Liam said. "It still had its angel swaying on top, and tinsel and strings of lights. The electric cord was trailing on the asphalt behind them. The two of them were doubled over in their bathrobes and scurrying across the street in this secret, huddled way."

He started laughing. He was laughing out of surprise as much as amusement, because he hadn't remembered this himself until now and yet it had come back to him in perfect detail. From where? he wondered. And how had he ever forgotten it in the first place? The trouble with discarding bad memories was that evidently the good ones went with them. He wiped his eyes and said, "Oh, Lord, I haven't thought of that in years."

Louise was still looking dubious. Probably she would have gone on arguing, but just then Kitty walked in and so the subject was dropped.

It didn't bother Liam that he would be spending Christmas Day on his own. He had a new book about Socrates that he was longing to get on with, and he'd picked up a rotisserie chicken from the Giant the day before. When he dropped Kitty off at Barbara's in midmorning, though, she seemed struck by a sudden attack of conscience. "Are you sure you'll be okay?" she asked after she got out of the car. She leaned in through the window and asked, "Should I be keeping you company?"

"I'll be fine," he said, and he meant it.

He waved to Xanthe, who had come to the front door, and she waved back and he drove away.

If only the roads could always be as empty as they were today! He sailed smoothly up Charles Street, managing to slip through every intersection without a stop. The weather was warm and gray, on the verge of raining, which made people's Christmas lights show up even in the daytime. Liam approved of Christmas lights. He especially liked them on bare trees, deciduous trees where you could see all the branches. Although he couldn't imagine going to so much trouble himself.

In his apartment complex, the parking lot was deserted. Everybody must be off visiting relatives. He parked and let himself into the building. The cinderblock foyer was noticeably colder than outside. When he opened his own door, the faint smell of cocoa from yesterday made the apartment seem like someone else's—someone more domestic, and cozier.

Before he settled in with his book, he put the chicken in the oven on low and he exchanged his sneakers for slippers. Then he switched on the lamp beside his favorite armchair. He sat down and opened his book and laid Jonah's bookmark on the table next to him. He leaned back against the cushions with a contented sigh. All he lacked was a fireplace, he thought.

But that was all right. He didn't need a fireplace.

Socrates said . . . What was it he had said? Something about the fewer his wants, the closer he was to the gods. And Liam really wanted nothing. He had an okay place to live, a good enough job. A book to read. A chicken in the oven. He was solvent, if not rich, and healthy. Remarkably healthy, in fact—no back trouble, no arthritis, no hip replacements or knee replacements. The cut on his scalp had healed so that he could feel just the slightest raised line, barely wider than a thread. His hair had grown back to hide it completely from view. And the scar on his palm had shrunk so that it was only a sort of dent.

He could almost convince himself that he'd never been wounded at all.

A NOTE ABOUT THE TYPE

This book was set in a typeface called Berling. This distinguished letter is a computer version of the original type designed by the Swedish typographer Karl Erik Forsberg (born 1914). Forsberg is also known for designing several other typefaces, including Parad (1936), Lunda (1938), Carolus, and Ericus, but Berling—named after the foundry that produced it, Berlingska Stilgjuteriet of Lund—is the one for which he is best known. Berling, a roman font with the characteristics of an old face, was first used in 1954 to produce the Rembrandt Bible, which won an award for the most beautiful book of the year.